BOTH

of Me

AMBER KELLY

Cover Design: Sommer Stein, *Perfect Pear Creative Covers*
Cover Image: Scott Hoover, *Scott Hoover Photography*
Editor: Jovana Shirley, Unforeseen Editing, *www.unforeseenediting.com*
Formatter: *Champagne Book Design*

To my "&" girls.
The world would be a dull place without your love, laughter, and friendship.
This book is for you.

Prologue

Gabby
Four Years Old

I AM GETTING ALL DRESSED UP LIKE A PRINCESS.

Papa and Mamma are expecting company for dinner tonight, so Nonna has dressed me in my prettiest dress. It is purple, and it has yellow butterflies on the front. Purple is my favorite color.

I twirl and twirl until I am dizzy.

"Hold still, so I can finish your hair, Gabriella," Nonna scolds.

She helps me get my shoes on as she explains that the Scutari family just moved two estates down from us. Mr. Scutari is in the same business as Papa. He and his three boys—Emilio, Atelo, and Christoff—as well as their grandparents are coming to meet us all tonight, and Papa wants me and my brothers to be on our very best behavior. She holds my hand and leads me downstairs.

"There is my *bambina*." Papa reaches out for me, and he picks me up and spins me around as I laugh with glee. He turns, and I see a group of people huddled in the foyer.

"Say hello to our new friends, Gabriella. This is Papa's friend Mr. Scutari and his boys and their grandparents."

"Hi." I wave shyly and lay my head on Papa's shoulder.

They all say hello in return, and Papa shows us into the dining room where Mamma and Nonna are placing food in the center of the table. My tummy growls loudly, and everyone laughs.

"My baby girl is always hungry." Papa smiles down at me as he places me in my seat between Nicco and one of his friend's sons.

I sneak a peek up at the stranger. He has long, dark hair that falls into his face. His eyes are dark green, and when he smiles down at me, he has a dimple in his cheek, just like Nicco.

"Hey, I am Christoff."

"Where is your mamma, Crisscross?" I ask.

"No, Chris-toff," he repeats.

I wrinkle my nose. That's what I said.

I mimic him, "Criss-cross."

He laughs, and so does Nicco.

"Gabriella, he said Christoff, not Crisscross. Crisscross would be a silly name."

"I didn't say Crisscross. I said, Criss-Cross," I state in aggravation.

"You just said it again."

"I did not."

Nicco is always mean to me, and he always tries to embarrass me.

"It's okay," Christoff whispers to me. "You can call me Crisscross if you want to."

"I don't want to call you that. People will laugh at me. I want to call you Crisscross."

Nicco laughs out loud again, and I don't understand what is so funny.

"It can be a thing just between you and me, okay?" he says. "I'll call you"—he scratches his head—"Gabby. You call me"—he stops, and his forehead crinkles like he is thinking—"Cross. What do you think?"

I look up into his green eyes, and I smile.

"Nicknames just for us?"

"Yes, ma'am."

I smile big at him. He is so nice. I think we will be the bestest friends ever.

Cross's papa tells us that his mamma was in an accident, and she is with Jesus and the angels now. His mamma's parents came to live with them afterward to help. I look up at Cross, and when his papa talks about the angels, his lips quiver. He is sad. I would be sad, too, if my mamma went to live with the angels and did not come visit me. I will have to love him extra hard for her, so he is not sad anymore.

After dinner, the adults have yucky coffee while we all enjoy dessert that Cross's grandmother, Una, made. Then, they excuse themselves. Nicco looks to Cross and asks if he wants to ride bikes, and I ask if I can come, too.

"No, you can't even ride your bike without training wheels." He rolls his eyes.

I start to get upset because I want to go with them. I don't want to stay while the older boys play video games and the grown-ups talk in the study.

Why can't I go?

"Tell you what, Miss Gabby." Cross bends down and looks me in the eye. "Next time I come over, I will help you learn how to ride without training wheels. Then, you can always go with us. Deal?"

"Okay," I say through my tears.

He wraps one of my curls in his finger and tugs. "Don't cry. We will have lots of time to spend together now that we live just down the street. I promise."

"Cross your heart?"

"Cross my heart." He slashes his fingers over his heart and winks at me as he follows Nicco out the back door.

I think he might be my prince, just like Cinderella. Prince Cross.

CHAPTER
One

Brie
Present

A s I step off the plane into the hustle and bustle of LAX Airport, anxiety kicks in. This is real. I am doing this. I left everything and everyone behind to begin again three thousand miles away from home.

I follow the horde of rushing travelers through the packed airport and into a surprisingly empty restroom. I look in the mirror at the weary face staring back at me. My chestnut eyes are slightly bloodshot, and my long, dark locks are a tangled mess from sleeping over half the flight from JFK. I splash some cool water on my face and run my fingers through my unruly hair. I pinch my cheeks and add a quick swipe of gloss across my lips. I take one last moment to gather myself. It's as ready as I am going to get.

I give myself a pep talk as I walk down to baggage claim to collect my luggage. "You can do this. You are Brie Masters. You are a single girl from the big city, here to experience life outside of your hometown bubble while finishing your degree." I work hard to convince myself as I grab my bags from the belt and head out into the warm California sun.

I take a deep breath to calm myself. Calm is something I haven't felt in a very long time. I am not exactly sure what Los Angeles has to offer a broken soul like me, but it has to be better than what I walked away from. It just has to be. Starting over is not something I thought I would be doing at twenty-two years old, but here I am. I have lived a thousand lifetimes in those twenty-two years, and I have cried over the past long enough. Time to chase—and hopefully catch—a few new dreams. So, I gather myself and walk into my future.

"Jeez, Brie, how did you manage to pack your life into two suitcases? I don't think I have ever known a girl to travel on vacation this light, much less move across the country."

With an emphasis on the name I now choose to be called, my cousin, Daniel, ribs me as he lifts all the belongings I cared to carry with me into this new adventure into the bed of his pickup truck.

"I told you, I am taking this moving-on thing very seriously. New everything. New name. New home. New friends. Even new clothes."

So far, I am happy with my decision to move west and reconnect with my cousin. We were great friends when we were children—before his parents divorced, and he moved to Cali with his dad, Matthew Taylor. Uncle Matt had done well for himself as the premier Dentist to the Stars. I assume well-maintained teeth are a fairly lucrative commodity in Hollywood. Every single face aspiring to be on stage, screen, or print has to have them after all.

Daniel and I kept in touch through the years as much as possible. Sending each other birthday cards every year and placing the occasional telephone call when we were younger and seeing each other when he came to visit his mom, my mother's older sister, in the summers. Once we were old enough for social media accounts though, it was like he had never left. That is the thing about sites like Instagram and Twitter; you feel like you are actively participating in the lives of people you haven't set your eyes on in ten or more years. It is the best and the worst thing about social media. Disconnected connection.

It felt good to be in the same space as him now. He has grown into a handsome man, tall and broad-shouldered, like his dad. His dark hair is a little wild, and he still has the scar that runs through his left eyebrow from when he fell from the tire swing in my backyard when we were about six years old. He is sporting a five-o'clock shadow; actually, it looks more like a seven-o'clock shadow at this point. And, of course, he has a smile that could blind you, courtesy of his dad. He is all grown up and an aspiring musician, still living at home in his dad's pool house in Beverly Hills while he lives his dream. He is a talented guitar player and singer-songwriter. I just know he is going to be famous one day. I wanted freedom and a fresh start, but I longed for a familiar face that wasn't vetted to the past in a way that it would keep popping up on me. Daniel is that face.

"You have certainly come to the right place. A lot of miles between here and New York. They are two completely different worlds, but don't worry; I am sure you are going to fit right in. Dawn and Kelsey have already gotten your room ready, and they are excited to officially meet you."

Dawn Martin is Daniel's current girlfriend and his stepsister, Kelsey Green's, best friend and roommate. Uncle Matt married Kelsey's mom when Daniel and Kelsey were already temperamental teenagers, so their relationship was strained from the beginning. Her mom was a former dental client and a wilting flower of an actress who had found fame in the early nineties, playing the sexy villain on a popular network soap opera. Daniel didn't take too well to the two female drama queens coming into and taking over his and his dad's easy bachelor lives. However, once he started dating his new sister's best friend, much to her chagrin, they were forced into a tentative truce. According to Daniel though, they grew on each other and settled into a love/hate, familial relationship.

The girls' former roommate, Tonya, just vacated her room and moved out on her own. That left them with a room for rent and hopefully room in their inner circle for me. I could use some friends.

Daniel told me all about the two—the good, bad, and ugly—and I feel like I already know them. My favorite part about them is the ugly. I know that sounds insane, but maybe my ugly won't seem so bad next to theirs. I guess we all carry a bit of it with us, but I am here to try to shed mine for good.

We pull up to a gorgeous stucco building in Santa Monica about thirty minutes later. It is a well-maintained place with a quaint court-yard and gated parking. It is close to the beach and the Third Street Promenade and definitely something I would never have been able to afford on my own, but with my savings and the money Una tucked into my hand as I left, I should, hopefully, be able to cover one-third of the cost until I can find a decent-paying job.

Enrolling in classes is my first order of business though. I gradu-ated high school a few months early and then took time off to spend a couple of years in Paris with my mom's younger sister, Aunt Mitzi. It was a glorious time in my life. Paris is a dream, and Aunt Mitzi is one of my favorite people on the planet. She took a heartbroken teen in and showed her a whole new world full of culture, food, fashion, and excitement that only Paris could provide.

I started taking classes at NYU the semester following my return to New York, but a little more than a year in was when everything in my life went sideways. Looking back, I probably should have stayed in France and gone to university. I loved it there, but something—or better yet, someone—kept calling me back home. Him. No, he is not allowed here. No thoughts of him in my new life.

Daniel parks the truck and hops out. I gather my purse and phone and open the door. A wonderful aroma of salt and sea envelops me, and I instantly love it here. Fresh air. Fresh start.

"Apartment number is three-B, and the girls are waiting for you. Go on up and say hi, and I'll grab your things and be up in a minute," Daniel instructs me as he types away on his phone.

I turn toward the courtyard and take it in. The space is a good size with a few large shade trees sprinkled about. There are cobble-stone sidewalks lined with flower beds bursting with purple salvia and bright yellow coreopsis along the path. A couple of people are seated on benches under the trees, reading or typing away on their laptops, and one girl is lying on a beach towel, soaking up a few late rays of sunshine. *Yes, I will definitely love it here.*

I make my way to the center building and climb the exterior staircase leading up to the third floor. It is insane how anxious I am to meet my new roommates. *Will they be able to tell by looking at me the hell I have been through this past year? Is my outside as tattered as my inside?* I know these are silly thoughts because my scars do not show on the outside. They are not physical scars, not all of them anyway.

I reach the third floor, and I see 3B right at the top of the stairs. A shadow is peeking out of the front window before my foot even hits the landing, so I assume Daniel texted to let them know we had arrived. As I raise my knuckles to knock, the door swings open, and a tall, slender girl my age with shoulder-length blonde hair that has bright pink tips comes barreling for me and wraps her arms around me.

Dawn, I think to myself. *This must be Dawn.*

"Brie, we are so glad you are finally here," she practically squeals.

She smells like coconut, and I allow myself to absorb some of her enthusiasm as I squeeze her back and look behind her into my new home. It's intimidating, but she hooks her arm in mine and leads me in like we have known each other for ages.

"We have your room all ready for you. The bed is made up with fresh linens, and it has been thoroughly cleaned. Tonya took everything with her that wasn't nailed down, but all of the furniture is still here, so we'll just have to go shopping to get you all the essentials, like pillows, blankets, and a lamp. Not that you need too many blankets here. It's always warm."

She is talking a mile a minute as she leads me through the apartment, past a nice-sized living space and down a hall. I instantly like her.

"This is your room. It's the smallest of the three, but it has the

8

best view. The ocean is across the street and down a couple of blocks. You have your own bathroom—well, sort of. It is the one across the hall, and it is also the guest bathroom when we have company. Kelsey and I have a Jack and Jill bath between our rooms, and we share it. Come on; I will show you the rest."

I follow her and check out both their rooms and the large-closet-sized space they use as a makeshift office with a tiny desk and shared computer and printer.

"Now, we come to our favorite spot in the entire apartment," she informs me as we round the living room.

She swings her arms wide in a dramatic game-show-hostess fashion. "Ta-da. The kitchen. This is where all the magic happens. We don't have a table or anything, but this island is massive, and the barstools are very comfy. It is the reason we rented this place. It is just so big and open. We like to cook, and we absolutely love to eat. There is a small deck through those sliding glass doors. It has an outdoor table and umbrella with a matching couch and electric fire pit. We sometimes like to sit out there and have coffee in the morning or dinner if it is a nice, cool evening. Or wine. We like our wine almost as much as we like our food."

She laughs, and I can't help but smile with her.

Kelsey, a petite girl with long blonde hair, is behind the island, cutting up what looks like bleu cheese and adding it to a board with other varieties, grapes, and crackers. My stomach growls at the sight.

"Yes, we do. We aren't exactly winos, but let's just say, we do our part to keep Napa Valley thriving." She looks up and adds, "Wow, look at you. You look like some exotic creature with your dark hair and olive skin. We don't see many Italian beauties around here. It's all bleached-blonde Valley girls with spray tans and fake tits. Present company excluded, of course." She slides her eyes to Dawn, who obviously has enhanced assets.

Dawn playfully sticks her tongue out at her friend. I can't help but notice that Kelsey is a natural stunner. Makeup free with a smattering of freckles across her nose. Her long hair is pulled back into a ponytail, and she is dressed in yoga pants and a tight tee.

I wonder if every girl in LA really is blonde and beautiful. It's very different from home. New York is a melting pot of ethnicity and culture, and everyone always seems to be made up to the max and in a hurry to be somewhere.

"I have some snacks here because we assumed you would be peckish after that long flight. We figured we would just call out for dinner later tonight after you had time to get settled in."

We hear Daniel enter the kitchen as I thank them for the warm welcome.

"No problem. We are happy to have someone new in here. Tonya was … well, she was …"

"She was the devil," Daniel finishes Kelsey's thought from the doorway.

Dawn walks over to him for a quick kiss and then admits, "Yeah, she was. I don't want you to think we are difficult to live with or anything. She was just in a bad mood most of the time and a bit on the lazy side. I mean, really, you are a twenty-three-year-old adult; wash your own dishes and pick your own clothes up off of the bathroom floor every once in a while." She rolls her eyes. "When she started hitting on Kelsey's boyfriend right in front of us one night, it was the straw that broke the camel's back. Girl Code. You never, ever break Girl Code. She had to go."

I get it. I have four brothers. *Tidy* is not a word in their vocabulary, and it drove me and my mother nuts. And I, too, have felt the sharp sting of a friend's betrayal.

"You guys do not have to worry about me. I like a clean and neat environment, too, and I have zero time or desire to hit on anyone at all. I am focusing on me right now. Only me."

A look of relief passes between my new roomies, and I know—I just know—I am home.

CHAPTER
Two

"COME ON, GABBY. IT IS YOUR BIRTHDAY. YOUR SWEET SIX-teenth birthday that both your parents and your bone-head brothers forgot. I am not going to let you sit here all night, crying into your pillow. Get up and get dressed. It's party time."

My best friend, Adriana, is standing above me as I lie on my bed, struggling to stop the tears.

Sixteen is supposed to be a big deal, right? I have been excited for weeks. When I woke up this morning, I fully expected to walk down-stairs and find my mother making birthday pancakes and singing "Happy Birthday" to me with her angelic voice, like she had done ev-ery single year before, but there was no one in the kitchen, except my brother, Nicco, eating a bowl of cereal while he waited for the coffee to finish brewing. He didn't even look up from his phone when I walked in. In fact, he didn't acknowledge me at all, except to grunt when I said good morning.

I asked him where Mamma was, and he said she had gone into the city with Papa on some kind of family business. I was disappointed but assumed, whatever the business was, it must have been urgent for her to miss seeing me off this morning. Perhaps it wasn't business at all.

Maybe my parents were out, making arrangements for us to celebrate later or buying my gift.

I spent the rest of my day at school, eagerly anticipating coming home to whatever my family had planned for my milestone. However, when I walked in the door, all I could hear was my parents arguing in Papa's study. I walked to the door, knocked softly, and peeked in. When Papa spotted me there, he immediately dismissed me and told me to go to my room and do my homework or something until dinner because the adults were having a grown-up conversation.

Funny how most of the grown-up conversations that happened in our house involved an awful lot of yelling.

Mamma, who had been trying to avoid eye contact with me, was standing behind him with tears streaming down her face. She finally looked up and gave me an apologetic look as I left, crestfallen. I could tell they were both extremely upset about something, but couldn't they have at least said happy birthday?

I checked my brothers' bedrooms as I made my way to mine, and they were all empty. *Where was everyone?*

Even though they were adults now, my brothers still lived here in the family home. Not that they ever actually slept here much anymore.

Tony, my oldest brother, is usually at his girlfriend's house. Stavros is usually wherever Tony is. Lorenzo is always crashing at a friend's house in the city after going out. And Nicco is either home or at his best friend, Cross's, loft, which is above the detached four-car garage on his father's property about half a mile from us.

Cross. My Cross. My Cross, who has been avoiding any contact with me for months now after an embarrassing encounter where he walked into the bathroom as I was coming out of the shower. I was using Nicco's bathroom because Mamma was having mine remodeled. I yelped when I walked out to find him walking in. He just stood there like a deer caught in headlights. It was mortifying.

I have been in love with Cross Scutari since I was four years old and his family moved in a few houses down from us. He and Nicco became fast friends, and he has always treated me like I am his little sister, too. However, the way he looked at me that day was anything but brotherly. At least, that's the way I recall it in my mind.

"You are right. I am not going to spend all night crying because of those selfish jerks. What do you have in mind?" I ask.

Adriana gets a mischievous look in her eye and replies with a sly smile, "I lifted a couple of bottles of vodka from my parents' bar, and I called a few new friends to meet us down at the hot springs. We are going to let loose and party our asses off to celebrate your birthday."

I am sure this is a very bad idea, but I am so angry with my family that I do not care.

Not one of my brothers showed up to dinner. Mamma and I ate in the kitchen, and Papa ate in his study. Apparently, he was very busy, and whatever had him busy had Mamma upset. She barely spoke a word while we ate takeout alone. Nonna and Nonno were suspiciously absent as well. They have their own little cottage in the back of our house, but they usually come up to the main house for breakfast and dinner. I haven't seen either one of them once today. *Weird.*

Mamma just stared at her plate of orange duck and moved the food around, not really eating. She didn't mention my birthday.

It is now nine p.m., and I only have three hours left of the day that I have looked forward to since … well, since forever.

I am hurt and angry. So, I get up and get ready for a fun night with a bunch of strangers and my bestie, who is apparently the only person who loves me enough to remember my big day. *Screw them all.* It is time to get drunk and forget them, too.

I have never had vodka before. Actually, other than a glass of champagne to ring in the New Year with my family, I have never had any alcohol before. It isn't pleasant. It tastes vile and burns all the way down. Why does everyone like this stuff?

Adriana keeps refilling our cups and adding enough lemonade to make it tolerable. We just keep forcing it down until we have enough in our system that we do not care how it tastes anymore.

The friends she invited are a few boys who attend the community college across town. I don't know any of them, but her older brother was in a study group with the one named Jamey. I can tell she likes him. I don't blame her. He is hot. He is three years older than us, and I assume his friends are about the same.

Adi has thought of everything tonight. She ordered pizzas and even has a cake that she put six candles on for me to blow out. It is store-bought and not the usual homemade German chocolate cake my nonna makes for me every year, but it is a cake, and she did the best she could.

We have music playing from Adi's iPhone and our drinks, and I am enjoying myself quite a bit, dancing around and singing along.

One of the boys, Dante, sits down beside me as I sit on the edge of the springs and place my feet in. He is handsome. He has black hair to match his black eyes. He is a lot bigger than the boys I am used to seeing in class. It looks like he spends a lot of time in the gym or maybe he plays football for his school. I think they were talking about football earlier. Weren't they? The night is getting kind of fuzzy. He sits so close to me; I can smell his cologne. I move over a little to give him some space, but he just moves with me.

"Where are you going?" he asks.

"Just thought I'd give you some more room."

He leans in and whispers against my ear, "Who said I wanted any more room?"

Goose bumps trickle down my spine, and in my compromised state, I cannot decipher whether they are from thrill or fear. He moves back and gives me an assessing look. Maybe he isn't sure either.

All of a sudden, he jumps to his feet and extends his hand to me as he suggests we all get into the hot springs for a swim.

"Um, it's November, and we didn't bring a bathing suit or towels or anything," I manage to get out as I stumble to my feet.

The hot springs is one of my favorite places. It is a natural spring out in the woods, about a quarter of a mile from the back of our family's property. It feeds into the lake further back, and it is always warm, January or July. It is like our own personal rock hot tub, hidden by the cover of the forest. When I was little, I thought it was a magical place.

I can still remember the day Nicco, Cross, and I found it.

They had been riding their bikes, and I was on mine, doing my best to keep up with them. Nicco was trying to ditch me. He was always trying to ditch me. I was a late-in-life "oops" baby, and I didn't think his thirteen-year-old self appreciated having to always entertain a five-year-old, especially a five-year-old girl. We were flying through the woods, and Nicco hit the bank. He flipped off his bike and went headfirst right into the springs. I screamed as I slammed on my brakes and skidded sideways to avoid going in after him. Cross jumped off his bike and came running to me.

"Hey, Gabby. Are you okay, Tesoro?" he asked as he lifted my bike off me.

"I think I hurt my leg," I cried.

He gently lifted my leg to inspect the damage. My right knee was busted open and bleeding.

"Yep, I think you did. It doesn't look too bad, but I think we'd better leave our bikes here, and Nicco and I will take turns, carrying you home."

I didn't like that idea at all. I was too big to be carried home like a sissy.

"See, this is why you shouldn't be tagging along with us in the first place. Boy play is too rough for little girls," Nicco added as he climbed his way out of the hole and shook the water from his hair.

Sure, riding bikes through the woods and falling into watering holes were very dangerous stuff.

"Man, Cross, this place is cool. That water is deep, and it's warm and bubbly. We should come back and swim once we get the baby home."

I jumped up and shouted, "I am not a baby."

Cross looked down into my angry face and said, "You are our baby, Gabby."

I was sure my heart broke for the very first time when he said those words to me.

I walked myself home that day. Refusing to let either one of them carry me a single step. Busted-up knee and a bruised forehead be damned. I wasn't about to let Cross see me act like a baby. I was a big girl. Big girls walked home without being carried and without crying.

Gah, Nicco was the worst brother ever.

I shake my foggy mind from the memory. "What did you say?" I ask Dante.

"I said, the water is warm, and we don't really need bathing suits. We can get in our birthday suits, since it is your birthday." There is a glint of excitement behind his eyes as he delivers his dare.

Is he crazy? We met a little over two hours ago. No way am I taking my clothes off and getting in the water without a suit in front of him or his friends.

I look to Adriana for backup. She is a few feet away in Jamey's lap, and he is kissing the back of her neck. She seems to be enjoying it very much. Adriana likes to make out with boys. Lots of boys. Well, maybe not lots, but she has had a couple of boyfriends, and she has let them round a few bases.

I have never been kissed. This is a fact that I am starting to get a little self-conscious about.

It isn't like I am ugly. I might not be a knockout like Adriana, but I know I am at least pretty. Genetics. All four of my brothers are gorgeous. A fact that every girl in my school makes very clear to me. They are always trying to befriend me in the hopes of finding themselves in the company of one or more of the Mastreoni boys. It is so annoying. Their bedrooms have had revolving doors since they hit puberty, which my parents pretend not to notice. What a double standard. I brought Philip Barns home from school to study for our Latin exam one afternoon, and with the way my brothers acted, you would have thought we'd started ripping each other's clothes off as we came in the door. I was so embarrassed, and needless to say, Philip never offered to help me study again. No boy ever offered to help me study again. Nor did they ask me out on any dates. I wasn't sure anymore if they avoided me because of my brothers or because they just were not into me.

"Hey, guys, you want to go skinny-dipping or what?" Dante asks before I get a word out.

"Yes!" Adi jumps off Jamey's lap and starts to undress.

All three of our guests follow her, and I stand there, a little dizzy, watching the show as they jump in.

"Come on, Gabby; don't be so uptight. Just keep your underwear on if you are that nervous and get your ass in the water. Be spontaneous for once. It's fun. We are having fun. Don't make a big deal out of it." She tries her best to convince me.

They are swimming and splashing around, and it does look fun. I mean, what could it hurt to let loose and do something wild for once? My head is swimming, and try as I might, I cannot think clearly enough to come up with a good reason not to jump in with Adi and our new friends.

So, I make my decision and lift my dress above my head.

CHAPTER
Three

MY FIRST TWO WEEKS AS A CALIFORNIA GIRL HAVE BEEN A whirlwind. Dawn and Kelsey have taken me shopping, helped personalize my room, introduced me around to their large, extended friend group, dragged me out for cocktails and dancing, and taken me to eat amazing food all over the city, and we have spent several lazy days on the beach. Needless to say, they took their responsibility of introducing me to my new home very seriously. It's been exhausting and wonderful.

I didn't have a lot of close friends back home. Only one really. My very best friend and partner in crime, Adriana. She is one of my dad's business partner's daughters I met when we were ten years old, and we were inseparable. She helped me get into and out of a lot of trouble through the years. Until now, that is. There is no way out of my latest trouble.

Even though she is one of the people I am most angry with, leaving her behind is one of the hardest parts of leaving for good. I miss her every day. No more so than now as I stare at the doors of California State University.

Today is the day that I start working toward my future goals. I have always dreamed of having my own restaurant. When I was a little girl,

I would be under my mamma's and my nonna's feet as they cooked these delicious meals for our large, loud *famiglia*. I am the baby of five. I have four older brothers, and my father's parents moved to America from Italy decades ago to live with us. So, dinnertime was always an event in our home. When I was younger, I was completely enthralled with the whole process—from growing the vegetables and spices in the garden to making pasta by hand, creating homemade marinades and sauces and baking cakes and cookies from scratch.

So, I find myself here, taking boring business classes because knowing how to cook is the easy and fun part of having your own restaurant. Time for me to settle in and do the work to learn the hard parts of owning your own business.

Somehow, I managed to complete enough classes the year before last and earned a few hard-fought online credits over the last ten months to enter the current year as a junior. I will buckle down and get this degree. No distractions. I can't allow myself to get off track ever again.

The first day is a success. Turns out, Dawn is in two of my classes, and Kelsey and I have the same lab hours. It is great to have familiar faces in class. All of my professors seem amicable. I took a full course load, trying to play a little catch-up. It will be a tough but hopefully productive year.

Now, onto the job search. I secured a position as a nanny for a four-month-old baby boy before I arrived. I have communicated with his parents and made all the arrangements via phone and FaceTime. Although I look forward to every moment with that little guy, that job will not pay the bills. So, I have a meeting at the local country club this evening. They are in need of a tennis instructor, and being as I taught youth tennis at our club back in New York, I was able to get Una to have my old boss call in a recommendation for me under my new name as a favor to her.

I really hope I get this job. I am in desperate need of it. Everything else is falling into place so well. Landing this would be the icing on the cake.

"Hello, Ms. ..." Mr. Cloniger, the head of HR for the club, extends his hand as I enter his office.

"Miss Masters. Brie Masters, but please call me Brie," I fill in for him as I take his hand.

He is a plump older gentleman with a graying comb-over and kind eyes.

"Yes, Brie, it is nice to meet you. Stan Morgan over at New York Golf and Country had a lot of great things to say about you."

We sit across from each other at his massive desk, and I wipe the sweat from my palms onto my slacks. I don't know why I am so nervous. I think because a lot is riding on this job. I only have enough money to last through the next two semesters. I am not comfortable with living so close to the edge. When I was growing up, money was not something I worried about. My father did quite well in his business, and he lavished our family with all the comforts one could want or need. Choosing to move out here on my own without any help from Papa was something I had to do, as scary as it was. I do not want his money or his business tainting my new life.

"I see you worked predominantly with youth, ages eight to twelve years old. Our need here will entail much of the same but a little broader age range from about six to sixteen years old. We have need of instructors for classes of four or more and then for a few one-on-one private instructions for adult beginners and youth. The classes pay a salary, as we discussed over the phone, and the private lessons are commission-based. We only offer insurance benefits for full-time employees, but we do have an opt-in 401(k) available for both full- and part-time. I understand you are in school as well."

This is where I am a little unsure. *Are my schedule limitations going to be a problem?*

"Yes, sir. I am in classes three days a week. On those days, I can take on any evening classes or private lessons you have. The other two days, I am available for either morning or evening sessions, and I am flexible all weekends. I am also working as a nanny for a couple in

Santa Monica, but the mother is a stay-at-home mom, and she is very flexible. I can work a schedule out with her once I know what your needs are. If you choose to hire me, that is."

He places the paperwork he was perusing on his desk and looks up at me. "I am going to be frank. Your résumé is impressive. Stan highly recommends you, but are you sure you want to take on this job? You are young and new in town. You are in college. Working a job already. Don't you want a little free time to hang out with friends and just enjoy life a little?"

Do I ever, but that is not an option for me at this point. Dawn and Kelsey both have parents paying their rent and tuition, so they can concentrate on both school and partying. I don't have that luxury. I am all I have.

"Trust me, sir; I will still have plenty of time to participate in the joys of life. I just really need this income. I promise, if you give me the opportunity, I will work very hard for you and do the best job possible for your members."

He thoughtfully stares at me for a few moments, and then he smiles. "You remind me of myself. I, too, had to work my way through school and climb the ladder all by myself. I respect that. Okay, young lady, you start Monday. I will get all the paperwork filled out and emailed over to you this weekend. Welcome to the team."

I fight the urge to release the tears of relief I feel at the backs of my eyes as he stands and rounds the desk. He extends his hand, and I ignore it as I reach up and give him a tight hug.

"Thank you, Mr. Cloniger. I promise, you will not regret this."

He pats me on the back and tells me to enjoy my weekend and to get ready for the madness. I leave his office, feeling lighter than I have in weeks … months actually.

When I arrive home, I open the door and walk into what can only be described as a Mexican luau. Mariachi music is blaring from Bluetooth speakers, and Dawn is dancing in the living room in a two-piece bathing suit and grass skirt with a colorful plastic lei around her neck and a huge sombrero on her head. Daniel is sitting on the couch with a bemused look on his face, and the aroma of tacos is wafting through the air. I think my roommates might be high. *Do they get high?* That's one question I never thought to ask.

"You're home!" Dawn shouts over the music and flies toward me as I close the door and walk inside.

"Yes, and you're drunk," I reply as I catch her in my arms.

"I am not drunk. I am pleasantly tipsy. Welcome to our celebratory Taco Tuesday! Well, I hope it's celebratory. How did the interview go?" She expectantly looks at me as she teeters backward toward Daniel.

"Good. It went really, really good. I start Monday."

She throws her hands in the air, giving the rock-'n'-roll horns as she shouts, "Celebratory Taco Tuesday it is, Kels. Woohoo."

Kelsey, who is dressed in the same attire, comes walking in from the kitchen, carrying a pitcher of margaritas and a glass for me. "Awesome. We always do Taco Tuesday here, but this time, we added a little extra pizzazz just for you. Hence the leis and the pineapple-glazed pork tacos. After all, it is your introduction to the tradition."

Dawn produces a sombrero from beside the couch and ceremoniously perches it atop my head. "Now, go throw on a bikini and start drinking as fast as you can. We are about two pitchers ahead of you."

Daniel smirks at me and explains, "The girls love tacos and margaritas, and Tuesdays are kind of an undeclared holiday around here. You will get used to it."

"Used to it? She will love Tuesdays as much as we do. It is an unwritten hard-and-fast roommate rule," Kelsey yells from the kitchen.

I decide right then and there that I will in fact love Taco Tuesdays, so I down my first margarita as fast as I can to catch up with everyone.

This is just what I needed. Normal, everyday twenty-two-year-old she-nanigans. I think I have felt thirty-five since the day I turned sixteen years old. It has been exhausting.

Stuffing the burden of my secrets down deep, I exhale and make the decision to try to be as exuberant as my new friends when it comes to life. I can do this. I just have to keep my head and my heart firmly in the present.

CHAPTER
four

Gabby
Past

I JUST GET MY DRESS ABOVE MY HEAD WHEN I HEAR IT.

"What the fuck is going on here?"

I turn to see Cross stomping across the clearing with Angelica on his heels. Angelica is his current girlfriend and the bane of my existence. They are wearing matching angry scowls across their faces, but Cross's is a little more lethal. In my inebriated state, I cannot wrap my head around the fact that my brother's closest friend has caught me partially undressed and very, very drunk. As he barrels toward me, my fight-or-flight instinct kicks in, and I drop my dress beside me and look for a place of escape. I take off toward the water. The water is a good place to go.

He catches up to me in a few long strides and grabs my waist before I have time to launch myself in the water and out of reach.

"Oh no, you don't, *Tesoro*."

I am not sure exactly what comes over me in that instant, but I am not happy he has ahold of me. He is here to ruin my fun. I start struggling in his arms, which only causes him to have to hold on to me in places he shouldn't be holding.

"Damn it, Gabby. Calm the fuck down."

I can hear Angelica interrogating my new friends, and then she turns to Cross and me and announces, "There are four empty vodka bottles over here. These kids are wasted."

I hate being called a kid. I especially hate it when she calls me a kid.

"Who are you calling names, you two-bit whore?" Adriana apparently doesn't appreciate it either.

"Oh, insults from a drunk teenager really bother me," she bites back.

I watch in horror as three very naked boys emerge from the water.

Dante speaks first with his hands held up in peace, "Hey, man. We are just having a little fun. Nothing illicit happening here. Yet." He grins over at me as he adds that last bit.

Does he have a death wish?

He looks back up at Cross, and the grin falls away.

"Just some good old-fashioned skinny-dipping."

Pure mortification washes over me. There is no way Cross is gonna let us slide and not rat me out.

"Skinny-dipping with minors," Cross spits out through gritted teeth. "Get your clothes on and get the hell out of here now before I call her brothers and let them deal with you."

I see the tinge of fear hit their eyes. They must know who my brothers are. One by one, they gather their belongings and start toward the trees.

Dante turns back a moment later and says, "Hey, Gabby. I had a great evening, getting to know you. Can't wait to see even more of you. Another time."

I hear and feel Cross's growl of anger against my skin.

"Angie, get Adriana home. Try to get her in the house without waking anyone."

Adi is not having it. "I don't need an escort. I can find my own way home, thank you."

"The hell you will. Those boys could be waiting for you in the woods. Do you understand what kind of danger you two put yourselves in tonight?"

Okay, I have moved from embarrassment to right the hell pissed off.

"Let me go, Cross." I start kicking and thrashing in his arms. "You do not get to come out here and start running off and insulting my friends. They are the only ones who gave enough shit about me to try to make my birthday special. In fact, they are the only ones who even bothered to wish me a happy birthday."

He goes perfectly still.

"Angie, take her home. Please make sure she gets inside safely before you leave. I am sorry our night has been cut short, but I really need you to do that. I'll call you in the morning. And, Adriana, if you give her any trouble at all, I will personally come over to wake up your father and inform him of what I found out here."

Adi huffs, but she gives in. No way does she want her papa finding out she stole his liquor and fed it to a bunch of underage teens.

I mouth, *I am sorry,* to her as she gathers her stuff.

Angelica comes over and kisses Cross before following Adi through the trees, toward her house. We stand here in silence with him at my back and his arms locked around me.

"It's your birthday?" he whispers.

"It's after midnight, so technically, yesterday was my birthday."

I hear a soft, "Damn it," uttered under his breath, and he releases some of the force with which he had my arms pinned against my sides. "So, your brothers forgot your sixteenth birthday?"

I turn in his arms, and with a quivering bottom lip that, try as I might, I cannot get to stop betraying me, I reply, "Not just my brothers. Everybody. Mamma, Papa, my grandparents … you. Not a single person, except Adi, remembered at all. So, she arranged this last-minute makeshift party to celebrate."

He just stands there, looking at me with pity on his face.

"Don't look at me like that. I am fine. It's just a stupid birthday. There will be another one next year. Maybe then I can swim with my friends in peace."

That wipes the pity right off his face. The pissed-off is back.

"Did you even know those guys? They seemed older than you and way soberer than the two of you. Were you really gonna get naked for them? Do you know what that says to a horny guy? Do you? You could have been attacked by any of them or all of them. How could you have been so careless? I expect shit like this from Adriana but not from you."

That does it. All the fight just flies right out of me. I start sobbing. Cross wasn't expecting the tide shift and picks me up into his arms.

"I didn't want to at first, but they all were doing it, and Adi seemed like she thought it was safe. All I wanted was to swim and maybe be kissed," I confess as I bury my face into his shoulder.

He was walking us out of the clearing when he stops dead. "You wanted one of those boys to kiss you? While you were drunk and naked in the water?"

It sounds really bad when he repeats it back to me. My head is getting heavier and heavier, and I am finding it hard to form words.

"I think so. I have never been kissed, and I think I'd like it. Though I don't think anyone wants to kiss me."

I hear his sharp intake of breath.

"Now, why on earth would you think a thing like that?"

I am starting to fade into the blackness that is pulling me under as I hear him repeat himself, "Why would you think that, *Tesoro?*"

What were we talking about again? Oh, yeah, kissing.

"Because nobody has ever tried to kiss me. I am the only girl I know who hasn't had her first kiss. It's starting to get embarrassing."

He is walking again.

"Please, don't take me home," I plead. "Papa and Mamma are fighting again, and I don't want to be there. Can you take me home with you tonight?"

My eyelids are so heavy, and so is my head, too heavy for me to hold it up any longer. I feel him change directions.

"I'll call Nicco. He is at Marianna's apartment. Maybe you can go there tonight."

I start softly crying again, and he stops once more.

"I don't want to go to Marianna's. I want to go home with you."

"That's not a good idea, Gabby."

"Why not? I miss you."

I do miss him. Since he decided to start avoiding me, I've felt like I am grieving a loss.

"Don't you miss me?" I whisper into his neck.

I don't hear his reply as I slip back into the darkness.

The next thing I remember, I am standing in Cross's bathroom in nothing but my bra and panties, and he has the shower running. I can smell the vomit in my hair. It makes my stomach turn, and the room starts to sway. *Or is it me? Am I swaying?*

Cross is holding me upright as he reaches his hand under the spray to test the water.

"Okay, in you go. We have to get you cleaned up."

I don't even bother to argue. I just step forward. The warm water hits my face, and I start to sink to the tiled floor.

"Oh no, you don't." Cross pulls me back up as he steps into the shower with me. He has on shorts and a T-shirt. "Turn around."

I do as I was told and turn toward the front of the spray. He is standing behind me, and I smell the shampoo in his hands as he takes my hair and starts to run his fingers through to build a lather. It feels so good. I lean back into him and sigh. He inches back, so we aren't touching, except where his hands are touching my hair. I let him wash and rinse me, and then he runs conditioner through my long locks, working the tangles out. I am very relaxed as he massages my scalp. I try to turn around and face him, but he brings his mouth close and commands me to stand still. His lips graze my ear, and I groan. He immediately reaches to turn off the water.

I stand here in the cold, unable to move. Cross just stands behind me, silent. Then, after a moment, he nudges me aside, reaches for a towel, and opens it for me to walk into it.

I stand and let him dry me off. It feels nice. Being taken care of. I look up at him as he is toweling my hair and decide that his jaw is the finest jaw I have ever seen. So, I lean up and press a kiss to the underside of it. He goes still.

"What are you doing, Gabby?" he asks.

I notice his voice is a little hoarse, and I look up at him.

"Kissing your jaw," I answer. I see the confused amusement on his face, so I explain further, "I decided it was the finest jaw I had ever seen, and it needed to be kissed as a reward."

He smiles a sexy little smile and shakes his head. Then, he takes a big step back. "Okay, drunk girl, we got your teeth brushed and the puke out of your hair. Now, hold your arms up."

I do as he asked, and he slides his hands behind my back and unfastens my soaked bra. I gasp at the unexpected move. He looks the other direction as he peels it off of me and drops it to the bathroom floor. Then, with my arms still in the air, he quickly pulls a way-too-large tee over my head.

"I will leave you to remove the rest and put these dry boxer shorts on, if you think you are steady enough now."

I just nod, and he turns and walks out of the bathroom, closing the door behind him. I quickly lose the wet underwear and pull on the boxers. They are way too big, and I have to get a tight grip on the front of them as I try to walk without them falling to the ground.

I can hear him on the phone as I shuffle into the open studio-style loft with a huge king-size bed in the middle, an open kitchen to the left, and a cozy living area to the right with a big stone fireplace and a large L-shaped couch. I love his place. It's big but cozy, and it fits him to a T.

I haven't been here in so long. For years, I would just pop in, and he and I would play video games or order pizza and binge-watch our favorite shows. Most of the time, Nicco was there, too, but sometimes, it was just the two of us. He has not invited me over since he started ignoring me. I miss it. It was an escape from my volatile home. I lost him that day. My friend, my bonus big brother. Gone.

Now, here we stand in the exact same room. He is right; I am still a little drunk. I can feel it, and my stomach is still very unhappy with me.

"Yep, every single one of us. I found her in the woods, drunk off her ass, with a bunch of older boys I did not recognize, about to go skinny-dipping in the springs. I know. Yeah, she's hurt, and I guess Adriana was just trying to cheer her up, but, for fuck's sake, they were getting wasted and voluntarily naked with complete strangers. Horny, drunk pricks."

Great, he is tattling on me.

"No, man, it's late. I will keep her here tonight. She has been puking up vodka for the better part of the last hour. I just wanted to warn you and see if you could intercept your mom when she realizes she is not home. Tell her she stayed with you at Marianna's apartment or something. Just put her off until tomorrow afternoon. I have a feeling she is gonna feel like ass in the morning. Yeah, me, too. I'll call you when we are up." He ends the call and looks up at me. "How are you feeling?"

I drop my eyes. "A little pathetic, to tell the truth."

I hear a chuckle, and then he says, "We have all been there before. Here, take these and drink this entire bottle of water."

My stomach churns at the thought, but I do as I was told.

"Now, bed."

I shuffle over, climb up the platform, and nestle in. It smells like him, and I sigh my pleasure. I love his smell. It is spicy and salty and all man.

A few moments later, I feel the dip in the bed, and I open my eyes to find Cross atop me. He has my arms pinned at the sides of my head, and his arms are locked in a push-up position. No part of him is touching any part of me, except his hands. I am confused and excited.

"What's happening?"

"Your first kiss," he answers as he lowers his lips to mine.

Just a gentle brush at first, and then a tug at my lower lip with his teeth. I gasp as a foreign sensation flushes my body. He takes the opportunity to enter my mouth. I don't know what to do. I can't think. All I can do is feel. As he moves his tongue with mine, gently at first and then with more urgency, I find my nerve, and I start to kiss him back. I don't even realize I am, but I start seeking his mouth more desperately. I want to touch him. I want to put my fingers in his hair and pull him to me, but he has my hands trapped, and my struggle is futile. He angles his head a little, and the kiss deepens. Every part of my body is on fire and longing to touch him or be touched by him. I plant my feet and arch up, so my aching breasts graze his chest, and I moan low in my throat at the pleasure that scores through me. Sweet agony.

Then, just like that, he is gone. He rockets off the bed and across the room. Disoriented and bereaved, I come up on my elbows and stare at him. He is standing there, against the wall, breathing heavy, with his hands in his hair. I have never seen anything sexier in my life. He drops his hands and meets my eyes.

"Don't go giving your kisses away to just anyone, Gabby. They are too precious, and you deserve better than some drunken make-out session with a random stranger. Promise me."

"I promise."

"Good. Now, get some sleep. That hangover is going to be intense in the morning," he says as he grabs a pillow and heads to the couch to settle in.

I decide right then and there that, that is the easiest promise I have ever made because I have no desire to kiss anyone else but him ever again.

CHAPTER

five

Brie

Present

I AM GETTING MY HANDS ON THAT BABY FOR THE FIRST TIME TODAY. I have looked forward to holding the tiny bundle in my arms all week. I love babies. I love the way they smell, the way they feel and sound, and I just melt when their tiny little hand wraps around my finger. God, I hope he likes me.

Little Cassian's mom and dad have a date night planned for his company's awards banquet, and afterward, they are staying at a resort hotel in Orange County for the night. That means, I am staying the night at their house, and I get twelve hours to bond with my new charge.

It is kind of crazy how excited I am to see a tiny human. It is like I am going on a first date.

Will he like me? Will he cry the moment he sees me? Is he gonna be traumatized when his mamma walks out the door? Am I going to know what to do if something goes wrong or if he gets sick in the night? All these questions are tumbling around in my head.

I have memorized both his parents' mobile numbers, the police department's number, the fire department's number, and the number to poison control. I can do this. Women take care of babies and live to tell the tale every single day. The fact that they are leaving their baby in the hands of a girl with zero experience in the childcare industry probably makes them nervous, too. I did, however, take a course back at home and became certified in infant care and CPR. I figured this was a good idea just in case the job at the club did not work out because California is full of mothers who either work all day or shop all day and need someone to raise their children for them, right?

Melanie White is neither of those moms. She and Rick are very nice, and I can tell she is a good mom and happy to be at home with her son, but everyone needs a break now and then. They are a good fit for me with my school and work schedule. I am so happy they are entrusting their baby boy to me. I do not take that gift lightly, and I will not let them or that little guy down.

"Oh my God, thank goodness you are here. I am running so late." Melanie opens the door as she juggles securing a sparkling earring to one of her earlobes. She is teetering on one stiletto heel. "Rick will be here any minute. Cassian was a little fussy and needed extra cuddles, so I wasn't able to get in the shower until fifteen minutes ago."

I can tell she is a bit frantic as I look around the living room strewed with discarded dresses and shoes. Being a new mommy has to be hard, even for the ones who stay home ninety percent of the time. Babies are time-consuming. I take a look around at the mess and decide I will help pick up once I get the baby down for the night. I can hear his unhappy cries coming from down the hall, and I follow the sound.

"I am going to go calm him down. You do what you need to do. Don't worry about us," I tell Melanie.

I receive her appreciative, "Okay. Thank you so much, Brie."

I find the nursery, and I am immediately enchanted. The walls are a pale blue-green, and one wall has a beautiful forest mural painted on it. It reminds me of my childhood. I loved the trees and earth and the sky and the animals. I walk over to the crib where all the scream-ing is coming from, and I look down into the most charming little, wet, bright red face. His tiny body is wiggling in discontent, and he is screeching his displeasure at being ignored loud enough for the neighbors to hear.

"Hey there, little guy. You sure seem a bit upset. Are you not getting enough attention from these stuffed lions and giraffes for your liking?"

He starts at the sound of my voice and then begins to settle.

His wails turn into whimpers as he looks up at me. I am not sure if he is old enough to be able to see my face clearly yet, but I know he can hear my soothing tone. I pick him up and snuggle him into the crook of my arm. I gently bounce him as I begin to sing an old Italian lullaby my nonna would sing to us when we were babies. He begins to coo up at me as his little eyelids start to droop. He is absolutely adorable. He has a dollop of dark hair on the top of his head and a deep dimple in his left cheek. I just want to pinch the cuteness. I am instantly in love.

"Oh, he likes you very much. Totally smitten."

I look up at Melanie, who is now completely pulled together and leaning against the doorframe, watching us. She looks stunning in her cocktail dress.

"The feeling is definitely mutual." I don't know why I was so unsure about this. I am certain this job is going to be the highlight of my new life.

After I have the baby fed, bathed, and peacefully asleep, I settle in on the oversize couch next to his bassinet and watch him sleep. I am vaguely aware that I won't sleep a wink tonight. I keep looking over to make sure his little chest is rising and falling like it should be. *How do new parents get any rest?* I am terrified to close my eyes.

I make my way to the kitchen to pop myself a bowl of popcorn, and then I grab the remote and settle in for a long night of late-night trash TV. I like this. Don't get me wrong; nights with my roommates are fabulous. They are fun. I finally feel like I am a part of a tribe. Living with them has been so much easier than I expected. I don't want to jinx myself, but between them, school, and this job, I am very content. That scares me because, every time I let myself fall into happy contentment, the floor always drops from beneath me. I don't want to be the girl who's always looking over her shoulder for the bad news lurking around the corner, but that is what this past year has reduced me to. What if it doesn't last?

I hear a little sigh from the bassinet and decide that I will not look for trouble anymore. If trouble is coming for me, it is going to have to look hard to find me.

The next morning, Melanie and Rick arrive home and regale me with stories of their adventurous night. I can tell they really enjoyed having some baby-free time together. It made me even prouder to be taking on this responsibility. I think parents who get plenty of planned alone time are able to recharge and be more focused parents. Little Cassian deserves nothing less than one hundred percent from all us adults in his life.

"How did it go with him last night?" Melanie asks as she scoops yogurt on top of a bowl of cut fruit and hands it over to me.

"It was wonderful. We cuddled and played a little, but he mostly just slept and pooped all evening, as four-month-olds do. He woke up at three a.m. and five a.m. for his bottles, and other than that, we had an uneventful night."

She nods. "He has been an easy baby so far. We are blessed. You know you are welcome to come by anytime, right? Even if we don't have anything in particular planned. Just come get a snuggle whenever you feel like you need one."

She knows this move has been hard on me. We talked in-depth about the changes I was making before I arrived. I like Melanie. She is easy to talk to, and she doles out sage advice. We became close friends while communicating before my move. She is more than my employer; she is a friend, and even though she is only ten years my senior, she is even kind of like a second mom.

As I say good-bye to the little family, I have a feeling of sadness wash over me. I miss my brothers. Yes, they are overbearing and even brutish at times, but they fiercely love me. All of them, especially Nicco. For all the grumbling and griping he did, being forced to have me tag along with him and his friends all those years, we actually grew to be quite close. He was my protector and my confidant. Families are hard sometimes. No one can make you happier or drive you crazier than your own flesh and blood. You know each other too well, and you know how to push each other's buttons. If only we could have stayed little. Chasing fireflies and wrecking bikes were our biggest worries. Everyone has to eventually grow up even if you have to be dragged into adulthood, kicking and screaming.

I take my phone out to call Nicco. I promised I would check in once I was settled. As much as I want as little contact as possible with them all, I still don't want them to worry. The call rings twice before my big brother's deep voice comes through.

"Hey, *cara*. Glad you finally decided to call your worried brother and let him know you were still breathing."

I knew he was going to get his shots in. Nicco is not a big fan of my life changes. He doesn't agree with running away from your problems. He thinks everyone should face them head-on and let them beat the absolute shit out of you in the process.

"Challenge makes you stronger, sis, and trying to outrun your problems isn't going to make them disappear."

That was his brilliant advice when my life imploded.

I never expected my problems to disappear. I wanted to disappear.

"When life flays you, you just stick it out and hope a thicker skin grows back in its place. It's our family's way," he said.

And he was right. It's how the women in our family have always lived. I have watched my mother turn the other cheek so many times, just to watch the shit get slapped out of the other a second later. I vowed a long time ago to never let that be me. I love my mother, but I do not respect her very much. Letting a man treat you like a piece of property he can rule over and letting him humiliate you time and again with his affairs and dismissal are not things to be proud of. She thinks it makes her a strong matriarch. I think it makes her seem weak. It is not something to pass down to your daughter like a fucking badge of honor. Although Lilliana Mastreoni likes to wear it like it is one. That would not be … could not be my life. I love my papa, and he has loved and doted on me my entire life, as I am his princess, but I hate so many things about him and the life he forces all of us to lead.

"Well, I am still breathing, big brother. Actually, I am quite happy here. I like my classes, and I have not one, but two awesome jobs and a couple of crazy-as-hell roommates. Life is shaping up pretty well here."

There is a long pause on the other end of the line. Then, "I am happy for you, sis. I just wish you had found that here. I miss your bratty face. We all do. I think Tony is eating his feelings. You should see the weight he has put on since you left. Total blubber butt now."

I laugh at his attempt to be funny. Tony is a gym rat. Completely obsessed with his muscles that one.

"So, you think you are there to stay, huh?" I can hear the sadness in his voice.

"Yeah, Nicco, I am here to stay. Be happy for me, please. You are more than welcome to come visit me. I wouldn't be opposed to that. Maybe in the spring?"

"A visit? You are going to allow me to come see you? Won't that blow your cover?"

"I am not in the Witness Protection Program, Nicco. I just changed my name and moved to a new city. I can have a brother visit. Just keep New York in New York."

"Got it."

"So, spring?"

"Yeah, sis, spring."

CHAPTER
Six

Gabby
Past

I STAND IN FRONT OF THE MIRROR AND STARE AT MYSELF. My long dark brown hair is in a cascade of curls flowing down my back. I am aglow with a smokey eye, and my high cheekbones are highlighted, courtesy of the makeup artist Papa hired to do my and Mamma's faces. The red two-piece cocktail dress I am wearing is halter style in the front and fits my figure perfectly, hugging my chest and cut low in the back. It shows a sliver of my stomach, and then the separate skirt swings out into a flattering, full A-line. I love it. I twirl around and let the skirt fly out around me. I feel beautiful.

Papa felt so bad last year when they forgot about my birthday that he has spent the last twelve months spoiling me rotten, trying to make up for it. It is no longer necessary. I forgave them all the instant I realized how truly sorry they were. My knucklehead brothers have done pretty much the same. I might complain about them, but nothing beats being their baby sister. They are overprotective and a little bossy sometimes, but they fiercely love me, and I am truly blessed.

Tonight, Papa is throwing me a Christmas/winter wonderland–themed party for my seventeenth birthday. I love Christmas, and being as my birthday is November 28, it's easy to combine my two favorite things. Basically, the whole of October through New Year's Eve is a celebration for me. Everyone is coming tonight. All of my friends and a lot of Papa's business acquaintances. He never misses an opportunity to schmooze them. I don't mind really. As long as I get to dance the night away, the more, the merrier is my motto.

I walk downstairs, and all of my brothers are waiting in the foyer, decked out in their black-tie best. What a ridiculously handsome lot they are. All of my friends are going to faint on the spot with the four of them arriving at the same time. Papa and Mamma come down a moment later. She looks splendid in her sapphire-blue gown.

Papa eyes me up and down as he walks over to kiss my cheek. "The wolves will surely be circling my baby girl tonight. You boys had better be on high alert." He gives his command. His thick Italian accent breaking through.

A chorus of agreement comes from the foyer, and I roll my eyes.

"Please, Papa, don't get them riled up before I have a chance to even dance my first dance. You will have me standing alone in a corner all night."

"Not a chance, *bella*. Your dance card will be most definitely full tonight; I am sure. Shall we?" He holds both his elbows out for me and Mamma to place our arms in, and he leads us to the awaiting car.

My brothers follow us in a car of their own, and I am buzzing with excitement as we make the trek into Manhattan to Papa's country club. He rented the entire club for the night and had a party planner do all the decorations. The club itself is catering, and my favorite local band will be playing as well as a DJ for part of the night. I am so happy. I just know this is going to be a night to remember.

"You are here. Wow, look at you!" Adriana is waiting for us as we pull up to the valet. She is in a mini black cocktail dress and mile-high heels. Her black hair is in an updo, and her lips are a startling bright red against her pale skin.

"I am. How does everything look inside?"

"Like a fairy tale. Your papa really outdid himself. I have been racking my brain, trying to think of something I can hang over my papa's head to guilt him into a shindig like this for my eighteenth next year."

"Your parents always spoil you rotten, Adi. You are crazy."

Never one to be outdone, she continues to brainstorm. "True. Maybe I will just ask for them to spring for all my friends and me to fly to Bora Bora or something for my birthday."

When we enter the club, we are met with an enormous Christmas tree glittering with red and green and gold ornaments and twinkling white lights. The banister of the grand staircase leading up to the ballroom floor is entwined with fresh garland on both sides and wrapped with large red ribbons. Christmas music is playing, and guests are meandering about with glasses in hand. We climb the marble steps and make our way into the ballroom, and my jaw drops.

The event planner really outdid herself. It's breathtaking from the ice-blue and snow-white floral arrangements to the enormous willow tree branches draped in icicle lights and faux snow sprinkled around the walkways between the tables and around the dance floor.

A winter wonderland, just as I pictured. I am so filled with elation; I can hardly contain myself. I turn, and Papa is propped in the entryway, watching to see my reaction. I run to him and into his arms.

"Are you pleased, *bella*?"

"Oh, Papa, it is more beautiful than I imagined. Thank you so much."

He kisses the top of my head. "You are so welcome, my dear. Now, go and enjoy your night, but remember to save your papa a dance."

He walks back out, and I make a turn about the room to say hello to everyone. I spot Dante at a table and stop.

After our first meeting last year, he called and asked me out on an official date, but my brothers instantly shut him down. As far as I know, Cross and Nicco kept the drunken skinny-dipping incident to themselves, but they felt a twenty-year-old was much too old to be dating their sixteen-year-old sister. Big brothers. What are you gonna do? Rather than be annoyed, I was kind of relieved they'd stepped in.

Dante is nice enough and quite attractive, but there is something about him that makes the warning alarms go off in my head. I can't put my finger on it. It is just instinctual. He is a little dangerous. Then again, it could all be in my head because Cross planted it there that night.

"Hi, Dante. Glad you could make it."

"Thank you for inviting me." He looks me up and down and wickedly licks his lips. "Don't you look stunning tonight?"

I blush at the compliment. I might think he is dangerous, but every girl likes to hear she has hit the mark when getting dolled up.

"Thank you. I hope you enjoy yourself."

"Oh, I intend to."

I start to walk away, but he reaches and gently tugs my wrist.

"Dance with me tonight?"

"Sure. I am going to finish greeting everyone and grab a glass of punch. I'll be right back."

I try to speak to everyone as I make my way back out and down the stairs. I want to powder my nose and then eat a little something before I go back up. On my way down, I run into Cross—literally. I trip on the step and stumble right down into his back.

"Whoa there. Steady." He turns and clasps my shoulders to brace me.

"Oops. I haven't drunk a drop either. Imagine once I am tipsy," I joke.

I haven't drunk a drop since he found me and nursed me through my first hangover. It was awful. Why would anyone continue to do that to themselves?

"Oh, I don't have to imagine."

"Joking," I concede as I put my arms in the air in surrender. "I gave up the life of reckless, drunken nights over a year ago."

I take him in. He is in a black tux that is tailored to fit him perfectly. His dark hair is still a touch beyond needing a cut, and the dimple on his left cheek is showing as he grins down at me. His green eyes are dancing in the twinkling lights, and they are mesmerizing.

"Scutari, look up!" someone yells from the bottom of the stairs.

Both our eyes follow everyone else's gaze up into the air where a mistletoe is hanging down in the middle of the staircase from a red velvet rope. Right above our heads.

I swear, I feel my entire body flush with embarrassment as they all start chanting, "Kiss, kiss, kiss," over and over.

My eyes return to Cross, and I am sure he can read the panic all over me.

He lifts his hands to the sides of my face and gently tilts it up to his. "Relax, *Tesoro*. It's just a Christmas tradition," he whispers right before his lips connect with mine.

I am instantly liquid. He moves one of his hands to the small of my back to support me, and the movement deepens the kiss. As his touch hits the skin above my skirt, an electric current slivers down my spine, and I instinctively lift my arms and wrap them around his neck. I open my mouth and melt into the kiss. He pulls me in even closer until I am tucked tightly against him. It's like our audience just fades away, and it's only us on the staircase.

I haven't been kissed since that night at his loft. I have been starved for it. I dream about kissing him every time I close my eyes at night. Every part of me has longed to be in his arms. I know it's wrong. I know he is twenty-five, and I am seventeen. I know he is my brother's best friend, and Tony would kill him. I know he only thinks of me as a little sister. I know all the reasons, and I don't care. I want him … want this so badly.

I am not sure how long we put on a show—it could not have been but a few moments—but the sound of catcalls from the people who have gathered draw me back to reality, and I pull back. Breathless and a little disoriented, I look around at all the cheering faces. All, except four, that is. My brothers are among the crowd gathered at the foot of the stairs, and their expressions are a mixture of anger and confused amusement. I guess that kiss looked as scandalous as it felt.

"Wipe that guilty look off your face and laugh for them, Gabby."

I do as he said as he addresses the crowd, "You guys just wait. I am going to stand at the foot of these stairs all night long and make sure every single one of you is forced into a kiss. Thank goodness Gabby here was the one caught with me and was a good sport. I hope you assholes aren't so lucky."

Everyone roars with laughter as he descends the stairs. I look around, and even my brothers' suspicious glares have dissipated.

Did I imagine how hot that kiss was? Because Cross doesn't seem the least bit affected. Maybe I did.

On shaky legs, I head down to the food to grab something to eat and drink and compose myself. I have got to get over this infatuation before I make a huge fool of myself.

CHAPTER
Seven

Present

WHEN I WALK IN FROM MY OVERNIGHT WITH LITTLE CASSIAN, Dawn is perched on the couch, still in her pajamas, waiting for Kelsey to wake up.

"My head hurts, and it's not even the good kind of *I partied my ass off last night, and I deserve this misery* headache," Dawn whines from her spot on the couch.

Apparently, the girls had as sleepless a night as I did with the baby, although theirs wasn't as uneventful. They went out to a nightclub on Sunset where Daniel and his band were scheduled to play as a last-minute replacement.

They just settled into their booth when Kelsey spotted her boyfriend, Bradley, across the room, waiting at the bar. He was supposed to be in Temecula with his parents at his aunt and uncle's thirtieth wedding anniversary party. Confused but happy to see him, she headed over to him. That was when a girl approached him from the side and whispered something into his ear. He wrapped his arm around her waist and pulled her up close before kissing her and handing her one of the drinks he had ordered.

Kels saw red, especially when the scantily clad companion turned her head toward the stage as the band was announced, and she got a good look at her face. Tonya. Kelsey barreled toward the pair. Bradley caught her before her fist connected with its intended target. He picked her up over his shoulder and fireman-carried her back up to the booth, leaving the seething backstabber at the bar. Chaos ensued, and Dawn, Kels, and Bradley were asked to leave halfway through Daniel's band's first set.

I make us a pot of coffee and sit with her as she fills me in on the rest of their night.

"It was a terrible Uber ride home. I felt so bad for the driver. I had hopped up front, and Kels and Brad were in the back. She was screaming mad. He told her that he had gotten the weekends mixed up and the anniversary party was actually two weeks from now. When he realized the mistake, he decided to get some study time in Saturday afternoon, so he could spend Saturday night with her. He lost track of time, and by the time he came by our place, we were gone. So, he headed to Sunset to see if he could catch up with us. He was at the bar about thirty minutes when Tonya came in. He said it was a coincidence. She asked him to buy her a drink while she went to the ladies' room, and that was when we came in. He said he saw us and that he was headed our way when Tonya came by to get her drink. She pulled him into an embrace and gave him a quick, friendly peck to thank him. He swore Kels had overreacted." She takes a break in the story to take a sip from her mug. Then, she continues, "He is such a lying sack of shit. Even if he really did mix up the weekends, why wouldn't he have just called Kels and told her?"

I stop her there. "Why didn't he take Kels with him to his aunt and uncle's party?"

"Oh, that's another thing. He told her his mom had said it was a small event space, and they were inviting family only." She rolls her eyes, as if to say, *Yeah, right.*

She gets up to grab a bagel out of the box I picked up on my way home.

She tears a piece off and pops it in her mouth as I ask, "Do his parents not like her?"

"They love her. That's why I am not buying the whole family-only thing. They consider Kels family. So, anyway, like I said, why not call and tell her about the mix-up? Then, he said he came by here and just missed us and headed to the Strip to catch up to us. First of all, how in the hell did he know where we were or where we were headed? We hadn't known anything about Daniel's gig until Saturday morning; plus, he was already at the damn club, ordering drinks when we arrived. We went straight there. No way he could have come here, found us gone, and then beat us to the club, much less in enough time to get there, accidentally run into Tonya—the traitor—and get drinks."

I just sit there, nodding in agreement at the twisted story.

"And, Brie, I saw that kiss, and that wasn't a friendly thank-you kiss. He pulled her into him, and he kissed her. They were there together. It was so flipping obvious."

Damn it, I hate this for Kelsey. She is crazy about Bradley.

They met when she changed high schools after her mom married Uncle Matt, and they moved from downtown Los Angeles to Beverly Hills. Apparently, he instantly liked her, but she was still seeing a guy from her old school at the time, so he was friend-zoned. They reconnected when he started working at the coffee shop his parents opened near the campus of California State. They started dating shortly afterward and have been together ever since. That was over a year ago, and she is now head over heels in love with him. He and Daniel have become friends, and the four of them do just about everything together. When Tonya moved in, she became the fifth wheel, and apparently, she wasn't happy with that position.

Oh God, I think to myself. *Am I the fifth wheel now?*

Dawn finishes with her story as we both eat.

"So, when we made it back here, I called him out on all his bullshit because she wasn't. He started backpedaling, saying he had heard somewhere that Daniel's band would be filling in, but he could not recall where he'd heard it, so he assumed that was where we were headed, and he hadn't called because he wanted to surprise her. It was all just more bullshit piled on top of bullshit, but I could tell Kelsey was trying to make it work in her head so that she could let herself believe him. She finally told him to leave because she needed a little time to think. He wasn't happy about it, but he got in a taxi and took off at about three a.m. Asshole probably had it take him straight to whatever evil lair Tonya lives in now. That fake bitch. I swear, I wish I had throat-punched her for Kels when we were in the club. I mean, hell, we ended up getting kicked out anyway."

As I sit here, listening to Dawn rage, I realize that maybe the ugly isn't my favorite part after all. My heart aches for my new friend. There is nothing like thinking your life and relationship are perfect and then finding out it is a lie. A girl gets a serious case of whiplash, going from blissfully happy to utterly devastated in a matter of seconds.

We finish our breakfast and watch three episodes of our latest Netflix obsession while we wait for Kelsey to emerge from her bedroom. She finally walks into the living room, looking like the walking dead, a little after noon. She doesn't say a word. She just sits on the couch and lays her head on my shoulder. I reach up and start running my fingers through her hair, and we start the next episode. The three of us watch mindless television for the rest of the afternoon. I know what it is like to need people close but to need them to give you space, all at the same time, so you can figure out your next move. I look over at Dawn, and we silently agree to do that for her.

CHAPTER
Eight

Gabby
Past

I AM STANDING AT ONE OF THE HIGH-TOP TABLES IN THE BALLROOM, resting my feet for a few minutes. I have danced the night away. Adriana keeps making her way to the band to make song requests. It's her sixth or seventh trip. She has her sights set on the lead vocalist, and she will find any excuse to go whisper in his ear. God only knows what she is whispering other than song requests.

"I have come to collect," a voice demands from behind me.

I turn to find Dante standing there with his hand outstretched to me.

"Collect?"

"Yes, ma'am. I do believe the birthday princess promised me a dance."

I stand there for a moment, debating on whether or not I should take his hand. There is just something about him that raises the hair on the back of my neck. Ever since that night in the woods, he has found reasons to unexpectedly show up where I am, and he always looks at me so intensely. I am sure it's just my imagination running wild because he has always been perfectly nice. Maybe it's my own embarrassment from that night that bothers me, and I am just projecting it on him. As the first notes of my favorite Ed Sheeran song start to play, I decide to just let it go, and I take his hand and follow him to the dance floor.

"You look stunning tonight." He gives me a quick twirl before pulling me in close to his body.

"Thank you. You clean up nice yourself."

He is a really good dancer, which is a relief. I have had the hardest time following the lead of most of the guys here tonight, and in some cases, I had to take over the lead. My poor toes have suffered greatly.

"To be fair, the last time we spent any time together, we were in the woods in November. Hoodies and jeans aren't my usual attire. If you would agree to go out on a real date with me, you would know this."

"I told you, I don't date."

"And why is that exactly?"

"It's called an overprotective papa and four large, scary big brothers." I laugh, but it is oh so true.

"Your brothers don't scare me, Gabby."

"Then, I worry about your sanity because they should."

"I am perfectly sane. I am just not afraid to go after something when I want it." He moves my hair and brings his mouth close to my ear. "And I very much want you. I haven't been able to stop thinking about you since that night."

The song ends as he makes his declaration, and everyone starts to clap for the band. We separate, and he gives me a little wink and kisses my hand before he turns to walk off the dance floor. I am a little taken aback by his boldness.

I turn to return to my table, and my eye catches what appears to be a very unhappy Cross standing against the wall, watching me. I begin walking toward him, and he stands up and puts his hands in his pockets. He glares at my approach, and then he walks right past me and out the door.

What is wrong with him?

I follow him out and down a dark hallway leading away from the ballroom and stairway. He darts out of sight, and I hurry after him.

About five feet in, a hand reaches out and grabs me, pulling me into a room about the size of my bedroom. It's dark, except for the faint glow of the Exit sign above the door. He shuts the door hard once he has me inside and whirls on me.

Angry. He is angry. Why?

I open my mouth to ask, and he starts to advance on me before I get a single word out. He wraps his hand in my hair at the back of my head and tugs hard. Then, he slams his lips on mine. This kiss is not like the one before. This kiss is wild and claiming. I open to him, and he starts to back me up until my back is against the far wall. He bends, and I follow as he places his hands on my waist and hoists me up. My legs instantly wrap around him. We are all hands and mouth and friction. I can feel his weight between my legs as he pushes deeper into me. I don't understand what is happening, but I do know that I don't want it to stop. I never want it to stop.

He wrenches his lips from mine, and he watches as his hand moves down the front of my halter top and across the silk bodice at the top of my breasts. My chest is rising and falling to meet his hand. He gently tugs the ribbon that is tied around my neck, holding the top in place, and it falls, exposing my lacy corset bra. He bites his bottom lip as he runs his knuckles across the swell. Then, he hooks a finger into the edge and pulls it low enough for my breasts to spill over the top. He dips his head and gently takes a nipple into his mouth. *Oh my.* I groan as pleasure shoots through me at the contact. He licks and then lightly blows a hot breath across each breast until my nipples are hard pink peaks. Then, he nips and sucks one breast as he kneads and caresses the other. He switches his attention from right to left. I am lost. No one has ever touched me this way.

I am writhing in his arms. I can feel pressure building in my center and a fierce need pulsing through me. I arch my back, and I start to move back and forth, reaching for connection where I need it the most. He places his hands under my ass and lifts me higher till we are hip-to-hip, and finally, I am where I want to be. I can feel him hard beneath me, and I start sliding against the seam of his trousers, using the wall at my back as support. He still has his mouth at my breasts, and the combination is mind-numbing. I start moving faster, reaching for something else and not knowing exactly what that is. He feels my need getting more and more urgent, and he moves his hand around and under my skirt.

He growls, "Fuck, Gabby. You are wet for me, baby."

For a moment, I wonder if that is a bad thing, but I am too far gone to care. I start moving against his hand and whimper. I need his hand to move. I need him to touch me. I need. I need. I need.

"Shit, baby, it's okay. I got you," he whispers as he pulls the hem of my panties aside and glides his finger through my folds.

It feels so good, and I think I might come right out of my skin. Then, he moves his thumb to the bud that is throbbing and gives it the attention it is seeking.

"Yes, Cross," I say shakily, "right there. I need you to—" My words die on a moan as he applies more pressure.

Then, he slides a finger inside me and starts to swirl it so deliciously. I rock on his hand. Reaching for something. My entire body is reaching. Then, he adds another finger, and it happens. I crest the wave that I have been riding. All of a sudden, my legs start to shake around him, and an explosion of sensations starts rocketing through the lower half of my body.

"That's it, baby. Take what you need," he says softly.

Then, he covers my mouth with his as I scream out his name in pure pleasure. Nothing has ever felt this good. Nothing could ever feel this good again.

He holds me tight against him until the quaking subsides.

We stand there, quiet, with nothing but the sounds of our racing hearts and the mingling of our heavy breaths.

"Fuck," he murmurs into my hair. Then, after a few heartbeats, he leans back and booms, "FUCK!" as he drops me on my unsteady legs.

He backs away and starts to pace with his head down and his eyes closed tight.

"Fuck, this can't happen, Gabby."

Tears prick the backs of my eyes as I take in the panic on his face. This did happen. *Did he not want it? Does he not want me?*

"I shouldn't have pulled you in here. I saw you dancing with that asshole from the springs, and I just lost it. He had you in his arms. He was holding you way too fucking close, and you were letting him," he accuses.

"We were just dancing," I whisper into the room as he continues pacing and ranting.

"I didn't like it. I don't like other men looking at you like that. I don't like them thinking they can touch you that way."

"He wasn't touching me in any way, Cross. We were just dancing."

"He wants to touch you."

"Doesn't mean he gets to."

"But he can. He can ask you out and take you to dinner and the movies. He can hold you, dance with you, and kiss you when he brings you home. I can't."

"Why not?"

"Because you are seventeen and I am twenty-five and your brothers would kill me and I wouldn't blame them."

I can feel my lips quivering as the weight of what he is saying settles between us. He thinks I am a child, and whatever this was, was just his reaction to Dante.

I have to get out of this room. I have to get out of the room right now.

I fly toward the door as he tries to stop me, and I burst into the hallway. I need air. I need somewhere private to let the tears out. I run toward the back stairwell and down to the ladies' locker room. It's empty, so I let my emotions loose. I sob for what feels like forever, and I realize I am too exhausted to go back out there.

I went from elated to broken in a matter of minutes. I think I am partied out, and I just want to go home and curl up in my bed. I gather myself and fix my hair and makeup as best I can. I head back upstairs to find Adi and tell her I am leaving.

I silently make my way toward the front of the club and back around to the staircase. I want to get in and out as quickly as possible, and hopefully, if I keep my head down, no one will notice my disheveled appearance. As I get to the bottom of the steps, I see a group of my brothers' friends congregated together.

Great. So much for getting out without being seen.

I dart to the side, out of sight, to come up with a new strategy when I catch a hint of their conversation.

"I don't know, man. That kiss looked like more than just a friendly Christmas kiss to me."

"Yeah, it was pretty hot. Looked like you were into it. For a minute there, I thought you might throw her over your shoulder and carry her out of the place."

"Hey, that's my sister you're talking about," I hear Stavros interject.

"Come on, Stav; you saw it. Your little sister doesn't look too little anymore in that dress, and I think our man Cross here noticed, too."

I know they are just teasing, but it's dangerous to tease one of my brothers. They can be volatile, and I worry a brawl is about to break out.

"Shut up, Conti. I only kissed her to save her from embarrassment after you jackasses pointed out that mistletoe. You guys know, she is like a sister to me, too. And don't get it twisted. I know she is just a little girl playing dress-up in that dress. Stop being stupid and acting like it was more. The thought actually makes me sick."

Every word out of his mouth hits me like a physical blow. I move slightly, so I see them better to make sure it is actually him saying these horrible things. His eyes fall on mine as I step out of the shadow, and I freeze. Just for a few beats. I stare at him, and the mortification washes over me as my heart breaks in two. I turn calmly on my stilettoed feet and make my way to the entrance of the club.

I have to get out of here right now.

CHAPTER
Nine

Brie
Present

BRADLEY CALLED KELS AND BEGGED HER TO GO TO DINNER WITH him and talk. She had been ignoring his calls all day, and they had been coming in about every thirty minutes for hours. She'd finally picked up and told him to come get her at six.

Dawn starts to protest, but Kels just holds up her hand.

"I have to face it eventually, and it might as well be tonight. I am not stupid, Dawn. I know when I am being lied to, but I don't know what I am going to do yet. I haven't decided if I can or will forgive him. Whichever I choose though, you will have to accept it and do the same."

Dawn groans and walks over to tightly squeeze her best friend. "I'll follow your lead on this one even if I don't like your choice. But, if I accidentally kick him in the balls as we pass in the hall one morning, you will have to accept it and move on as well."

I can see Kelsey's shoulders shaking with laughter, and I know, whatever she decides, they will be just fine. I really hope she walks away now. I can tell Dawn doesn't trust him anymore, and if she were honest with herself, Kelsey probably doesn't either. In my experience, your friends are usually a better judge than you are when blinded by your feelings, and the longer you wait, the harder it is to let go. Trust is something we give pretty freely, but once someone destroys it, it takes an act of God to repair.

I talk Dawn into getting out of the apartment, so she won't be tempted to do her kicking-balls-in-the-hall trick when Bradley comes to pick Kels up. She accompanies me to the country club, so I can check out the lay of the land.

It is a beautiful club. A bit larger than the one we are members of in New York. It has a couple of enormous and elegant ballrooms for events, a restaurant, a full bar, large outdoor patio space with options for dining, his and her locker rooms for members, an indoor pool, two outdoor pools, four tennis courts, and an impressive golf clubhouse, pro shop, and pristine golf course.

Everything the upper echelon of greater Los Angeles could want in a club.

I find my employee locker and pick up the parking pass for my assigned space. Then, we grab dinner. I can't wait to get started tomorrow night. It has been a while since I lost myself in any good physical activity, and this is the perfect way to get back at it. Being paid to do so.

"Are there any famous members here—you know, like movie stars?" I ask.

"A few." She shrugs. "To be honest, if they are famous enough for you to know who they are, then they probably have all the amenities this place has to offer at their own home."

"Makes sense."

"You aren't one of those creepy celebrity stalkers, are you?" she asks with wide eyes.

"No." I throw a grape at her. "Unless we are talking Jason Momoa because I'd climb that man like a tree. I wouldn't even mind paying the bail money."

"Touché," she agrees, and we clink our wine glasses.

As we are leaving, we are stopped by a guy who obviously knows Dawn.

I learned on our way over that Dawn and her parents have been members of the club for as long as she can remember, and apparently, so are Kelsey and her mom and Uncle Matt and Daniel.

Great, just my luck that I get to work for them.

Not really. Kelsey's mom is the only one who has any interest in tennis, but the point is, I will be wearing an employee name tag, and they will be wearing swimsuits and lounging by the pool. It's crazy how the tides in your life can switch directions so drastically. Luckily, I am sure my friends will never make me feel beneath them in any way. Besides, Daniel worked at the club as a lifeguard for a few summers when he was in high school to earn extra cash. It's nothing to be ashamed of.

"Hey, Jake. This is our new roommate, Brie. She is the club's newest tennis instructor, so we came by to let her get a look around before she gets started tomorrow after class. Brie, this is Jacob Mason. He is the son of Oscar Mason, the producer, who happens to be the president of the club's board."

Jake takes my hand. "It is very nice to meet you, Brie. Good to see that Cloniger is hiring a few people in our age group to liven the old, stuffy place up a bit."

He smiles a brilliant smile at me, and I have to admit, I am dazzled for a moment. He has a chiseled jawline and sky-blue eyes. His hair is golden with streaks of light blond that I am sure have come from the sun and not the salon. He is tall with broad shoulders, and he is in fantastic shape. Courtesy of the racket I see in his left hand I am sure.

"Maybe I should take a lesson or two once you get settled. I am a racquetball man myself, but some time on the tennis court could only improve my game."

I find myself liking that idea very much, which is dangerous.

"Sure thing," is the only reply I can manage as I turn to Dawn. "Let's go. I think we should check in on Kels."

"Yes, ma'am. See you later, Jake. You behave yourself."

"I always do."

"Sure you do."

We say our good-byes and head back to Santa Monica. On the drive back, I silently berate myself. I will not be sidetracked by a single smile.

When we arrive at the apartment, we find Kelsey and Bradley on the couch, watching a movie. I guess the talk went in his favor after all. I sure hope she knows what she is doing. Dawn is not in a very accepting mood at the moment, so after a few niceties are exchanged, she excuses herself to her room to study. Not her usual Sunday evening activity. I open a bottle of Sancerre and settle in to finish watching the movie. I figure Kelsey needs the backup, and honestly, as much as I hoped it would go the other way, who am I to judge anyone for the relationship choices they make? I just hope that Bradley uses this opportunity to get himself in check. Sometimes, the possibility of losing something you love can kick your balls into your throat as easily as a pissed-off roommate's foot. After the movie is over, I gather our empty glasses and head to the kitchen. Kelsey follows me, out of Bradley's earshot.

"I guess Dawn is pissed at me now. I was expecting it, but I figured she would just give us both some shit and then sit down and get over it."

I can see the unease etched on her face, and I assume that she and Dawn probably do not have disagreements very often.

"I don't think she's so much pissed off as she is worried. Well, at least, not pissed at you. She doesn't want you to get hurt. That's what true friends do. They worry when they think you are going down the wrong road, and truthfully, that is what you want in a friend. One who cares that much about your happiness because, if they don't, then you end up with a friend like Tonya. I wouldn't worry. You guys are going to be fine, and as long as that man of yours keeps whatever promises he made to you tonight, they will be fine, too. He'll have to prove it to her, but after a while, she'll forgive him if you forgive him."

She smiles a relieved smile. "Thanks, Brie. I think you have gotten to know us all pretty well in the few weeks you have been here. We sure are lucky you needed a place to stay. A sane voice of reason is nice to have around."

She returns to Bradley, and the pair of them head off to bed. She is wrong; I am far from the voice of reason. I am usually the one making the wrong choices. Isn't it funny how we are all so wise when dispensing advice to our friends and all shit at taking it when we are the ones in need of it?

CHAPTER
Ten

Gabby
Past

I RUN ACROSS THE FRONT ROOM OF THE CLUB AND TOWARD THE EXIT. I need to get out of here. Now. I can feel the hot, angry tears streaming down my face. I don't want anyone to see me. When I reach outside, the valet stands from behind his podium.

"Miss Mastreoni, are you ready for your car, ma'am?"

Papa and Mamma left the party about an hour ago and sent the car and driver back for me.

"Yes, please."

"Joe went to grab a snack across the street. I don't think he expected you to be leaving for some time. If you wait here, I will go get him. It will be just a few moments."

"Please tell him I am sorry, but I am not feeling well and think it's best if I go now. Thank you."

I bend at the waist and start gasping in the cool air. I am so upset; I actually feel nauseous. I hear the doors swing open behind me, and I turn to face him. I knew he would follow me.

"Don't. Just go back inside and leave me alone."

"Damn it, Gabby. That wasn't what it sounded like."

"Really? Because I am pretty sure you just told everyone that kissing me was like kissing your own sister and that it made you want to vomit."

He holds his hands up in a placating manner as he starts to approach me. I start walking backward so that he can't reach me until I am up against the curb.

"Yeah, I did, but it was to protect you. They were getting the wrong idea about you, and I didn't want them spreading rumors about you or for untrue gossip to reach your father's or your brothers' ears."

"You weren't protecting me. You were protecting yourself. You don't want your friends to think you actually like this silly little girl."

"That is not true."

"You know what? You don't ever have to worry about this silly little girl again. I hate you. You've ruined everything. This night was supposed to be special. I got all dressed up in this pretty dress that my papa bought me. I love it, and I feel beautiful in it even if you do think it looks like I am just a child playing dress-up. All I wanted to do was dance the night away, and now, all I want to do is go home."

"Don't go. Come back in and enjoy your party."

The car pulls up to the curb.

"Please, Gabby. Stay. Let's sit down and talk. I know I handled it poorly earlier. I was angry with myself for letting things go that far, not at you. I just ... you twist me up. I needed to get out of that room before I did something I couldn't take back. I got carried away. Fuck, you drive me mad, and you are worth more than a dry-hump in a fucking coat closet."

About that time, Nicco comes bursting through the doors. "What's going on? The driver called and said he was picking you up because you were sick."

"She's fine now. I am trying to talk her into rejoining the party. Can you give us a minute?"

Nicco looks back and forth between us. What a sight I must be. With my hair all a mess and makeup smeared with tears streaming down my face. If he hasn't already figured us out, I bet he is about to.

"No, I don't think I will."

"Please, Nicco. Five minutes. We need five minutes."

"No, we don't. I am done. So done." And, with that, I hop into the back seat of the car and tell the driver to take me home.

Mamma is waiting in the kitchen when I walk in the back door. She changed out of her gown and into a silk pajama set. She opens her arms wide, and I walk into them and start to cry once again. She smooths my hair and holds me until the tears begin to subside.

"There, there, now, baby. No boy is worth this kind of misery."

"How did you know?"

"Joe called and said he was bringing you home and that you said you were sick, but you appeared to be upset and crying. I assumed it was because of a boy. Most tears are."

"Oh, Mamma, I feel so stupid. I thought … I thought …"

"You thought Christoff would take one look at you in that dress and fall madly in love."

I purse my trembling lips and look up at her.

"My dear, it's no secret to any of us. We all know how you feel about him. At first, it was the cute little crush of a four-year-old. I thought it would go away, but I have seen how it has grown stronger and changed into more than a crush the past few years."

"He thinks I am still a silly little girl."

"Oh, but he doesn't. He sees you. But he is also eight years older than you. He is an adult, and he has been one for quite some time. You just turned seventeen. He is a man, and you are technically still a girl. I know it hurts, but he is trying to do the right thing."

"But I am not a little girl anymore. I am growing up, and no one wants to see it. Not him. Not my brothers. They can't keep me little forever."

"You are on the cusp, darling. We all see it. The boys are never going to like it. You will always be their baby sister, but they will learn to accept it. Now, Christoff is different. He sees it, and it's confusing him. It's written all over him."

"I love him, and I don't think he is ever going to love me. Not the way I want him to. I wish I could fall out of love with him, but I can't. I don't know how. How do I do that? What do I do, Mamma?"

She pours us each a cup of hot chocolate she has simmering on the stove. Ever since I was little, she would soothe my pains with homemade cocoa.

"Gabby, you are a young woman, and I am going to be frank with you. You know that Christoff's father and your father are in business together. You also know that what your father does for a living isn't exactly on the up-and-up. Your brothers and, one day, Christoff will join the family businesses, as sons are supposed to do."

She is looking at her hands wrapped around the handle of her mug and not in my eyes as she continues, "I have always loved being your father's wife, and being your and the boys' mother has been my greatest joy. But I will not lie to you. It is not easy to love a man in this world. I know you see the way he hurts me, and you wonder why I put up with it. I was raised in this life. I was taught a woman takes good care of her family and her husband and looks the other way when he does something she doesn't like. To always bend to his will and always show him respect.

"I do not want this life for you, my darling girl. I want you to find a man who will love you and always put your happiness before his own. Before everything. Christoff is a good man ... for now ... but I am afraid that, if his father gets him involved with the business, he, too, will become someone you do not recognize.

"I think you should get away for a little while. Separate yourself and get some perspective. The world is vast and full of potential. Maybe time and space will help you fall out of love with him. I think we should send you to your aunt Mitzi for a year abroad. In fact, I think you should go right away. I can have a ticket booked for you tonight and have you on a plane first thing in the morning. You already have enough credits to finish high school at the end of December, and we can have anything you need to finish up forwarded to you in Paris. I think a fresh start is just what you need."

I don't want to go. I don't want any of this, but she is right. As long as I am here, I will never be able to let go of him. Seeing him almost daily. Watching as he dates other girls. Feeling that pull between us, knowing that he doesn't feel the same or he doesn't want to. It just breaks my heart over and over again. I need time and distance.

"Okay, Mamma. If you think that's for the best, I will go."

"I think, once you are there, you might fall in love with Paris and never want to come home."

I can tell my decision has thrilled her, and she is right about one thing. I will never be the woman who allows herself to be mistreated. I will never be the one waiting at home while my husband is out, doing dangerous or illegal things. I will not be the one broken by his affairs or his dismissal. If that is Cross's fate, I need to get far, far away from him right now. I have to.

I head upstairs to pack for my new adventure. I am emotionally spent, and I just want to crawl into my bed and sleep for days; however, my flight leaves at dawn, so I have to get ready. Mamma said to pack a light suitcase, and she would send everything else I needed next week. I am almost finished when I hear someone knocking at the back door. I sneak down the stairs and hide out of sight.

"Come in. I was expecting you."

"Mrs. Mastreoni, I know it's really late, but I was wondering if I could speak to Gabriella for a moment."

"Sit down, Christoff. Let's have a chat."

I hear the scrape of the barstools across the floor. I turn to walk back upstairs and let Mamma deal with him. I don't have the energy.

After what feels like an eternity, I hear the back door shut, and I move quietly to my window and look out. He is walking toward his car with his head down. Right before he reaches it, he stops and turns around. He looks up and scans the second floor until he finds my window. My lights are off, and I move slightly to the right to make sure I am out of sight. He stares at me, not seeing me, but still looking right at me for what feels like forever. The look on his face is sheer agony, the same agony that is slicing through me. He lifts his hand and waves. Then, he tightens it into a fist and brings it to his chest. Then, he turns and gets into his car and drives away.

I don't sleep a wink.

CHAPTER
Eleven

Brie
Present

"HEY, BRIE. WANT TO GO TO MAX'S AFTER YOUR LAST lesson tonight?" Julie, a server at the club, pokes her head in the locker room as I change into my tennis skirt.

"Sure, I'd love to. I won't be done with the kids until about nine. Is that okay?"

"Perfect. The kitchen doesn't close until ten, but Wednesdays are usually slow, and Scott will let one of us go early. It's my turn. Have a good session, and I'll meet you after."

I grab my bag full of rackets and balls and head out to the court. I have a group lesson tonight with the sweetest six-year-olds I have ever met. They don't really pay attention, and I am lucky to get a serve a piece out of them, but I enjoy every minute I get with them. Their parents don't care if they actually learn anything anyway. They use the lesson time as a reprieve to go into the club's bar and drink a few cocktails and socialize with other members. I am basically a glorified babysitter. Who am I to complain though? It's damn good pay for babysitting.

After the children are picked up by their parents, I quickly change into my jeans and meet Julie in the parking lot. We drive over to Max's Bar and Grill near the Third Street Promenade and grab a few cocktails before heading home for the night.

"How are classes going for you?" I ask as the waitress places our ridiculously fancy cocktails in front of us.

"Ugh, I think I might drop my Economics class. My professor hates me. I was late a couple of times last week, and this week, he locked the door and refused to let me in."

"Really? Maybe you should just go to class on time instead of dropping?" I suggest as I take a sip from my glass.

The drink is a little sweet for my taste, but it is the Wednesday night special. Who turns their nose up at a half-priced cocktail?

"Yeah, I guess. I just wish he were understanding about the choice us working students face every day. Promptness or sleep? I am telling you now, sleep wins every time."

She is not lying. I am constantly fighting to stay awake in my Business Law class. Mr. Bolin lectures in the most sleep-inducing, monotone voice I have ever heard. He lulls me right into a drooling mess.

Our appetizers arrive, and we dig in as the place starts to fill up. Just as we are about to flag the waitress down to get our check, she arrives, carrying two more cocktails.

"I am sorry. We didn't order these," I inform her of the mistake.

"No, you didn't. The gentleman at the bar sent them to you."

"Which one?" Julie asks as she scans the seats behind me.

"The hot one on the far right."

"Nice. Please tell him to come by so that we can thank him." She is all smiles as the waitress scurries off to do her bidding.

"I can't believe you invited him over here. What if he is a serial killer? Or better yet, what if he is trying to roofie us?" I hiss under my breath.

"Damn, no wonder you are single. If you accuse every guy who buys you a drink of being a serial killer, you'd better start applying to the local convents now. Paranoid much?"

"I am not paranoid. I am cautious. You should be, too."

A deep chuckle sounds over my left shoulder, and I turn to see a familiar face.

"Hi, ladies." He extends his hand to Julie. "Your friendly neighborhood serial killer at your service."

I look up into the amused face of Jake Mason.

Great. I think I would have been happier if it had actually been a serial killer.

Putting my foot in my mouth in front of my boss's son was not part of my plans for the evening.

Julie eagerly offers for him to join us, and he accepts. He comes to my side of the booth, forcing me to slide over to accommodate his size. It's a tight fit.

"Thank you for the drinks, and I am sorry for accusing you of being a potential murderer or rapist," I try to make amends as he settles in. "Although, until we have finished these drinks and make it home alone safely, it remains to be seen if my assumption was accurate," I add.

He just looks at me like he thinks I am the cutest thing he has ever encountered. Julie starts to immediately fill the conversation with tales from the club while I sit and sip my drink. I take the time to study his face. It's annoying how handsome he is.

"How about you, Brie? Are you enjoying instructing at the club?"

"Yes, I am. Very much. It is a bit more laid-back here than it was at my last club. I like the change of pace, and the kids are adorable."

"Are you doing private adult sessions yet?"

Julie chokes on her drink at his phrasing of the question.

"Um, sure. I mean, if you arrange it with Mr. Cloniger, I am sure they will add it to my schedule. Are you certain I am the instructor for you? I usually teach children and adult beginners. You aren't a beginner, are you?"

I have had a chance to observe him in action on the racquetball court since the first time we met. He is a machine and definitely not a beginner. Not that I am going to admit that to him.

"Oh, I think brushing up on the basics is exactly what I need."

Julie decides to order actual food. I guess we are staying awhile. I really wanted to get home early tonight and get in a little study time and a soak in a hot bath before bed. This is my nightly dilemma. To enjoy a night out like a normal girl my age or go home and study and sleep. I resign myself to hanging out and just getting up early in the morning to study. I rejoin the conversation. Julie is telling Jake about her brother winning some surfing competition last weekend before he turns his attention back to me.

"So, tell me more about yourself, Brie. All I know is that you are new in town and living with Dawn and Kelsey and working at the club."

"Not much more to tell really. I am originally from New York, and I got tired of snow and crowds, and I decided to follow the sunshine here and finish my business degree at Cal State." I shrug nonchalantly and hope that he leaves it at that.

"What about your family? Do you come from a big or small one? Are they still in New York? Left a boyfriend behind maybe?"

I am not going there with him. My life before I stepped off that plane is no one's business. I changed my name so that no one could trace me back to my family, and I have only revealed enough vague details and half-truths to keep people from being suspicious so far. Daniel, who only knows part of my story, warned Dawn and Kelsey before I arrived to just leave my past alone. They have respected that so far. If I refuse to let them in, then I am certainly not letting this guy in.

"So curious, are you writing a story on me?"

"Evasive. Hmm, what are you hiding, Brie Masters? Can't a guy just want to get to know a pretty girl better?"

"Yes, some of my family is still there. We are scattered. Daniel Taylor is actually my cousin. You probably know him. Nothing else really to tell."

"I do. I know him and his dad." He skeptically looks at me as if he knows there is a lot more to my story than I am sharing.

I can see the moment he decides to just let it be, and I am grateful.

About that time, a shapely redhead approaches our table and purrs, "Jake, are you ever going to make it to our table?"

She gives him a little pout, and I have to keep from laughing out loud at her antics. *Does that approach really work for her? Pouts and purrs? Is that what boys are looking for nowadays?* I am so screwed when I decide to dive back into the dating waters. I have never purred in my life. I am not a cat.

"Carlie, of course I am. I was just distracted by my new friends here. Brie and Julie, this is Carlie. She's an old friend from school."

She looks a little offended by the *old friend* comment but recovers quickly and smiles a fake smile at us. "Hi, ladies. I hope you don't mind if I steal him. He promised me a meal and drinks, and he knows patience is not one of my virtues." She giggles as if to play it off as a joke, but we all know it's not.

"No problem. We are all finished here," I say sweetly.

"It was so nice seeing you both again." He turns to me. "Brie, I will contact Mr. Cloniger tomorrow. I look forward to our private time together."

He exits our booth, and Carlie instantly latches on to his arm.

"Well, that was interesting to watch ," Julie notes.

"Yeah, she is something."

"Not her. You and Jake. He is so into you, and you are totally playing it cool. I bet he doesn't get that from a lot of women. Jacob Mason is a hot commodity around here. Everyone fights for his attention, and you act all aloof when he is showering you with it."

"He wasn't showering me with anything. He just wants some help with his tennis game. That's all."

She gives me a look that clearly says I am insane.

"That boy grew up in the club. Do you honestly think for one second that he needs tennis lessons? He is willing to pay for them to see you. I will add that I have worked there for three years, and he has never once bought me a drink or asked about my family. Damn, what a waste. I wish he were looking at me that way. Unlike you, I wouldn't squander the attention. I would bask in it."

Julie is stunning. All long legs and tight, toned body. She and Jake would actually make a very handsome couple.

"He is all yours. I am not interested."

"Oh no, my friend, he is definitely all yours, and I bet he will make a valiant effort in changing your mind."

God, I hope not. The last thing I need is a charming guy trying to get into my pants. They are closed for business for the foreseeable future.

CHAPTER
Twelve

Gabby
Past

PARIS IS A DREAM. AFTER A WEEK OF STAYING IN MY PAJAMAS ALL day and crying myself to sleep every night, Aunt Mitzi has had enough. She forces me up and out the door.

She works at a pastry shop a few blocks from her apartment, and now, apparently, so do I. We get up with the sun and make our way to the shop where she gets all the menus changed with the day's exclusive creations, and I head into the kitchen to help Sacha, the big bear of a pastry chef. He could see immediately that I had a natural talent for baking. I love everything about it. The smell of vanilla and almond lingering in the air. The feeling of my hands kneading the dough. The sound of the mixers whirling. The rhythm of cutting out shapes for cookies. It does not seem like work at all. So, he has become my mentor, allowing me hands-on experience. It is invaluable and better than any culinary or pastry arts course I could have taken this year. I leave every afternoon, delighted and covered in chocolate or powdered sugar.

On our days off, she introduces me to the sights and sounds of Paris. The city is chock-full of history and culture. It is as if the city were alive. It has a pulse and a heartbeat, just like New York. It is on the cutting edge of cuisine and fashion. Everything girls my age covet.

We eat all the things, and being as the drinking laws in Europe are a little more relaxed than in America, she has taught me the finer points of a good wine-and-food pairing. I find that I very much enjoy Sancerre and pinot noir.

Slowing but surely, I have begun to acclimate to my temporary home, and my heart has indeed started to mend. It didn't happen overnight, but I have started thinking about Cross less and less as the days progress. By spring, I hardly think of him at all.

Adriana came for a visit after graduation, and I felt my first real pang of homesickness. I missed her. She stayed for almost three weeks, and I didn't want her to leave, but she had to get home to ready herself to move into the city. She is going to NYU in the fall and sharing a fifth-floor walk-up in Hell's Kitchen with two roommates. Her papa thinks it will be a good learning experience for her to live as other college students live. I wanted to go with her. We were supposed to move into the city together, but I knew it was too soon, and I truly was starting to like my life here.

The plan is to stay through the end of the year. I promised Mamma a year. I can start NYU at the beginning of winter semester, and I am sure Adi will have run at least one roommate off by then.

By the time November rolls around, I have met a boy. Antoine lives in the Montmartre area of Paris, which is a very eclectic mix of historical town charm and the evolving modern scene. The streets are lined with independent boutiques and old-world shops. The atmosphere is energetic, and it is filled to the brim with pubs and bistros and live music. For the first time in my life, I feel free. Free to sing and dance and date and kiss and just be a teenage girl without the men in my life breathing down my neck and trying to control my every move. It is magical, and yet I still feel this pull from back home.

I have plans to go back by Christmas, but Aunt Mitzi falls in the shop one evening and breaks her ankle. She has been so wonderful to me, and I don't want to leave her alone and helpless for the holidays, so I decide to stay at least until she is back on her feet. This thrills Mamma and Antoine even though it means missing the holidays with my family for the second year. To ease the sting, Mamma comes to stay with us the week after Christmas, and I am so happy to see her. We have talked on the phone every day and video-chatted, but nothing compares to her wrapping her arms around me. I missed the way she smelled and the sound of her laughter. She and I spend the week shopping and seeing the city. At night, we cook together, and the three of us just enjoy each other's company.

Antoine charms Mamma the night he takes us out on the Seine River for dinner. He treats her with the utmost care and respect. He is beautiful inside and out, and I really do like him.

Still, something is missing. I don't lie awake at night and miss him when he is off to London for work. I don't dream of him when I drift off to sleep. My dreams are still reserved for one person.

It is less painful to think of him as the time passes, but I miss him. I can't believe that he has not attempted to contact me. Not even once in over a year. How very little I meant to him is a bitter pill to swallow, but the pain carries me and helps me to move forward.

By the time Aunt Mitzi is back to her old self, I have talked myself into staying in France the rest of the year. Antoine is extremely pleased, and I keep to my mission to fall completely out of love with Christoff Scutari.

Home. I am home. As I unpack my suitcase and look around my bedroom, I realize how much things have changed. I am no longer that seventeen-year-old girl. Two years abroad have changed everything. I am older and wiser and will no longer allow myself to be held under my brothers' thumbs. They aren't going to like the new me, but they are going to have to get used to her.

"Welcome home, brat." Lorenzo engulfs me in a tight bear hug.

"We have sure missed you around here."

I just stand there, wrapped in his arms. He doesn't let go until I start wheezing.

"I missed you guys, too."

"I was beginning to think you had forgotten all about us and were never coming back."

"As if I could ever forget my brothers."

"Tony moved out, you know. Got himself an apartment in the city. Stavros is crashing there most of the time, which Tony hates but lets him do it anyway. So, it's just you, me, and Nicco."

"For how long? I can't see you living here much longer."

"Me? I will be here forever. I have a great room. The maid does the cleaning. Nonna does my laundry, and between you, Mamma, and Nonna, I eat like a king. Why would I ever leave here?"

He is not wrong. It is not a bad life at all, living in *Casa di Mastreoni.*

"Come on, sis," he says as he throws his arm across my shoulders. "The folks planned a welcome-home dinner in your honor. Let's go eat."

The entire family is seated at the table. All my brothers, my grandparents, and Papa and Mamma. I am so happy to see them all. I want to cry, but I don't. New Gabby doesn't leak as much as she used to. We eat and drink until I am completely sated, and Adriana shows up just as dessert is being served.

"I am stealing you."

"Adi, I am exhausted. I had a really long flight home. Give me a day or two to recuperate, please."

"No way, bitch. You have been gone for two years. You owe me. I am here to collect," she says as she starts rummaging through my closet. "Surely, you purchased some sexy clothes while you were in Paris. Aha! Score!"

She pulls a slinky black dress with a dangerously low neckline and high hem from the hanger. It has thin spaghetti straps, and the back is so low that it skims the top of my ass. I purchased it with every intention of wearing it out to a dance club with Antoine, but when I put it on and realized I couldn't bend over in it, for fear of exposing my top and bottom, I changed my mind. I have no idea why I still have it.

"No, ma'am, I am not going out in that thing. It barely covers my ass. I can't."

"Oh, yes, you are. We are going to show everyone what a vixen Paris turned you into."

"I am hardly a vixen, Adi." I laugh.

"Cross will be there. He is always there. With Angelica," she says over her shoulder while holding the dress up to her reflection in the mirror. "Did I tell you they were back together? Have been for over a year now. I think it's getting serious."

"It is none of my business who Christoff is or isn't seeing or where he hangs out, for that matter. I have a boyfriend." I yank the dress from her hand and strut to the other side of the room. Then, I start to change.

"Uh-huh. Not your business."

"Shut up."

I slip on a pair of black slingback stilettos and do my hair and makeup. I give myself a once-over in the mirror and swipe on some red lipstick before we leave. I might be over him, but that doesn't mean that I don't want him to see what he is missing.

When we make it to the Black Flamingo in Brooklyn, I am brimming with anticipation. Adi has secured us fake IDs, which just makes me feel silly. In France, I could get in and drink anywhere. Now, I am home and have to pretend to be someone else to get in. The bouncer at the door doesn't even bother to card us though. He grins from ear to ear when he sees us approaching.

"I was wondering when you were going to show. This must be the friend you told me about. Welcome," he says as he takes my hand and kisses the inside of my wrist.

"Thank you, Marcus. I promise to find you before we leave, baby."

Once we are inside, I ask, "Are you doing the bouncer just to get in?" I do not put anything past her.

"No. I am doing the bouncer because he is gorgeous, and I like him. Jeez, why do you think I got the IDs, Gabby?"

The place is loud and crowded, and we squeeze our way past the dance floor to the bar.

"What'll you have?" the bartender asks when he spots us.

"I'll have a vodka martini. Dirty, please, with extra olives."

"You are so highbrow now," Adi accuses. "I'll just have a beer. Whatever is on tap, handsome."

"Coming right up."

After we get our drinks, we head to the dance floor. I am a little tired and a lot jet-lagged, but once the martini starts coursing through me, all I want to do is dance with my friend. I missed her.

We are on the floor, laughing and enjoying ourselves, when Adriana ends up in the arms of a sexy man who looks to be about thirty years old. I decide to leave her to it, and I move to the middle of the floor, alone. I just start moving my body to the music. I feel light as a feather and completely lost in the beat when a pair of hands settles on my waist from behind. I should protest and move away, but why? Can't I dance in the arms of a stranger for a while? I lean back, and I start moving with him. He is a good dancer, and he pulls me closer as he rests his chin on my shoulder. I can feel his breath on my neck and smell the scotch on his breath. The song slows down, and he snakes his arm across my stomach. I dissolve back into him with my eyes closed as my hips sway instinctively to the music. It's very warm on the crowded dance floor, and I feel the sweat beading and rolling down my spine.

I am completely engrossed in the rhythm when I hear a whisper against my ear, "Welcome home, *Tesoro*."

I instantly halt dancing.

"No, you don't. The song isn't over yet," he says as his arm grows tighter.

"I am sorry, but it's too hot in here. I need some air."

I want to escape his grasp right now. Yes, I came in hopes of seeing him, but I wanted to see him at a safe distance because, even though I am sure I am over my infatuation, I do not want to tempt fate.

"Okay, baby, let's get some air."

He leads me off the floor, out the back entrance, and onto a low-lit patio. Other patrons are tucked in corners, talking or leaning against the railing, smoking. I walk to the farthest end and turn to face him. He looks good. More than that, he looks somehow maturer and rougher around the edges. His jaw is covered in a light stubble, and his intense green eyes are dark and dangerous and focused on me. I think he must have put on about twenty pounds of pure muscle since the last time I saw him. His arms are barely contained by the sleeves of his Henley, which are pulled up to his elbows, revealing a new tattoo curled around his right forearm. He stands there, towering over me, and I try to find my words. When I finally do, I wish I could snatch them out of the air and put them back into my mouth.

"Did you miss me?"

CHAPTER
Thirteen

Brie
Present

"THIS BABY IS THE CUTEST THING I HAVE EVER SEEN." DAWN has Cassian raised in the air above her, cooing at him.

"Be careful. He just had a bottle. He is going to spew all over you if you keep shaking him up." The words barely leave my mouth before he projectile vomits formula all over her face.

"Oh my God, I think some went into my mouth."

Kelsey and I are both howling with laughter as I claim the baby from her, and she runs to the bathroom, gagging.

"Oh, a little bit of baby spit-up isn't going to kill you," I shout through my laughter.

The girls have fallen as hard for him as I have. His chubby little legs and arms and his angelic face just melt us into a puddle. Thank goodness he is a very chill baby, too. I am able to take him with me just about everywhere with ease, which means I am able to spend more time with him. He even lets me study without complaint. He just lies there, playing with his toes, unless he is wet or hungry.

"All right, give him up." Kelsey has her arms open wide. "Now that he has that out of his system, Auntie Kelsey wants some baby snuggles."

I hand him off and grab my purse as I hear my phone start to ring inside.

"Hello?"

"Hi, Brie. This is Mr. Cloniger at the club. I was wondering if you were free this afternoon for a private instruction."

"Sure." I look at the clock on the wall. "I am on baby duty until five p.m., but I can head over after I drop him home, say around six thirty. Will that work?"

"I will schedule it at seven just to make sure you have enough time to eat dinner before you arrive."

"Thank you, Mr. Cloniger."

I end the call and look over at Kelsey as she blows raspberries on Cassian's belly to make him giggle. He sure is a blessing. When my days get stressful or I get upset or homesick, all I have to do is go pick him up for an hour or two, and everything just fades away to bliss.

"Another lesson?"

"Yes. I think the private lessons are starting to pick up, which is great."

"Commission. Yay!" She lifts his little hands in the air, and he squeals.

After dropping the baby off with his mom, I head to the club. This pace is exhausting, but honestly, idle hands and idle thoughts are not my friends, so staying busy really doesn't bother me.

After getting a quick bite to eat in the bar, I head to our assigned court and wait for my new pupil. I start warming up and hear a low whistle from behind me.

"That's a killer serve."

I turn to see Jake standing there, watching me.

"I see you made good on your threat to rent me out for fake lessons."

"Fake lessons? What are you talking about? I am in desperate need of your services." He places his hand over his heart, like my words have wounded him.

"Sure you are. Don't worry; I am not complaining. I'll take your money to just play and kick your ass in a couple of sets."

I continue to warm up by emptying a can of balls in a succession of rapid-fire serves. I feel him approach me.

He brings his mouth close to my ear and says low, "How else am I supposed to get alone time with you? You keep blowing me off."

"I am not blowing you off." My words linger in the air between us, and I flush from head to toe when it dawns on me how that came out.

He grins a wicked grin.

"Don't." I point my racket at his chest as I warn, "Don't say a word."

He raises his hands and declares, "I didn't. You are the one with the dirty mind, not me." He makes a lock-and-key motion against his lips, and then we both burst out laughing.

"Let's get started, and you'd better bring your A game, buddy, because I am not taking it easy on you."

"Bring it, gorgeous."

He's the one who brings it. Three hours later, we are exhausted and sweaty. We sparred hard. Playing three sets. He won. I wasn't the least bit surprised that he did, but I am not going to lie; it stung a little.

"Dinner?" he asks as he is toweling off.

"You just paid to play tennis with me. Now, you want to buy me dinner? Either you are really bad with money or you are trying to trick me into the strangest date in the history of dates."

"What if I let you buy dinner? Would that make you feel better?"

"No, it would not. You just beat me in the sport I was supposed to be teaching you. By virtue of soothing my wounded pride alone, you owe me a meal. And, just so you know, I might be small, but I eat a lot. I mean, *a lot*, a lot, and I am ravenous after that beatdown." I scowl at him.

"Damn, you are cute when you are angry. Calm down, sore loser.

Dinner is on me. Let's go."

He leads the way, and I follow him off the court to the locker rooms. He stops in front of the girls'. He turns his head to glance at me and winks. "You were easier to trick than I'd thought."

Bastard.

We leave my car at the club and get into his fancy-as-hell Maserati. It's a matte gunmetal gray, and I have to stop myself from drooling as I slide into the soft-as-butter black leather passenger seat. I love cars. I especially love fast, foreign imports. It is impressive and sexy, and it suits its driver to a T. His blond hair is still wet from his shower, and he smells of fresh soap. He has his arm out the window, and the music blaring. For a moment, I let myself get lost in the fantasy of being young and free and on a date with a gorgeous, charming guy in a hot, fast car. It's a carefree feeling I have rarely had the pleasure of experiencing before, and just for tonight, I wish I could let go.

We pull up to The Beverly Hills Hotel about twenty minutes later. It's an old hotel but legendary and still a beacon of old Hollywood glamour. The original iconic sign greets you as you pull up. Not exactly what I was expecting, but I have to admit, a little thrill jolts through me as we approach.

"This looks a little too fancy for my jeans and tee," I inform him.

"Don't worry; it's casual."

Somehow, I don't believe him as we exit the car and round the hotel to a back entrance. We are met at the door of The Cabana Cafe by the maître d'.

"Right this way, Mr. Mason. We have your table ready."

"You know, if you are trying to impress me between the car and your dinner spot of choice, it's totally working."

He glances at me over his shoulder and gives me an incredulous look that says he hasn't even begun to try to impress me. This is just who he is.

"You'll know when I start trying to impress you," he confirms.

The maître d' passes us off to a server who leads us around the hotel's massive pool to a private cabana booth. He places menus in front of us and starts listing off the drink specials.

"I'll have The Pink Drink."

I snicker at his choice, and he gives me a quizzical look.

"What? It's their signature cocktail. And it's yummy. Don't knock it till you've tried it."

"Challenge accepted. Make it two, please."

A few minutes later, the server returns with two elegant and, I have to admit, delicious cocktails and takes our order for burgers and fish tacos.

"Awfully fancy burger joint you brought me to."

He looks around and then brings his eyes back to me. "I like it here. It's comfortable and quiet and pretty private for a burger joint."

It is lovely. The pool area is subtly lit in an array of soft colors. Everyone is lounging in their cabanas or seated at low-lit wicker tables. Very nice indeed.

"So, Jacob Mason, tell me all about yourself."

I decide to start the personal interrogation so as to keep it from being pointed at me.

He leans in super close. "What do you want to know?" I can feel his breath on my cheek as the words leave his mouth. That's too close for my comfort.

"Everything. Start at the beginning."

Our dinner arrives quickly, and he spends the next hour filling me in on all things Jake Mason as we enjoy our food. He is twenty-four years old, and he works full-time for his dad's production company. He has lived in or around Los Angeles all his life. His dad is a television producer, and his mom was a stay-at-home mom. He has two siblings, both girls. Aspiring actresses slash waitresses. He shares a house near

LA with two roommates. One is a college buddy, and the other is a guy who answered a Roommate Wanted ad. He is a stoner, but he pays his rent on time, so they don't really care.

"I am also very much single in case you were wondering."

"I wasn't."

"Ouch. You sure know how to hurt a guy's ego."

"Oh, I have no doubt your ego is just fine, Mr. Mason."

"I like the way you call me Mr. Mason."

I look up at him, and he has a sexy gleam in his eyes. He thinks I am a challenge, and he is very much up for the chase. This is exactly what I didn't want to happen. Although I will admit, Julie was right about one thing. It sure is nice to bask in his attention.

"Stop looking at me that way."

"What way is that exactly?"

"Like I am a puzzle you want to solve."

"You are a puzzle I want to solve."

"Nothing to solve here, Jake. I am just a girl working her ass off to pay her way through school. No mystery. I am the least interesting person on the planet."

"Funny thing, you keep telling me that, and yet I don't buy it. Why is that?"

"I don't know." I shrug. "Maybe you're just pigheaded."

"Perhaps, or maybe I can see right through your charade."

God, I hope not. A sliver of fear runs through me. If he could, he would not like what he saw. I might look all clean and put together on the outside, but my insides are a mangled mess. I am not the girl he wants to get involved with. Trouble will eventually come looking for me. I cannot outrun it forever.

"There is nothing to see through."

"Evasion will get you nowhere, Brie. I am on the line now. Hook. Line. Sinker."

"Then, don't blame me when I toss you back out to sea. I warned you. I am not playing a game of hard to get. I am just not interested.

It's not you. I am not interested in any relationships outside of friend-ship right now."

"Then, we will be friends."

I look him dead in the eye. "Are you capable of that?"

He stares right back at me. "Baby, I can be the best damn friend you have ever had."

That's what I am afraid of.

CHAPTER
fourteen

Gabby
Past

CROSS JUST STANDS THERE, ACROSS THE PATIO FROM ME. NOT touching me. Not responding to my question. I feel so stupid for asking it. Of course he didn't miss me. If he had, he would have called or texted me or sent me a damn telegram. Something. A brief pang of pain hits me, and then I straighten my spine and remember that I am not the same girl who left New York.

"Never mind. Don't answer that. It was nice to see you again, Christoff, but I have to go find Adi before she runs off with a bartender or something."

I move to go around him, and he blocks my path. He is still just looking at me. *What is his deal?*

"Let me by."

He just shakes his head and stands there.

"I am serious. I need to go."

He looks off over my shoulder for a moment, like he is trying to find his words, and then he meets my eyes again. He reaches out to touch me, and I brace myself as his hand glides down my bare back. Goose bumps crawl up my flesh. I forgot how scantily I was dressed. *Damn it, Adriana.*

"I like your dress—what there is of it, that is."

"Excuse me?"

"Your dress, Gabby. Where is the rest of it?"

He must be drunk.

"This is all there is to it. Are you about to go all brother on me now? Is that what all this is about? Because I am not a little girl anymore. Whether you or Nicco or Tony or any of my brothers wants to see it or not"—I raise my arms and slowly turn around, so he can see all of me—"I have grown up."

He incredulously shakes his head. "You think I haven't noticed? I see you, Gabby. I have always seen you. That doesn't mean I like you putting yourself on display, so every other fucking guy in here sees you, too. You don't have to act like Adriana to get attention."

"Go to hell!"

"Right back at you, baby girl."

"You know what? I am done. I thought we could … I thought …" I trail off, trying to remember what exactly I did think Cross and I would be when I came home. *Friends? Faux siblings?*

"You thought we could what?" he roars, and it catches me off guard. I blanch at his tone. "You left. For twenty-seven months, you fucking left."

"Yeah, I left."

"And you want to know if I missed you?"

"No, I don't. I don't know why I even bothered to ask."

"Right."

He looks away again, and I seize the opportunity to slip past him. He swings his arm out to catch me around the middle and stop my progress.

"Please let me go," I demand, so only he can hear.

"Why? So you can run away again? You are awfully fucking good at that."

Anger hits me like a ton of bricks. *What did he expect me to do? Stay and suffer through him treating me like I was a kid? Stand by and watch him with his parade of women? Is he really so cruel that he would wish that on me?*

"Go to hell," I spit out again because my mind won't let me think of anything else to say.

I jerk free of his hold and try once again to escape his presence. He is on my heels, and his arm goes above me and rests against the door as I try to pull it open.

"Why did you leave?"

"I had to."

"Why, Gabby?"

"Because I needed to fall out of love with you, and I could not do that here," I confess as tears fill my vision. I had no intention of ever telling him that.

"Did it work?"

I stand there, caged in by him, surrounded by his scent with his hot breath on my neck, and I know that, if I don't get away from him soon, I am going to cave and confess all of my true feelings.

"Yes. It took a while, but I finally managed to step back and see that you were right all along. My feelings were just the foolish crush of a little girl."

About that time, through the small window in the door, I see Angelica approaching from inside.

"Time's up. Here comes your girlfriend."

He sighs and moves back just a fraction. Then, he turns me around, backs me up against the door, and leans in.

"Do not put words in my mouth, Gabby. And do not pretend to have the high ground here. You left without so much as a word to me. For twenty-seven months, not a word. You want to twist what you think I did or did not say in that pretty little head of yours? Fine. But this conversation is not over. Not by a long shot."

He releases his grip and backs away just as a thud sounds, and I feel a push against the door at my back. I move aside in stunned silence, and two seconds later, Angelica is there.

"Hey, babe. I have been looking for you for fifteen minutes. Didn't you get my text that I was here?" She heads straight to him and wraps her arms around his waist. She doesn't even notice that she shoved right past me.

His eyes don't leave mine. His stare is intense, and the dimple in his cheek is jumping with fury. I don't understand why he is so angry. He got what he wanted. I left him alone. I fell out of love with him—kind of. Now, we can be the brother-sister-whatever relationship he wanted from the beginning. Shouldn't he be happy?

"Oh, hi, Gabby. I was wondering when we'd see you. Marianna told me you were back in town. She also told me all about your new French boyfriend. What is his name?" Angelica expectantly looks at me.

"Antoine."

"That's right, Antoine. Cool name. Is he going to be joining you here?"

"He'll be here on the fifteenth, and he plans to stay a couple of weeks, but after that, we aren't sure on what the plan will be for us," I answer her but keep eye contact with Cross.

"Great. We can't wait to meet him. Right, babe?"

She looks up at Cross, realizing just then that he hasn't said a word or moved a muscle since she walked outside.

"Right?" she demands.

That's when he finally decides to acknowledge her. He looks down at her and smiles his brilliant smile. He says, "Right."

Then, he places a kiss on her lips, and she sways into him. I have to look away. I might be over my infatuation, but that doesn't mean I like Angelica any more than I used to, and the last thing I want to do is stand here and watch them make out. I turn and flee through the door in search of Adi without so much as a glance back at them. *What was I thinking, coming here? They can have each other.*

I tear through the club, looking for Adi, and I spot her in the corner with the bouncer who let us in earlier.

"I think I am going to call an Uber and head home," I tell her as I approach the two of them.

She looks up, and her eyes start scanning the room behind me as she tells her friend, "Come find me at closing." She pulls me back into the club behind her. "Where is he?"

I stop. "Where is who?"

She spins on me and narrows her eyes. "Do not even try that bullshit with me. You know exactly who. Cross. Where is he?"

"He is out on the patio with Angelica. So?"

"So, you are not taking off because of him!" Exasperated, she throws her hands in the air and yells above the music, "You have been gone for years because of *him*. I lost you for years because of him. You can deny it all you want, but you aren't fooling anyone. I know it was him. Now, you are back, and you are two inches taller and ten pounds lighter. Your hair has grown down to your ass, and you look like a fucking runway model. So, you are going to stay right here in that hot-as-hell dress and dance with every single guy here and Cross fucking Scutari is going to watch the whole damn thing and eat his heart out because he fucking deserves it."

"He doesn't care what I do or who I do it with, Adi."

"Oh my God, you cannot be that blind. Why do you think I brought you here? I was there when Nicco told him you were coming home. I swear, he got a boner as soon as your name was mentioned."

"Ugh, he did not."

"Yes, he did. He has been nothing but a hot, brooding mess since you left, and he's not fooling anyone, especially me. I have got his number and yours, too."

"I am just tired, Adi. It's been a long day, and I need a hot bath and some sleep."

"Liar. You are still running. Time to be the badass bitch that you are and stand your ground."

"I don't know if I can. I am not feeling very badass at the moment."

"Please, for me. It's not even midnight yet. Drink with me, dance with me, have a little fun."

"One more hour," I concede because I really did miss her, and I have to build up a thicker skin when it comes to him. He is not going anywhere.

"Deal!" She bounces on her heels. Then, she pulls me onto the dance floor.

About an hour later, I am tipsy and chatting with a guy from Tennessee who is in New York on business. He lives in Nashville, and I am picking his brain. I might be a Yankee, but I love country music. It's all love songs or breaking-up songs or down-home songs. Luke Bryan is my favorite, and this guy lives about five miles from him.

"So, what you are saying is that, if I were to come visit you, we could possibly run into Luke and his family in the local coffee shop or, say, the grocery store or pharmacy?"

He grins and brings his beer to his lips. "Darl'n, anything is possible. I have been known to bump into him a time or two."

"Well then, you might have just convinced me that I need to come to Nashville soon."

He puts his beer down and puts his hand on mine. "You are welcome anytime, sweetheart."

I probably blush from head to toe. Good thing the lights are so low in here.

"Do you want to get out of here?"

"Out of here? And go where?"

"There is a quieter café around the corner, or my hotel is a few blocks away."

"We just met twenty minutes ago, and you want me to come to your hotel room?"

"Of course I do. What red-blooded male wouldn't want a beautiful woman to come back to his hotel room?"

"Sorry, cowboy, but you see that girl right there in the white halter top?" I point to Adi on the dance floor. "She is the only one I will be cuddling up to tonight."

"Uggghhh," he groans. "You really had to put that picture in my head before sending me off on my own? You are a mean one."

I throw my head back and laugh while he just shakes his head and grins at me. I take my glass, empty it in one last swallow, and stand up. "Well, if you will excuse me, I have to go powder my nose."

"I'll keep your seat warm and order you another drink."

"Thanks, but I think I am done. It was very nice meeting you, and I will be sure to look you up when I finally make it to Tennessee."

He gives me a nod, and I walk back toward the restrooms. I dart in and do my business. Then, I wash my hands and check my lipstick in the mirror. I am glistening from the dancing, but other than that, it's not too bad. I head back out to find Adi. I promised her an hour, and it's been almost two.

When I make it to the hall, Cross is standing there. *Just great. Time to let him know who he is dealing with now.*

"Enjoying yourself?"

"I sure am."

"Be careful, *Tesoro*. Lots of predators out there."

I laugh. "Maybe I want to be hunted."

He looks me up and down and then smiles. "You couldn't have made that more obvious if you had worn a neon sign around your neck."

That is it. How dare he.

I advance on him and raise my hand to slap him across his stupid face, but I am too slow, and he catches my wrist inches from his cheek, stopping the blow.

"Uh-huh. You want to dress and act the part. Don't get pissed when you get cast in the role."

I snap my wrist out of his hold and stomp off to gather Adi. I am so done with him. I thought we could be friends, but that's not going to happen. He can fuck right the hell off.

CHAPTER
fifteen

Brie
Present

"**D**ON'T FORGET, IT'S TACO TUESDAY, SO GET YOUR ASS home right after class today, biotch," Dawn yells out her bedroom window as I run down the staircase to the parking lot.

"Nowhere else I'd rather be," I yell back before hopping in my car and racing across town.

I have my first fall exam today, and I have been pulling some all-nighters. I haven't been able to spend much time with my girls, and I can't wait to unwind with a few too many margaritas tonight. Taco Tuesday has become my favorite night of the week. Each week, they get a little bit weirder than before. Last Tuesday, I arrived home to find Dawn with a bedsheet belted around her, wearing Birkenstock sandals with her hair in an elaborate Roman goddess braid and gold leaf jewelry, topped with a sombrero. Kelsey served up soft shell tacos filled with marinated grilled chicken, red pepper hummus, and smothered with green goddess dressing and feta cheese. It was so strange and so delicious. They called it a Mexican Toga Party. I honestly can't wait to see what they come up with next.

After class, I am light as a feather as I head to Melanie and Rick's for a celebratory baby squeeze. I am pretty sure I aced my Accounting exam. My brain hurts from all the numbers rattling around, and all I want is to hold that little bundle close and breathe in his baby-powder scent. It always calms me.

Melanie greets me at the door with a sleepy Cassian in her arms.

"Gimme, gimme, gimme," I demand as I skip up to them.

She relinquishes the baby, and I follow her inside.

"Hey there. How is BB's favorite boy in the whole wide world?" I ask as I cuddle him in my arms.

He reaches his hand up and grabs at my nose, and I pretend to gobble his hand as he cackles with glee.

"How did it go today?"

"I think I did pretty well. For all that concern, it was a simple and straightforward test."

"I figured you were overthinking it."

"How did he do today? Is he acting any better?" I ask.

He was running a fever the night before, and worrying was half the reason I was up all night.

"Better. The pediatrician saw him this morning and said it was an ear infection. He told me to give him infant Tylenol every four hours and to keep a check on his temperature."

"Do you want me to stay in case he is fussy again tonight?" I offer.

"No, ma'am. You are a zombie. You need to go home and rest tonight, or we are going to have two sick babies on our hands."

"Are you sure?" I worry my lip with my teeth as I try to decide if I want to stay or go home for tacos with my friends and sleep.

"I promise to call you if there is any change at all. I got this. You go home to your friends and celebrate surviving the past week."

"Okay, but I'll come by in the morning to check on him, if that's all right with you?"

I give him one last kiss on his perfect little nose and hand him back to his mother.

"Of course it is."

Confetti assaults me as I walk through the apartment door. Daniel is standing there in jeans and a T-shirt that reads *Voodoo King*, and he has on a purple-, green-, and gold–jeweled king's crown. Purple, green, and gold beads are strung around his neck.

"Come on in, and welcome to Mexican Mardi Gras," he says with an eye roll.

Really? Mexican Mardi Gras?

New Orleans–style big-band music is playing, and I can see Kelsey in the kitchen, wearing a purple-green-and-gold swing dress and, of course, a sombrero.

"I can't wait to see what's on the menu."

"Crawfish and Creole shrimp tacos with hurricane margaritas!" she yells above the music.

"How do they come up with this stuff?" I ask Daniel as Dawn comes in from the deck.

"Just go in your room and grab your party dress and get your ass in here. You are on margarita duty," she informs me.

I do as I am told and head toward my room, but then I run head-first into a rock-hard body coming out of the bathroom.

"Whoa there. Steady." He places his hands on my waist as I rock backward from the collision.

"Jake Mason, what are you doing in my bathroom?"

"Daniel invited me for dinner. I didn't realize it was a theme party, so I had to change when I got here. Apparently, Dawn always has extras in case someone brings home a stray guest."

"So, you're a stray, huh?" I lift my eyebrow in question.

"Sure am. See, there is a contest for which girl can accumulate the most beads tonight. I couldn't miss that," he explains.

"Yeah, she is kinda nutty when it comes to her Tuesdays, just warning you."

The hallway is small, and his massive frame is making it hard for me to get past him.

It seems impossible, but he moves even closer to me and whispers, "I am already thinking of creative ways you can earn all my beads."

Dear Lord, I am both intrigued and terrified of what he has up his sleeve for the night.

"You are just going to have to surrender them, Mason. I am not a monkey; you cannot make me dance," I say as I squeeze right up under his arm and escape to my bedroom.

By the time I come out, fully in costume with my sombrero on my head, the party is in full swing. The girls invited a couple of guys from the apartment complex and a couple of people from school. No one else has on a sombrero.

"Hey, where is everyone's hat?" I protest.

"Kirk pointed out that taking beads off their necks and placing them around our necks is not conducive to sombrero-wearing, so we nixed them," Dawn explains.

"Doesn't seem very Mexican without them," I grumble.

"Oh, please, we still have tacos and margaritas. We are Mexican enough. Now, get your ass in here, so I can explain the game."

I join everyone in the kitchen, and Dawn explains the rules and the rewards. All the girls start out beadless, and all the guys have the same number of strands around their necks. The girls' mission is to get the guys to give up the beads. The guys can ask any price they want. The girl can refuse or accept. At the end of the night, the girl with the most beads gets a prize Dawn has wrapped in a box in the living room. However, us roommates have a side bet. Whichever of the three of us has the least amount of beads at the end of the night has to do the other two's laundry for a month.

"Not fair, Dawn," I protest. "You will do anything for beads. You already know you will win!"

She looks at me with a wicked gleam in her eye and shrugs. "Then, I suggest you loosen up a little and get those beads."

Ugh, I guess I'll be cramming extra laundry into all the free time I have lying around. I resign myself to my fate as I head into the kitchen to take my post as the head of margaritas.

Turns out, hurricane margaritas are exactly what they sound like. You take the premade hurricane drink mix, loaded with both white and dark rum, and use it in lieu of the normal margarita mix. And, of course, add tequila. In others words, we are all shitfaced a little over an hour later.

With the alcohol sloshing around in my gut, I get somewhat brave. I am indeed losing our battle because Dawn has shown just about everyone in the house her almost-see-through bra all night to get loaded down with beads. I keep looking over at Daniel when she lifts her top, and he just shrugs and laughs.

"It's just cleavage, Brie. Nothing everyone hasn't already seen in a bikini on the beach."

I still can't bring myself to expose my body like that, only to be ogled by complete strangers. It just feels icky. Maybe I am a prude.

Kelsey also has a handful of beads around her neck. She went to lift her shirt up earlier, and Bradley immediately shut it down. He took all the beads from around his neck and transferred them to hers. Payment for services to be rendered at a later time.

I only have two strands, and that is because a couple of the guys felt sorry for me and gave me a strand for refilling their glasses. Something has to be done. I cannot go down like this. If I can talk just one guy into giving up his beads, I can still take Kelsey down.

I walk out on the deck and find Jake lounging on the outdoor couch. He still has what looks like every single strand of his beads around his neck. I take a deep breath, and with liquid courage coursing through my veins, I approach him.

"Okay, Mason, name your price. What does a girl have to do to get you to give all of those up?" I point nervously at the shiny strands.

"You know what the normal going rate for a single strand of beads is, right?"

Grr. I knew he was going to say that.

"Fine, forget it."

I turn to walk away, and he catches me and pulls me back.

"Tell you what. How about a friendly kiss, and you can have them all?"

"Friends don't kiss, Jake."

"You kiss Daniel."

"Daniel is *la mia famiglia*. We are Italian. Italian relatives kiss. You are not family."

He gently tugs me, and I fall into his lap. I sit up and steady myself. I am now straddling him on the sofa. He leans in and rests his forehead against mine.

"Just one kiss. I just want to know what your lips feel like. I have been dreaming about these lips," he says as he raises one finger and runs it across my bottom lip.

Now that I am this up close and personal, I see the flecks of gray in his blue eyes. They are nice eyes. He has long eyelashes and bushy, unruly eyebrows. Manscaping is obviously not his top priority, which I like. Too much manscaping, and you take the man right out of the scape.

"Okay"—I take a deep breath—"one little kiss; that's all."

I give in. What can I say? I am drunk and I am weak and he smells good and he feels good.

He leans back, so he can look in my eyes, searching for permission. I balance myself by placing my hands on his shoulders, and before I can chicken out, I bring my lips to his. It's a chaste kiss—at first. Then, he moves his hands to grasp my hips, and he leans back against the couch. I follow him. My body is flush against his, and I can feel every muscle in his body tense and then relax. He starts to nibble at my bottom lip and coaxes my mouth open. His tongue glides in, and he starts caressing mine with it. It's slow and sensual, and I get lost in the feel of it. It has been a while since anyone kissed me. A while since anyone touched me intimately. I did not realize until this instant how much I wanted this. I bear into him and deepen the kiss. Just like that, we are a frenzy of lips and tongues and teeth. I moan into his mouth, and all of a sudden, he pulls back and disconnects his mouth from mine. He stares at me, wild-eyed for a minute, and I can see his Adam's apple bobbing as he swallows hard.

"Brie, baby, you have to get up."

"What? Why?"

"Because you win. I got my kiss, and you get your beads."

I am a little stunned at the sudden shift as he picks me up and deposits me on the couch beside him, and then he stands. He removes the beads from his neck and places them over my head. Then, he dips low and places one more quick kiss on my lips.

"Better than any damn dream I could dream," he whispers. Then, he turns and walks back in the house.

I am not sure what just happened, but I am pretty certain I am in big trouble. I should have just taken the laundry duty. I guarantee it would have been a lot less aggravation in the end.

CHAPTER
Sixteen

Gabby
Past

T HE NEXT FEW MONTHS ARE A WHIRLWIND OF ACTIVITY. I AM FI-
nally heading to NYU with Adriana. I am so excited. We are
both business majors, but I am a year behind, so I am opting to
take a couple of extra online classes to catch up.

Just as I expected, both of Adi's roommates have already bailed,
so we now have her apartment in the city all to ourselves. Papa wanted
to move us to the Upper East Side where we would be safer, but I protested. I like the apartment in Hell's Kitchen. Everything, except the
walk up, but I figure doing five floors up and down several times a day
will at least keep me from gaining the freshman fifteen. To appease
him, I promised him I would take the train up to New Rochelle with
Tony every Sunday for family dinner. Tony lives about five blocks from
us, which is probably the only reason Papa relented.

In the middle of this madness, Antoine is scheduled for a visit. He
flies into LaGuardia tomorrow. I cannot wait to see him. Keeping up a
long-distance relationship is challenging, and about a month ago, we
agreed to see other people, but we continue to talk. We'll see what
happens in a couple of years when I am out of school. So, the pressure
is off with this visit. We get to just enjoy each other without all the
heavy talk and emotional upheaval.

I am upstairs, packing, when I hear footsteps coming down the hall.

"Hey, Nicco, do you mind helping me carry some of this down to my car?" I call out as I tape another box closed.

He pops his head in and looks around. "Wow, that's a lot of boxes," he says. Then, he turns and yells downstairs, "Cross, man, come up here and help me load up Gabby's bedroom."

Then, he scoops up one box and heads out the door. A few seconds later, Cross is coming in. I haven't spoken to him since that night at Black Flamingo. He's been here to the house a few times, and I ran into him and Angelica at a restaurant in town, but I have stealthily avoided being caught alone with him or having to engage in any one-on-one contact every time. I guess it was bound to happen sooner or later.

"Can I come in?" he asks before stepping all the way in.

"Sure. I am not going to turn down the help."

He fully comes in and glances around at the floor. "I can't believe you are headed to college. Seems like just yesterday you were all pigtails and Barbie dolls."

"Yeah, well, my brothers have said pretty much the same thing more than once this week. I get it; I will always be stuck at five years old for you guys."

He bends down beside me to lift the box in my hands from me. "You haven't been five years old in my eyes in a very long time, *Tesoro*. Just feeling nostalgic, is all. It's like you are leaving all over again." He just stays there, squatting beside me.

The tension is thick, and I don't know what to say. I am tired from packing all night, and I don't have any fight in me today.

"I am just moving into the city this time."

He shakes his head and looks me in the eye. "You might as well be moving across the ocean again. It feels like you never came home." With that, he picks up the box and walks out.

He and Nicco continue to load my car until all the boxes are out of my room. I come down, and they are in the kitchen, rummaging for snacks.

"Want me to make you guys something to eat? My way of thanking you for all the help."

"Yes, sis, that would be amazing. I am going to run and jump in the shower really quick while you cook." He looks to Cross. "Sorry, man, I know you wanted to be on the train by now. Thanks for helping though."

"No problem. Go get your shower. We will still be there in plenty of time."

I get out a few slices of prosciutto, a loaf of sourdough bread, Gruyère cheese, tomatoes, fresh spinach, and a bottle of olive oil and start on their sandwiches. Cross stands there in silence while I start to cook.

Then, he comes over and asks, "Can I help?"

"You can slice the tomatoes for me."

He takes them to the sink and starts washing them. Then, he comes and stands beside me, elbow to elbow, while I slice the cheese and bread.

"Are you scared of moving out into the city, alone?"

"I am not going to be alone. I am moving in with Adi."

"Yeah, she will be about as useful as a trout if you get into trouble."

He cuts his eyes to me, and we both start laughing because it is kind of true.

"I can handle myself, Christoff."

"Why do you do that?"

"Do what?" I ask as I brush the bread with olive oil.

"You call me Christoff now."

"It is your name."

"It has never been my name to you."

"I am a grown-up now. I can pronounce your real name."

"I liked you calling me Cross better."

"Let's not do this, okay?" I say as I face the oven and not him. "It's different now; we are different now. Today was nice; don't ruin it by getting bossy or intense or whatever mood it is you are in today, please."

He finishes his task, brings the plate of tomatoes over, and sets them beside the pan. Then, he moves in close. "Call me whatever you want to call me, Gabby."

I turn to face him. "Are we going to be friends?"

"You tell me."

"I want to be. I came home, thinking we would be. I mean, isn't that what you wanted all along? I went to Paris, so I could sort myself out and come back and just be your friend again, but you act like that's not good enough either. I don't know what you want from me. I am so confused."

He is standing close, and his eyes don't leave mine. He is pensive and looks at me like he is trying to assess my words. He still has the finest jaw I have ever seen, and more than anything, I want to reach up and run my hand over the stubble on it, but I don't.

"I do, Gabby. I want us to be friends again. If you can forgive me for everything that happened before, I will forgive you for taking off, and we can start over right here."

"No more angry Christoff."

"No more angry Christoff," he agrees.

"Deal."

"Deal."

He kisses the top of my head like he used to, and I feel like everything is going to be okay again.

Nicco comes back down, and I load up three plates with gooey grilled cheese sandwiches and chips. We sit together and eat and laugh, and it feels good.

When they leave, I decide to turn in early and enjoy my last night's sleep in my childhood bedroom.

Adriana and I pull up to International Arrivals to pick up Antoine the next morning. I see him standing there with his suitcase, and the cars can't get out of my way fast enough. I finally make it to him, and I jump out of the car and into his arms.

"*Mon amour,*" he says as he catches me.

"Hey, babe, I missed you." And I did. I didn't realize how much until right this minute.

We load him and his bags and head to my parents' house. Mamma insisted on a family dinner to welcome Antoine.

"So, French Hottie, how long are you gracing us with your presence?"

I believe Adi is as excited about his visit as I am.

"For now, the plan is to stay for three weeks. That's how long my office expects for me to work remotely."

"Oh, we can show you the entire New York experience in three weeks." She is conspiratorially rubbing her hands together.

Antoine has no idea what he has gotten himself into with us.

When we pull up to the house, I am surprised to see all of my brothers outside, playing basketball. They used to play every evening, and I loved sitting on the sideline and watching them. I would always cheer for Tony to win. The others would act hurt and pout, but they all knew I was Tony's biggest fan. I always have been. He is the oldest of the four and fourteen years older than me. In a lot of ways, he was more like a second father to me than big brother. He doted on me, and he was my hero. He still is.

When we stop in the circular drive, the game halts, and all four of my sweaty brothers descend on us. *This should be fun.*

"Antoine, these are my brothers—Tony, Stavros, Lorenzo, and Nicco. Boys, this is Antoine."

They all crowd Antoine as they shake hands. I have to hand it to them; they are polite and a little less intimidating than I was expecting. I am sure Mamma had a nice long talk with them before we arrived. She is a huge Antoine fan, and having her as an ally is no small thing.

"It is a pleasure to meet you all. Gabriella speaks so highly of you."

"Damn, that accent is sexy as hell. I bet you cream your panties every time he calls you," Adi says out loud.

All four of my brothers cut their eyes to her, murderous glares on their faces.

"What? I just call them like I see them. It is hot as hell." She shrugs off their ire.

"Come on." I drag her toward the door. "Let's go in before they strangle you."

The boys rope Antoine into a game, and Adi and I head inside to help Nonna and Mamma finish in the kitchen.

About an hour later, Nonna sticks her head out the back door to call the boys in to wash up. I am setting the table and smile as I hear them all coming in the door.

"Ew, get your smelly pits away from me," I hear Adi exclaim. "Who invited you anyway?"

I peek around the dining room entrance to see whom she is talking to, and there stands Cross with his arm raised above her head, shoving it into his sweaty shirt. *Great.*

"I am always here for family dinners."

"Yeah, he is just as much family as you are," Nicco interjects.

"Whatever. You guys had better not give French Hottie a hard time tonight."

"French Hottie?"

"Told you, I call them like I see them."

Dinner is a success. The food is amazing, and everyone seems to like Antoine, even Papa. They talked business and international politics, and I could tell Papa was impressed with Antoine's knowledge of foreign affairs. Vincenzo Mastreoni is not a man easily impressed. Nonno is able to talk to Antoine about "the old country," as he and his family have spent summers in Capri every year for as long as he can remember. He is even able to slip in and out of *Italiano* while they speak of my grandparents' island home. He complimented Nonna's food and ate three helpings, which thrilled her. That is how Nonna shows her love—through food—and that is why I want to own my own restaurant one day—to pass down the love she has taught me. I kept catching Cross looking at me across the table with a curious look. He would smile a small smile just for me and then rejoin the conversation. I also noticed Mamma watching us all carefully.

After dinner, we all head out to the veranda for coffee and dessert, and the boys smoke cigars and drink an expensive bottle of whiskey Papa opened. It is a wonderful evening.

I get up and walk over to the outdoor fireplace to escape the cigar smoke while Mamma and Adriana are talking of redecorating our apartment.

"I like him." Cross joins me, away from earshot of the others. "I tried not to, but he is charming."

I turn and face him. "He is wonderful, isn't he?"

"You deserve a man like him in your life, *Tesoro*."

I laugh a humorless laugh. "You mean, one who will actually get on a plane and fly across the ocean for me?"

His expression changes from sincere to offended. I just had to open my big mouth and ruin a nice moment between us.

"Gabby, I didn't know where you were."

"What? That's ridiculous."

"It's not. I came here the night of your party to talk to you and to make sure you were all right. Your mother wouldn't let me see you. She said you were upset and had gone to bed with a headache and that, if I wanted to talk to you, I could come back the next day for Sunday brunch and talk to you then. I didn't want to leave, but I looked up, and your bedroom lights were out, so I thought maybe you actually were sleeping. I went home that night and figured everything out in my head and what I was going to say to you.

"Then, when I got here the next day, you were gone. All your mom would tell me was that you'd decided you needed time away and that, if I cared about you at all, I would give you the space you needed. I expected you to be gone a week, or two at most, not over two years. I called you every damn day until your voicemail was full, and I could not leave any more messages. You never returned any of my calls. Then, one day, the number was just disconnected. I asked Nicco where you were, and all he would say was that you were staying with a relative overseas. And, by the second month, I just gave up. I thought maybe it was for the best."

My mind is whirling with all this new information. Mamma got me a new phone with a Paris number about a week after I left. My old phone didn't have international calling. I never understood why she didn't just add that to my old number. I guess I know why now.

"What did you figure out?"

"What?"

"You said you went home and figured everything out and what you wanted to say to me. What did you figure out?"

"Does it even matter now?"

"It matters to me."

He looks around the patio. We have caught the attention of several people. Mamma, Adi, and Tony in particular.

"Not here. This is Antoine's time."

Nicco stands with his phone in hand. "Hey, Cross, Angelica just texted that she and Marianna are on their way. We should probably head out."

With that, he gives me one more small smile. "Have fun tonight, *Tesoro*."

Then, he and Nicco head inside.

I turn my eyes to my mother. *What did you do, Lilliana?* I cannot decide if I am angry with her or grateful. *Was he going to crush my heart even more that day? Did she save me from that, or did she ruin everything?*

She looks back at me and smiles, and I know that, either way, she did what she did out of love.

CHAPTER
Seventeen

Brie
Present

After the Mexican Mardi Gras party dies down and everyone leaves, Dawn and I are left to clean up since Kelsey and Bradley retired about an hour ago.

"She owes us," Dawn grumbles as she empties half-full cups and throws them away.

"Oh, she is going to be paying all month long."

After all the beads were tallied, I barely squeezed out a victory with one strand more than Kelsey. She is now on roommate laundry duty for the next four weeks. Victory is sweet.

"Yeah, congratulations, by the way. Exactly what happened out there for you to walk in after Jake, wearing all his beads, huh?" She wags both eyebrows at me as she perches on the arm of the couch and waits expectantly.

"Nothing scandalous, so don't get too excited."

"I don't buy it for a minute. Spill."

I give in and settle on the couch next to her. It's only the two of us for now. Daniel gave a guy who had obviously drunk too much a ride home. He'll be back soon though.

"A kiss."

"He gave you all his beads for a kiss?" She whistles low. "Must have been some kiss."

"It was pretty amazing, but I am not sure he thought so."

"What do you mean?"

"I don't know. He practically ran back into the house to get away from me."

She starts laughing incredulously. "Are you serious? That boy has been doing everything in his power to get your attention for months. No way he was scared away by a kiss. I bet he just didn't want to take advantage, being as he was completely sober and you, my friend, were swaying."

This is true. He has been very persistent even though I throw up walls at every turn. Him taking off so abruptly made no sense at all. Perhaps he was just trying to be a gentleman.

"It's better this way anyway. I was only kissing him to get out of having to do you heifers' laundry. I do not have the time or energy for any romance in my life."

She pensively looks at me for a moment, and then she places her hand on my knee. "Look, Brie, I don't know what went on with you in New York before you got here. Daniel just said you had been through some bad shit and that you wanted to get away and start over. The way you acted when you arrived, I figured it'd had to be pretty bad, because you were so shut off and had this fort around you. We didn't want to pry, so we let you have that and assumed that, if we provided a safe place for you in our friendship, you would open up when the time was right. But, in the last few weeks, you have let your guard down more and more, and I have seen you smile and laugh and enjoy your life a little. I think you might be healing, and maybe Jake Mason is supposed to be a part of that healing."

"I cannot let him be a part of anything."

"Why? You know what? Maybe that's too much responsibility. Maybe he is just supposed to be a fun, sexy distraction. Dating doesn't have to be so serious and heavy, you know."

"Maybe ..."

"My point is, you are too damn young to let whatever happened before steal all your joy. Have a fling, or hell, have a couple. Kiss all the boys. Just live, Brie."

It all sounds so simple. Maybe, if she knew my whole story, she would understand why I am so protective. Why I can't act like every other twenty-two-year-old on the planet. I am not ready to divulge all my secrets yet though. I want to, but I just can't. Not because I don't trust her. I do not trust myself. I have dammed off my past, and I am terrified that, if I open the gate even the tiniest bit, the floodwater is going to start rushing in and drown me. So, I lay my head on her shoulder and give her what I can.

"You might be right, but I am not that girl. I am the girl who gets her heart all tangled up in every relationship. It was mangled the last time, and it just hasn't had time to heal properly. But I hope it will one day."

"Just promise me, you will try. Baby steps is all I ask."

"Okay, Dawn, I can give you baby steps."

She pops a kiss on the top of my head and stands back up. "Good. Now, let's get this mess cleaned up and get to bed. I have a feeling we are going to be nursing some major hangovers tomorrow. Junk food and Netflix all day long for us, missy."

I love her. I really love her.

"He's doing much better; don't worry."

I called Melanie to check on the baby as soon as my eyes opened this morning.

"Does he still have a fever?"

"A low-grade one, yes, but that's probably because he is fighting the ear infection. We have to give the antibiotics time to work."

"I don't know. He is so little. How does a seven-month-old even get an ear infection? I don't like him taking antibiotics either."

Truth is, I don't know much about infant sickness. I took the infant care classes, but that's all I have to go on. All I know is that he started acting a little lethargic when I was babysitting the other night, and he wouldn't take his bottle. Then, about an hour later, he was very warm to the touch. It terrified me. I kept thinking maybe there was something I did or didn't do that he needed from me. I feel so guilty that he is unwell.

"You worry too much, Brie. This is normal. If I were concerned, I would take him straight back to the doctor."

"Okay. As long as you are sure."

"I am, and I have got everything covered here, so you enjoy the day with your friends. And, if he is feeling better by Friday, you can come keep him while Rick and I go to dinner. Deal?"

"Sounds like a plan. And I am available if you need me anytime before then."

"Thank you. He is such a lucky little guy to have so many people who love him."

We disconnect, and I head into the kitchen to grab some breakfast. My head is pounding, and I can definitely feel the residual effects of the hurricane margaritas. Maybe not the brightest idea we have ever had.

Dawn and Daniel emerge from her room about an hour later, looking very much worse for wear.

"Why are you being so loud in here? Are you angry with those pots and pans or what?" she asks as she slides into one of the barstools at the island, holding her head.

I place a plate of bacon, eggs, and toast in front of her, and she groans.

"Eat. You'll feel better."

"I do not think I ever want to eat again," she says as she pushes the plate away.

Daniel pushes it right back in front of her. "Oh no, you don't. It's your fault everyone is in this condition in the first place. Now, eat this greasy breakfast, so you can recover."

He is not hungover. He stayed sober last night, so he could watch over us girls. I guess he saw the repercussions of the hurricane margaritas coming a mile away. Smart man.

We hear yelling coming from Kelsey's bedroom a few minutes later. Bradley comes storming out the door, pulling a T-shirt over his head and grabbing his shoes from the mat beside the door. Kels is hot on his heels.

"I am not putting up with this accusatory shit, Kelsey. Just because I say I need a weekend to myself does not mean I am cheating on you."

"It did the last time you needed a weekend," she throws back at him.

"I told you, I did not and have not cheated on you. I haven't spoken to Tonya since that night at the club."

"Then, why was she blowing your phone up last night?"

Dawn and I give each other an *eek* look, and then we move closer to the living room entrance, so we can hear and see the fight better. Daniel just continues to stuff his face, unfazed by the commotion.

"I have no idea. Maybe she is delusional. Maybe she was texting the wrong number. How the hell should I know? By the way, I am still pissed you were going through my phone while I was passed out. I do not do that to you. Want to know why? Because I fucking trust you."

That's a low blow. Of course he trusts her. She hasn't given him a single reason not to trust her. He, on the other hand, has been squirrelly as hell lately.

"I looked at your phone because it was going off rapid fire at three a.m., and I thought maybe it was an emergency, you jackass." She is now throwing his wallet and keys at him from her bedroom doorway. "What I find instead is a text from Tonya, saying how much she misses you and wants you to sneak out and come to her apartment. Then, she sends a titty pic and offers to let you make good use of them."

I look at Dawn with wide eyes, and she just starts shaking her head.

We knew this was coming. We hoped we were wrong. Apparently, we had him pegged. I just hope Kelsey is able to stay strong this time.

"I told you, Kels, she is delusional. How is that my fault?"

"I am not buying the innocent act this time, Brad. God, I cannot believe I was so stupid. I knew you were lying, and I chose … I actually chose … to pretend like you weren't. I have become one of those pathetic women I hate."

He starts to walk back toward her. "I am innocent, baby. I love you. Only you."

"Stop," she commands as she throws her hands out in front of her and tightly closes her eyes.

At that, Daniel finally gets up. I can see that he has been paying attention the entire time and is more than ready to intercede if Kelsey needs him to.

"This is not love. Get out!"

He just stands there, looking like a lost puppy, and for a split second, I actually feel bad for him.

"Get out of my house!" she screams at the top of her lungs.

That sets Daniel in motion.

"Come on, Brad. You heard her; it's time to go."

"Stay out of this, Daniel. It's between me and Kelsey."

"It's over for now, buddy. She wants you out; you have to go. Now."

He stands there, staring at her for a few more seconds. Then, he turns to go. His parting words are harsh. "Fine. You know what? I was getting tired of you anyway. You are doing me a fucking favor." He grabs up his things and steps out the door.

"Oh, and, Kels, don't bother calling and trying to get me back. Remember, when you are lonely and crying in your pillow because no one else wants your high-and-mighty ass, that you wanted this."

So the wrong thing to say.

Dawn jumps to her feet. "Her?" She laughs hysterically and then turns to me. "Did you hear that, Brie? He thinks she is the one who is going to regret this?" She bends over, laughing dramatically. "You think no one will want the beautiful, sweet, blonde homecoming queen? Are you still drunk? Buddy, she will have ten guys lined up outside this door before you pull your tired-ass Mazda into your driveway. Good luck getting any respectable girl to touch you once she learns any part of you has been up inside that whore Tonya though."

Seething, he turns and stomps down the stairs and out of sight.

Dawn walks over and shouts after him, "Good riddance, asshole," and slams the door.

We all just stand there, silent for a moment.

Then, Kelsey says, "Netflix and junk food, right?"

"Yep," we all say in unison.

"Great! Let's do this."

So, we all pile in the living room in our pajamas and start a *Game of Thrones* marathon.

CHAPTER
Eighteen

Gabby
Past

CLASSES STARTED THIS WEEK. IT FEELS GOOD TO BE IN THE CITY ON a normal schedule again.

Antoine stayed for three weeks. We had a fantastic time, showing him around New York, taking him to Broadway shows, going to Yankee games, and just enjoying our time together. When he left, we reaffirmed our decision to see other people but to stay in touch. It was hard seeing him off because I think we both knew that this could be the last time we saw each other. In a lot of ways, he was my first love. The first love who loved me in return, that is. So, he will always be dear to my heart.

Now, Adi and I are headed to the Hamptons for one last weekend getaway. The warm weather will be coming to an end soon, so we are soaking up all the lazy, sunny days we can. Tony and Stavros have rented a beach house for the weekend, and just about everyone we know is coming out for the party.

When we reach the house, we claim one of the rooms upstairs and dump our bags. We change into our swimsuits and head straight for the ocean. A lot of guests are already set up on the shore, and Tony has music playing and the grill going. There is a line of coolers filled with chilled bottles of beer and wine, and a few of the boys are playing volleyball in the sand. I throw my towel onto a lounger and remove my cover-up. I hear a whistle and look over to the volleyball net. The game has stopped, and all their eyes are on me and Adi.

"Hi, fellas." Adi lowers her sunglasses and waves.

They all grin and resume their play.

We lie there all afternoon, soaking up the sun and enjoying the party.

At one point, I am lying on my stomach, and I drift off to sleep. I awake to a pair of hands on my back. I yawn as I come up to my elbows and look back. I see one of Lorenzo's friends, Jeremy, sitting on the edge of my lounger.

"Hey, Gabby. I think you fell asleep. You need to turn over soon, so you don't burn."

"Thanks," I say as I bring my hand up to shield my eyes from the sun, so I can look at his face.

He is handsome in a boyish kind of way.

"Want me to rub some sunblock on your back?"

"Sure."

I hand him the lotion from my bag, and he gently smooths it over my skin.

"I was wondering," he says while he is applying the block, "if maybe you would like to go to dinner with me sometime."

I look over in Lorenzo's direction and say, "What does Lo think about that?"

"He said, over his dead body or mine."

"But you asked me anyway?"

"Yes, ma'am. The way I see it, a date with you is worth the bodily harm."

"Well, how can I refuse when you are willing to risk a painful death?"

"Is that a yes?"

"That's a yes. For dinner. Just dinner."

"Awesome. I'll call you when we are back in the city."

"Okay."

I look over to see Lorenzo and Cross watching as Jeremy finishes his task of reaching the places I can't with the sunblock and then heads back toward the house. Neither looks very happy. They will just have to get over it.

We all eat, and the party starts to slow down as the sun sets. Some of the crowd starts dispersing to their own rentals, or they're heading back into the city. Adi and I, Tony and his girl of the moment, Stav, Lo, Nicco, Marianna, Cross, and Angelica are staying at this house.

Adi has snuck off to the neighbor's house with him. He is the son of one of her mother's friends, and the two of them hook up every chance they get. I probably won't see much of her the rest of the weekend.

After a quick shower to wash away the sweat and the sand, I rub myself down with after-sun lotion, throw on a pair of bike shorts and a tank top, and head downstairs. It's late, and almost everyone has crashed for the night, but I am still wide awake. I decide to make a snack and curl up on the huge sofa in the den to watch a movie. I settle for a scary movie about possessed dolls, cut off all the lights, and grab a blanket. The movie is intense. Just as one of the dolls is about to wrap its hands around the neck of a sleeping child, a hand reaches over the top of the sofa and tugs my ponytail.

I scream a bloodcurdling scream. I mean, I scream so loud, the foundation of the house shakes. Thank God the den is in the basement, and the houses in the Hamptons are miles apart, or the cops would probably be showing up. I jump to my feet and throw my hands into a *Charlie's Angels* fight pose. How I think that will benefit me in a fight to the death with a bloodthirsty china doll I have no clue. When my eyes adjust, I see Cross standing there, laughing his ass off in the dark. *Bastard.*

"What in the hell are you doing, sneaking up on me like that?"

"I wasn't sneaking. I couldn't sleep and came down here to watch a little television without waking Angie. I saw you curled up and thought you were sleeping. I did not realize I would freak you out so much." He is still laughing at me. "Please don't karate-chop me to death. I am truly sorry."

I drop my arms and plop back down. "Ugh, you ruined a good part. Now, I have to go back."

"How far are you in?"

"About twenty minutes. Why? You want to watch it?"

"If you don't mind starting it over."

I grab the remote and start the movie over. Then, I pass him my bucket of popcorn as he sits on the sofa. He picks my feet up, puts them in his lap, and settles in. It reminds me of all the times we used to do this before things got weird between us. On Sundays, I would walk or ride my bike to his place, and we would make food and lie around on his couch, watching videos all day. I cherished that time together.

When the movie ends, we stay there in silence and in the dark. Neither of us wanting to get up and head back to our rooms upstairs.

Finally, he starts to talk. "So, Jeremy, huh?"

"It's just dinner."

"What happened to what's his name, French Hottie?"

I laugh at his use of Adi's nickname for Antoine.

"Antoine. And we still talk almost every day, but I did not want to be worried about maintaining a long-distance relationship while I was at school. So, we agreed to see other people."

"I thought maybe he would move here."

"He talked about it, but he loves his job, and his family is very close. I didn't want to be the reason he left either."

He nods at my revelation.

"I guess he was not the one after all."

"Why do you say that?"

"Because, if he were, he would have moved here whether you asked him to or not. He would not have been able to stay away."

Maybe he is right. After all, I wasn't able to stay away. Hard as I tried.

"Are you ever going to tell me?"

He is rubbing my feet now, but his mind is far off.

"Huh?"

"What were you going to tell me when you came to see me the night before I left? Or the next morning when you came for brunch?"

He keeps kneading my foot, and he's looking down, watching his hands and not meeting my eyes. "I wanted to apologize for what happened in the coat closet. I should have been able to control myself better than that. I didn't mean to ruin your party for you. I felt like shit."

"That all?"

I am disappointed. I wanted it to be more than just that.

"I wanted you to know that I hadn't meant what I said to the guys. They were teasing me, and I let them get to me. I wanted to divert their attention from you, and I did not realize how what I was saying would sound to you, especially when I had just had you pinned against the wall upstairs. When you rounded that corner and I saw the look on your face and realized you had overhead us, after what we had just done, I was sick."

"It's fine. I was really upset that night, but I think I get it now."

"No, you don't, Gabby. You were seventeen years old. I was twenty-five. It was all kinds of wrong for me to touch you that way, but I was so fucking jealous when I saw you dancing with that punk from the woods. Jealous over a fucking kid. I knew though, once I crossed that line with you, there was no going back. When I held you in my arms while you came on my hand … fuck me, I knew everything had changed."

I grow warm at the memory. I have played that moment over and over again in my mind. It still gets me as excited as I was then.

"I chased after you when you left to tell you we could not do that again. No matter how I tried to spin it and make it okay, it wasn't. You were too young. I needed two more years."

"You needed two years? What does that mean?"

"Fuck, Gabby, you were underage. But you wouldn't be forever.

I needed you to be patient and give me time. Time to work on your brothers and time for you to not be underage anymore, but when I got there the next morning to explain, you were gone. Lilliana said you had decided a while ago that you wanted to spend some time abroad. Then, she ran down for me all the reasons I was not good enough for you and why I needed to leave you alone. My age, my family, the fact that I hurt you so badly. She was very fucking convincing."

Oh, Mamma, you got what you wanted. You ruined everything.

"I guess we were not meant to be, huh?"

He looks over at me then and smiles a sad smile. "I guess not."

"Hey, at least you never had to endure being beaten to a bloody pulp by my brothers."

"True."

He just sits there with that faraway look again, so I playfully kick him in his side, and he catches my foot and starts to tickle it.

"Noooo, stop."

I start laughing, and he doesn't let up until I am unable to catch my breath, and tears are streaming down my face.

"Babe?" we hear a sleepy voice calling down the stairs.

"I'll be right up, Angie," he yells back.

He looks over at me like he is sorry he has to go.

"Go on. I am probably going to sit here and watch one more horror flick. I don't think I have been thoroughly scared yet tonight."

He gets up and stretches. "You know, Jeremy is actually a pretty good guy."

"That's good to know."

"Pretty lucky guy, too."

With that, he kisses the top of my head and heads upstairs to his girlfriend.

CHAPTER
Nineteen

FALL BREAK WAS A WHIRLWIND. DAWN AND I HELPED KELSEY PACK up all of Bradley's belongings into a box, and we sent it to him via UPS. She didn't want to see him and give him the opportunity to try to change her mind. We had saved up a little money and decided to go to Laguna Beach for a long weekend as an early twenty-third birthday celebration for me. Just us girls. We rented a convertible and drove the PCH the entire way. It was glorious. Four days on the beach, playing volleyball and drinking frozen cocktails. I came back with a closer bond to my roommates and some impressive tan lines.

I've received a ton of calls from Jake, which I let go to voicemail because I am slightly embarrassed and a lot confused about the kiss.

Finally, I decide to stop avoiding him.

"Hello?"

"Hey, pretty girl." His cautious voice comes across the line.

"Hey, Jake. Look, can we go ahead and get it out of the way? I don't handle awkward situations very well, and honestly, I have been sending you to voicemail on purpose all week because of it."

I hear the relief in the chuckle that comes across the line.

"Have I ever told you how much I love how matter-of-fact you are,

Miss Masters? I don't like awkward either. So, do you want to start, or should I?"

"You go," I reply quickly. I am anxious to hear what he has to say, and I believe in just ripping the Band-Aid off.

There is a sigh and a long pause.

I think that maybe he is going to change his mind, and then he starts, "Look, I like you, Brie. I really like you. And, Tuesday night, I was just trying to be funny and charming when I asked for that kiss. I assumed you would let me have a quick peck or a kiss on the cheek and bolt. When you didn't, I was afraid that maybe you were a little drunker than I thought. So, I was warring with myself. Because that kiss was …" He trails off for a second, like he is trying to carefully choose his words. "It was fucking everything, but I did not want to take advantage of you. I was sitting there, exactly where I wanted to be, with you in my lap and your mouth on mine, but I wasn't sure if it was truly where you wanted to be. So, I did the most douche-worthy thing I could; I picked you up and set you on your ass, and I walked off instead of staying and talking to you and making sure you were okay. All because I did not trust myself enough to keep my hands off of you."

When he finishes, he lets out a long breath and waits on the line. I did not expect him to be so honest. I expected him to laugh it off as drunken fun and accuse me of overreacting to the entire scene. He didn't do that.

He nervously clears his throat, and I realize I have just been sitting here, giving him no response.

"I appreciate that more than you know."

"Appreciate what?"

"You stopping it where you did. You are right. It was a great kiss, but I would have been upset with myself if it had gone beyond that."

A heavy sigh comes across the line. "Yeah," he confirms.

I make a decision. It is a reckless, in-the-moment decision, but maybe it's time to let go.

"I like you, too," I whisper. "Maybe we can explore that a little more. If you still want to. I can't make any promises, Jake, but I wouldn't be opposed to spending some more time together, off the court."

"How about now?"

"What? Right now? I just got back from Laguna, and I have to unpack and shower."

"Tonight then?"

"Okay," I relent before I have a chance to overthink it and chicken out. "Tonight around seven. See you then."

I hang up the phone, and I lie across my bed. My heart is racing. From excitement or maybe a little bit of fear. Perhaps a mixture of both. I made a promise to myself that I would not get distracted by a boy, and here I am, going out on a date with Jake. A feeling of foreboding washes over me. *This is a bad idea. A very bad idea.*

Panic quickly sets in. *What am I thinking?* I unpack, and I frantically start to toss clothes onto the bed, trying to decide what to wear. Jake didn't say where we were going, and the last time, he took me to The Beverly Hills Hotel. I settle on a light sleeveless dress and a pair of flat leather sandals. It is dressy casual, so I should be okay either way. I keep my long hair down and flowing in a beachy wave. The mocha locks now have a few caramel highlights running through them, courtesy of the Laguna sun. I skip any makeup other than a few coats of mascara and a pale rose lip gloss. When I emerge from my room, Dawn is lying on the couch with Daniel, watching television.

"Wow, you look nice. Where are you headed?" Dawn asks.

"Um, I am not sure. Jake is taking me somewhere."

At that, she darts straight up. "Jake? You are going out on a date with Jake?"

"I guess you could call it a date. I don't know. I just agreed to spend some time with him, and we'll see where it goes."

"Kelsey, get your ass in here!" she yells.

"Oh my God, please do not make a big deal out of this. I am

nervous enough." I stand there, wringing my hands and trying to think of a good excuse to call him and back out.

"Girl, it is a big deal. You are finally tearing down some of those walls you have built up. I feel like such a proud mamma bear at this moment."

Kelsey comes out of her room, looking like she was in the middle of a nap. "What's going on?"

"Brie is about to go out on her first date with Jake Mason."

That declaration pulls her right out of her drowsiness. "You are? Oh my goodness, this is so exciting. Where are you guys going?"

"She doesn't know. He didn't tell her."

"A surprise! Even better." She claps and hops up and down.

Daniel can see the panic building inside me, and he decides to intervene. "Ladies, do you mind if I have a moment with my cousin?"

Both of them look like they want to tell him to fuck off, but he gives them both a look that says to back down. They relent and head to the kitchen, and Daniel pats the seat beside him. I sit down, and he wraps his arm around my shoulders.

"You okay?"

"Not really. I am scared to death, to tell you the truth."

"Brie, I am going to lay some honesty and a little big-brother advice on you now."

Great, just what I need—another big brother.

"Not every relationship is going to be as heavy as the one you left behind, okay? Things here are very different than in New York. There are no family ties here. You are just a normal girl. Going out on a simple date with a nice guy who happens to think you are worth the trouble of getting past your boundaries to get to know you. It doesn't have to be more than that. Relax. Have fun. Jake is not going to push for more than you are ready to give. I promise you that. If he does, I will break his kneecaps."

At that, I bust out laughing. Daniel is no enforcer.

"No family ties, huh? Sounds like you keep a few in your pocket."

He shrugs. "They are there if I need them."

"Thanks, Daniel." I take a deep breath. "I know I am overthinking this. I am going to try to relax and have fun. I promise."

About that time, the doorbell rings, and Dawn and Kelsey race out of the kitchen and hurl themselves at the door. Jake is standing there in slacks and a white linen shirt with three pink roses in his hand. He looks at the two of them with a smirk. He knows what they are about. He hands a rose to each of them as he says hello, and I can see the cartoon hearts appear in their eyes. Oh, this guy is good. Win the friends over, and you win the girl over. I don't think it's going to be quite that easy this time.

We end up at the Santa Monica Pier. It's beautiful, and I love the lights and the people-watching. This is exactly what I needed to make the anxiety disappear. No pressure, just two people in the sea of others at the pier, enjoying a gorgeous fall night. We eat at The Albright, which is a great little seafood restaurant where you can get buckets of beer and low-country boil. It is amazing, and my simple dress is just fine.

"You aren't afraid of heights, are you?" he asks as we approach the ticket booth.

"No. Why?"

"Because I am about to take you on the Ferris wheel and show you my favorite view."

He grabs us both tickets, and we stand in line. The Ferris wheel is stunning with large multicolored cars. We see a bride and groom crawl into the car ahead of us with what appears to be their wedding photographer. How fun and unexpected. We get settled into the car that we are sharing with a couple of teenagers, and I feel the excitement build inside me. I love Ferris wheels. I have since I was little and my nonna took me on the Wonder Wheel at Coney Island. Now, any new city I visit, I always seek out the Ferris wheel, if they have one. I can't believe I have been here over three months, and this is the first time I have been on this one.

The wheel keeps climbing slowly as they load all the cars. Once we are at the top, I look around, and he is right; the view is spectacular.

He starts to point all around us. "Look that way, up the coastline, and you can see the cliffs of Malibu. This way"—he points to the side—"and you can see the lights of LA. Of course, out there"—he points to the water on the other side—"is the Pacific Ocean. This is why it's my favorite view." He leans in and whispers, "It's a little more breathtaking tonight though because you are in it."

The wheel finally starts to move, and we get a wonderful breeze as we go round and round. I look over to the two teenagers across from us, and she is practically in his lap. Then, all of a sudden, they are making out hard-core. Like we aren't even in the car with them. My mouth falls open, and I hear Jake's roaring laughter.

Once we are back on the ground, I muse, "Wow, I don't think they came up for air the entire ride."

"You've got to love young love. I mean, when you live with your parents, you have to take every semi-private opportunity you can to cop a feel."

I elbow him in the side.

"Ouch. What? You know it's true."

He is right. I do. I remember fighting for privacy when I was in a house full of nosy relatives. Maybe that's why everything feels so much more intense at that age. You have to fight so hard for a single touch or a single kiss. You dream about it. Fantasize and build it up in your mind, and once you have a moment to act on it, all that pent-up emotion and angst just explodes out of you. It's the best feeling in the world.

After we walk around the rest of the amusement park and Jake makes an ill-fated attempt at teaching me how to bait a hook to fish— honestly, I can't kill anything, even a gross worm—we head back to my apartment. I am fidgety the whole way.

What does he expect when we get there? Does he think I will invite him in? Should I invite him in? Do I want to invite him in? I am not sure of any of the answers. This is why first dates suck.

Turns out, I shouldn't have worried. Jake makes it easy on me. He gets out and walks me up the stairs to make sure I get in safely, and as I unlock the door and turn to invite him in, he places his hands on either side of my face and leans in for a sweet, lingering kiss. Just one.

"Thank you for going out with me tonight. I hope you had a good time."

"I did."

"Good, because I plan to take you out many more times."

"Okay."

He gives me one more quick kiss. Then, he starts backing down the stairs. "I'll call you in the morning."

"All right."

"Be sure and lock the door behind you."

"I will."

Then, he is gone, and I can finally let out the breath I have been holding since we left the pier. I walk in, and Dawn and Kelsey are on the couch in their pajamas, waiting up for me.

"Come sit and tell us all about it," Dawn says as she scoots over.

So, I sit, and I tell my friends all about my wonderful night. Just like any other girl.

CHAPTER
Twenty

Gabby
Past

SCHOOL HAS BEEN TOUGH. I THINK HALF THE PROBLEM IS LIVING with Adriana. I love her dearly, but buckling down and doing the hard work is not her forte. I swear, that girl talks me into putting off studying and going out more than I should allow.

My date with Jeremy went really well. He is sweet and funny, and even though I have no desire to settle down with anyone at the moment, it is nice just to go out without any strings attached.

Tonight, I have a study date with one of the guys in my Critical Thinking class. We are meeting at a local coffee shop, then we plan to walk down to the Wine Cellar for the live music and a light meal. I love New York City in the fall. Warm days and cool nights.

After a few hours of studying and several cups of coffee, we are seated at a comfy couch in the corner of the wine bar, we give our server our drink order, and Wes excuses himself to the restroom. The acoustic guitarist is setting up, and I take a moment to look around. I spot Dante across the room with a couple of guys and a beautiful blonde. His head is bent to her, and she is whispering something in his ear, but all of his attention is focused on me. I smile and give him a little wave, and he winks at me. Then, he says something to his table as he stands and then heads my way.

"Hi, gorgeous," he says as he sits down beside me.

"Fancy seeing you here. Are you following me, Mr. Calvacanti?"

We laugh because it has become an inside joke how often we run into each other. It seems we have the same taste in food, music, dance clubs, and apparently, wine.

"I am beginning to think you are following me," he says with a smirk.

"Hardly. My date actually picked this place out. I think he knows the owner."

"Date, huh? I guess your brothers have eased up some?"

"Oh, I don't know. They would probably like to keep me in their pockets forever, but they can't."

"So, when are you finally going to agree to have dinner with me?"

It's a brazen move to ask me out on a date while I am in the middle of my current one. That's Dante though, and as much as it is a ballsy move, I admire his confidence.

"Well, I am free this weekend. Perhaps we could meet somewhere for coffee?" I offer.

"Coffee? All right, I will take it. All I need is an inch, Gabby."

So damn cocky.

Wes makes his way back to us, and Dante gets up and shakes his hand as he bids us a good evening.

"I'll call you this week and confirm our plans."

With that, he makes his way back to the blonde, who is obviously put out by the attention he was giving me.

"He seems … determined."

"What?"

"Looks like he was trying to pick up my date while he himself is on a date."

"No, he is an old friend; that's all," I lie. No reason to make Wes feel awkward.

"Really? He looks at you like he wants to take a bite out of you or something. Not that I can blame the guy."

I laugh and tell him he is crazy, and we settle in for a great night. The music is amazing, and so is the wine. Dante and his crowd leave about an hour later, but we stay and close the place down.

I walk into the bakery to meet Dante.

He wasted zero time in taking me up on my offer to meet him for coffee. By the time I made it home from my night out with Wes, I already had two voicemails from him, trying to nail down a time and place. He wanted to pick me up, but Adi and I have a hard-and-fast rule that no new guy in our life is allowed to know our apartment address until at least the third date. It helps to ferret out the creepers, and even though I have known Dante for years now, I still feel like the rule should apply until I decide if there will be a second date.

"Hi, gorgeous." He kisses my cheek as I arrive at the table and sit in the chair he has pulled out for me. He is nothing if not a gentleman. He stands behind me with his hands on the back of the chair, and he looks down at me. "You wore pink. I fucking love you in pink. Stunning."

I look down at the simple pale pink off-shoulder linen jumpsuit I have on. It's nice, but I didn't realize it looked that good on me.

He runs a finger over my bare shoulder and adds, "It looks so good against your olive skin and dark hair."

"Thank you."

"Thank you for coming."

He takes his seat across from me, and we order a couple of pastries and two lattes.

"I do like a girl who eats."

"I'll tell you a secret," I say as I pop a big bite of a fresh croissant into my mouth. "All girls eat. Some just do it in hiding for some weird reason."

"Is that so?"

"Yep, but those girls are nuts. I am not going to sit in my room, eating stale crackers, when you can bring me to this delectable place with all this goodness on the menu."

I moan as the next bite melts in my mouth and then proceed to lick the buttery goodness from my fingertips.

He chuckles and calls the server back over to our table. "We will take one of everything on your menu."

"One of everything, sir?" she asks, surprised by his request.

"One of everything."

I look at him, wide-eyed. "We will never be able to finish all of that."

"Probably not, but I will enjoy every second of watching you try, and then you can box up whatever we don't finish. I can't have my girl living on stale crackers."

"Your girl?" I question with a raised eyebrow.

"Working on it," he says as he sips his latte.

"So, how did it go?" Adi asks as I waddle my way in.

I am thoroughly stuffed, and I have two boxes of goodies in tow. "It was nice. Actually, it was really nice. He is taking me to dinner tomorrow night."

"Thank goodness. That boy has been hounding me to talk you into going out with him forever. I swear, I was about to have my number changed if you didn't agree soon."

"Maybe we can double date with you and Jamey sometime."

"Jamey?"

"Yes, Jamey, Dante's friend that you were into that night at the springs before Cross and Angelica showed up to break up the party."

She stops and wrinkles her forehead, like she is trying to recall the night. A night I could not forget if I tried. The night of my first kiss.

"Oh, him. Girl, I haven't talked to him in ages. I let him feel me up one night, and he was all thumbs. He couldn't find my clit if I drew him a map. No, thank you."

"Jeez, Adi."

"What? I am not training a man to pleasure me. It's their one job. If they suck at it, then I am out. Aren't you?"

Sometimes, I wonder how we are best friends. We are so different. I blush. "Sure. I mean, who wants to deal with that?"

"Damn straight."

Dante and I have been out on two more dates. I think I might actually be starting to really like him.

Tonight, we are headed to dinner at my favorite Cuban restaurant, Havana Central, and then to a party at one of his friends' apartment. It's the first time I am meeting any of his friends, so I made an extra effort when getting ready tonight. I am wearing a short winter-green swing dress with some long, beaded silver chains around my neck and black high-heeled leather ankle boots. I have my hair down, and I used a wand to create long, wavy curls down my back. I went a little heavier than usual on the makeup, doing a smoky eye and nude lips. When I meet him at the door, I can tell he appreciates the effort.

"Damn, you look amazing."

I spin for him, and then I ask if I should bring a coat. The nights are getting colder here, and I am not sure how much walking we will be doing.

"No, ma'am. I have my car, and I am more than willing to keep you close and warm."

On our way to dinner, he pulls me next to him and slides his hand in my hair. He always finds a way to do that. It's one of the reasons I wore it loose tonight. I know he likes it. He brings my head to his and presses a kiss to my mouth. This is new, the kissing, but I like it. His mouth is soft and gentle with mine. I open for him and let his tongue glide with mine. He tastes of tequila and lime.

"I am excited about the party tonight," I tell him.

I have been so engrossed in fall exams that I have had very little time for much more than late-night study sessions and sparse sleep.

"Me, too. I have a feeling it's going to be a night neither one of us forgets."

He kisses my lips one more time before we hop out of the car, and he hands the keys to the valet. My stomach growls as we head into the restaurant.

"My girl," he whispers in my ear, "always so hungry. I'll tell you a secret; the way you look tonight, I feel a little ravenous myself."

CHAPTER
Twenty-One

Brie
Present

"**Y**OU ARE MY SUNSHINE, MY ONLY SUNSHINE. YOU MAKE ME HAPPY *when skies are gray. You'll never know, dear, how much I love you. Please don't take my sunshine away,*" I sing to Cassian as I walk and bounce him.

He is snuggled into my bosom, and his little eyes are growing heavier and heavier with sleep. He has had a rough go the past few nights because he is teething. I insisted Melanie leave him with me tonight. I don't have class tomorrow, and I can stay up and walk the floor all night with him if that is what he needs. She was exhausted, and she relented fairly quickly. So, here I am, up with a fussy infant, and there is nowhere else I'd rather be. As soon as he finally falls off into a fitful slumber, I tightly swaddle him and lay him in the bassinet beside my bed.

The next morning, the girls take turns in walking the screaming baby around the apartment while I make breakfast and guzzle coffee. They love him just like I do, but I can tell they are weary from lack of sleep. The baby was up every couple of hours, and try as I might to calm him, he always managed to wake one or the other up. I am feeling a bit guilty now. I think that, from now on, when I want to give Melanie and Rick an overnight break, I need to do it at their house.

It's not fair to bring my nanny troubles to my roommates' doorstep. Neither complains though, and it's one of the many reasons I love them so.

After breakfast, I get Cassian bundled up, and I take him home. Melanie looks like a new woman when she answers the door. Rested and vibrant.

"Hi, Brie. How did he do last night?"

"Not too bad. He was up and down and a little fussy, but nothing I couldn't handle."

"Liar. I can see the dark circles under your eyes. Thank you for keeping him. Honestly, I don't think I realized exactly how sleep-deprived I was. That good night's sleep has completely recharged my batteries."

"You're welcome, and you know, anytime you need that reprieve, all you have to do is tell me, right?"

"I do."

I leave the baby with his mother, and I head to the club. I am not working today, so I thought I would hit the pool with Dawn and Kelsey for a while. I can even catch a nap while I am floating around.

The girls are already there and have our lounge chairs reserved when I arrive. I peel off my dress, exposing the bikini beneath, and I begin to layer myself with sunscreen. The pool is lively this morning for a weekday. Lots of mothers relaxing while their children are in school I surmise. I feel a little out of place here, which is crazy. Back home, my parents were club members, and I spent most of my childhood summers in swim or tennis lessons. My mother loved to lie by the pool with a daiquiri in hand and gossip with her friends while we swam till our hands and feet were pruned. But here is different. Here, I am an employee of the club, and I could never afford a membership. I am only allowed to use the pool as a guest of Dawn, Kelsey, or Daniel, and I feel like the other employees are judging me when they have to bring me a drink or a towel or anything.

I am lying on my stomach, letting the sun hit my back, and drifting in and out of sleep when Jake sits down on the lounge beside me. I jump when his hands tickle up my bare sides.

"Sorry, I didn't mean to scare you. You just looked too irresistible, lying there, for me not to touch you."

Ever since our first date to the pier, we have been seeing each other pretty steadily. He's kept to his word, and he hasn't been the least bit pushy, so I am now very comfortable with him and his touch. In fact, I find myself seeking his touch more and more.

I lean over and plant a kiss on his lips. "I didn't know you were going to be here."

"Well, I wasn't planning on it, but when I got your text, saying you and the girls were heading this way, I thought I would drop by and say hello while I was at lunch."

I get up and gather my things. "You want to head inside and get a bite to eat then?"

"Yes, ma'am."

I ask Dawn and Kelsey to save my spot, and I pull my dress back over my swimsuit. Then, I take Jake's hand, and he leads me into the club's restaurant. We pass a table full of girls, who are drinking pitchers of mimosas and laughing as they chatter away.

"Jake?" one of the girls from the table, a gorgeous redhead, calls to Jake as we pass. Then, she gets up and comes over to wrap her arms around him before placing a kiss right on his lips.

What in the hell? I am standing right here with my hand in his. Jealousy flares, which catches me off guard. I do not know exactly when I became territorial over him, but here I am, one second from tearing her arms from her body if she doesn't remove them from around his neck.

"Carlie. Hey," he says, and he sounds a bit startled by her ballsy attack.

"I haven't seen you in ages, baby. Why haven't you returned my calls?" she purrs at him.

And it dawns on me. She is the girl he was meeting the night Julie and I ran into him. They must have been dating.

"Sorry. I have been busy. You remember Brie Masters, don't you?"

She turns to look at me as if she is just now noticing someone else is standing with him. "Oh, yes. Brie, is it? Don't you work here?" She gives me a once-over, and I can feel the disdain dripping off of her.

"Yep, I sure do, but today, I am having lunch with my boyfriend," I say sweetly as I innocently bat my eyelashes at her.

The blow hits the mark because her face instantly turns as red as her hair.

She turns to Jake. "Can I have a word—alone?"

Jake is obviously amused by our little confrontation.

"I don't think my girlfriend here would appreciate that, and she is obviously a bit hangry, so I'd better get her fed. It was good to see you. Tell the girls hello for me."

He leads me away and to a table out of sight.

"Ugh, she has some nerve. I mean, who does that? She could clearly see you were holding my hand. It takes a major bitch to walk up to a man who is with someone else and kiss him. Right in front of me. She is lucky I like my job, or I would have punched her right in her high-dollar nose job for being so disrespectful."

I keep ranting as we are seated, and the waiter fills our water glasses. I look up to find a very amused Jake grinning at me.

"What?" I snap.

"So, I am your boyfriend. I knew I would eventually wear you down."

That's when the weight of what I said comes down on me. *Oh my God. Oh my God. Jake and I are officially a couple.* I did this. I just declared it out loud to him, and I can tell by the way he is looking at me that he is not going to let me take it back. *Oh well. In for a penny, in for a pound.*

"I … well, I mean … do you want to be my boyfriend?"

He looks at me like I have gone mad. "Baby, I have been yours for a while now. I have just been waiting for you to realize it."

We order, and I wait for the panic to rise, but it doesn't. All I feel is content and happy. We finish our food, and Jake walks me back toward the pool, but before we make it there, he stops and guides us into the sauna. It is empty, and he clicks the lock but doesn't turn on the heater. Then, he backs me up to one of the benches, and he fists the hem of my dress and pulls it over my head.

"You know, I really love this bikini on you," he says hoarsely as he peppers kisses down my neck and across my chest.

I lie back and relax and give him full access as he follows me down. I start clawing at his shirt to free it from his pants and pull it over his head. I love his chest. I love how hard and defined it is. I run my hands across it as he comes back down on top of me. His lips take mine in a heated kiss as his hands skim down my sides and under my ass, and he lifts me to him. Um, delicious contact. I press against him and kiss him harder and deeper. He glides his hands into my bottoms and grasps my ass with both, kneading and pulling me up to meet him. I gasp at the sensation, and I lift my right leg and wrap it around his back to bring us more fully together. My need is great.

For the past few weeks, he has been so patient with me. Never taking more than I have been willing to give. Never pushing. But I think my declaration at lunch just gave him permission to take the lead, and I find that I want him to. I want him. I want to feel him. All of him.

I reach between us, and I glide my hand down the front of his pants. I feel him hard against my palm, and I start to stroke him. He lets out a gurgle and breaks his mouth from mine.

Then, he places his forehead to mine and whispers against my lips, "Damn, baby. I want you so bad right now. I wish I didn't have to go back to the office. I would pick you up and carry you to my car and drive us straight to my house and make love to you until we both dropped from exhaustion."

My breath hitches at his words, and my body wants to start moving again.

"But I can't," he adds, his words dripping with remorse. "I have a meeting I have to attend, and I am not gonna be inside you for the first time in the sauna at the club. Honestly, I am about to come in my pants like a sixteen-year-old."

I giggle up at him.

"You think that's funny, huh?" he says as he swipes a piece of hair out of my eyes.

"No, but I guess you'd better let me up, so you don't have an embarrassing accident on your hands, Mr. Mason."

He kisses me hard one more time. Then, he helps me up, and we get dressed again. When he opens the door to exit the sauna, Carlie and her friends are standing outside, waiting to get in.

Jake ignores the looks on their faces and just takes my hand. He nods in their direction. "Ladies, it's all yours," he says and leads me away.

"So, where have you been?" Dawn asks.

I settle back into my lounger beside Dawn and Kels, and Jake heads back to work.

"I told you I was going in to grab lunch with Jake."

"Yeah, you did, and Mr. Cloniger came by looking for you. He said something about an instructor canceling and needing you to take on a youth group class tonight or something, so I went to get you, and you were nowhere to be found. That was forty-five minutes ago ," she informs me.

Crap. Busted.

"I don't know. We took a walk."

"Uh-huh. Sure, you did. Is that why you are blushing from head to toe right now?" Kelsey teases.

"Okay, so maybe we took a detour into the sauna for a quick make-out session before he had to leave." I look over at their grinning faces. "Happy now?"

"We will be as soon as you spill some hot details on us ," Dawn adds.

They both look at me expectantly.

"Not gonna happen here, guys. Big ears everywhere."

Kelsey starts pouting, and I promise to fill them in later. The pool is starting to get crowded with all the parents showing up with their children after school, so we decide to pack up and head home. Carlie and her friends walk past us as they claim a couple of loungers down from where we were. I look back, and I see the anger on her face, directed right at me. I know that she is going to be a problem. I just know it.

CHAPTER
Twenty-Two

Gabby
Past

I LOCK MYSELF IN THE BATHROOM WITH THE PHONE GRASPED TIGHTLY in my hand. I splash some cold water on my face and try to calm down. I don't know what is wrong, but something definitely is. I can feel my heart racing, and I am burning up. Dante is refusing to take me home. He says I just need to eat something, and I'll be fine, but I don't think so. I ate quite a bit at dinner, which was only an hour or so ago, and the two drinks I have had since we arrived should not be hitting me this hard. Maybe I had bad pork empanadas at Havana Central. My skin is crawling, and I feel a little dizzy.

I look at the phone in my hand and try to think of who to call. I don't know many numbers by heart. Everything is stored in my phone, which is in my purse that Dante locked in his trunk. I try Nicco's number. That one I know. He is going to be upset that I am calling so late, but I know he will come get me. The call goes straight to voicemail. *Damn it.* I am not going to call 9-1-1. That would be overreacting. I decide to call the only other number I know by heart.

"Hello?" His sleepy voice comes over the line.

"Cross," I say hesitantly.

"Gabby? What time is it? Did you get a new number?"

I let out a little sob of relief.

"What's wrong?" He sounds more alert now. "Talk to me, baby. Are you okay?"

"No."

"Are you hurt?" I can hear him rustling around now, like he is up and dressing.

"I don't think so"—I sniffle—"but I don't feel right."

"Where are you?"

"I don't know. I came to a party in SoHo with Dante. We have been here about an hour, I think, and something is wrong. I am dizzy, and my heart is racing. He doesn't want to leave and he won't let me leave by myself and my phone is in my purse in his car in the parking garage. I grabbed the phone off the wall downstairs and came to the bathroom upstairs to splash some cold water on my face, but it is not helping. I only know your number and Nicco's number, and he isn't answering his cell."

"What do you mean, he won't let you leave?"

"I told him I didn't feel well and wanted to call a cab to go home, and he said I just needed to eat and that he wouldn't call a cab for me to leave alone this late because it's not safe or something."

"Fuck."

"Cross?"

"Gabby, I am on my way. Do not leave that bathroom. Stay locked in there, okay?"

"How will you find me?"

"I will; trust me. Baby, stay locked in there. Do not leave that bathroom. I have to hang up now."

"No, please don't hang up," I cry into the phone.

"I have to let you go, so I can make a call to someone who can help me find you."

"What if you can't find me?"

"I promise you, I will."

"Please hurry."

"I promise I will get there as fast as I can. Stay locked in that bathroom, and don't come out until you hear my voice."

He hangs up, and my legs start to shake, so I sit on the floor with the phone clutched in my hand. After about twenty minutes or so, a banging starts on the door.

"Gabby, what's taking you so long in there?"

It's Dante. I knew it would not be long before he started missing me and came searching.

"I don't feel very good."

"Are you getting sick? Open the door."

"I think I need to go home now."

"Okay, come out, and I'll call down for my car."

"Really? I thought you didn't want to leave."

"I'll take you home, and I'll come back."

For some reason, I don't like that idea. Alone in a car with him is not something I want right now.

"Can we just call me a cab?"

He doesn't say anything for a few minutes. Then, he relents. "Okay, come on out, and we will go downstairs and call a cab for you."

Relieved, I stand up, and I hide the phone in the bathroom drawer. I don't want him to know I freaked out and tried to call my brother. When I open the door, he is standing there in the hall, looking very put out. I am sure this is not the date night he had in mind, and for a moment, I feel a little guilty for ruining his night.

"I am sorry our evening is ending this way. I really don't know what's happening. Maybe I ate something bad at dinner."

He comes closer and starts to stroke my hair out of my face. "Maybe. You know, my friend offered us a room here for the night, and I think, if you just lie down for a little while, you might start to feel better."

"That's nice of him, but honestly, I just want to go home and go to sleep in my bed."

"You can sleep here. I will hold you all night, and I will take care of you. Doesn't that sound nice?"

It does sound nice. He is stroking my arms up and down now, and it feels amazing.

"I can rub your back," he says as he slides his hands behind me and starts to trail them up and down my back, kneading lightly, "and other things."

"I … maybe … another time? I don't think I am going to be much fun tonight," I protest as I actually arch into his touch.

"I disagree, baby. I think you are going to be a lot of fun tonight," he growls as he nips at my earlobe.

Why is he being so difficult? It's one ruined date. We can go out another night.

I pry myself out of his hold. His hands are distracting me, and I keep losing my train of thought.

"Come back here, Gabby, now," he demands in a low, angry voice.

Confused by his anger, I slowly step back to him, and he grabs my arm and wrenches it behind my back. It hurts, and I let out a surprised yelp. Then, he backs me against the wall.

"I have been chasing you for years now. Ever since you teased me with your little show at the hot springs. Do you know how many nights those pink lacy bra and panties of yours have haunted me?"

He has me pinned with his hot breath on my face. It smells of vodka and makes my stomach turn.

"Now, I finally have you right here, and in a few more minutes, when the ecstasy your drinks were laced with kicks in, you are going to let me do all the dirty things I have been fantasizing about to you, and the best part is, you are going to enjoy every single depraved thing."

"What? You drugged my drinks?"

He smirks. "Baby, you asked for those drinks, and everyone here knows the drinks are laced with X," he says as he skims his hand down my side.

My own body betrays me, and I shiver because it feels so good.

"I did not know. Please, let me go. We can finish our date another night. I promise."

He continues to caress my body and starts to move my hair, so he has access to my neck.

"Please, Dante, you said you would call me a cab. Please let me go home."

"Mmm," he says as he presses even closer to me, "I like it when you beg, baby. That sweet little mouth of yours will be begging me all night long."

Then, he takes his hand from my side and moves it under my dress. I am paralyzed with fear.

"What do we have here?" he asks as he glides his fingers between my thighs. "Oh, your panties are so wet. I think our party favor is starting to kick in."

I moan, and I am so embarrassed by my reaction to his touch.

"I love that sound. Tell me, Gabby, are your panties pink tonight?"

He licks my neck, and I try to bring my hands up to scratch his face.

"Uh-uh-uh, you can scratch your nails down my back later while I am inside you," he says as he grabs both hands and pins them above my head and returns his other hand under my dress. He hooks his finger in my panties and is just about to pull them down.

"Stop. Please stop and let me go. I don't want this."

"Your body is saying something different."

That is when we hear footsteps thundering up the stairs.

"Listen to her fucking words and get your fucking hands off of her!" Cross roars.

Dante immediately grabs me and throws me down behind him. I catch myself at an awkward angle and cry out in pain as my head hits the table in the hallway, and my arm is twisted beneath me. I reach up and feel the blood trickling down my forehead. Cross dives for Dante. He is murderous, and for a second, I am scared he is going to kill him. He keeps repeatedly hitting him, and Dante fights back as best he can, but he is no match for Cross's fury.

I want to leave. I want to leave now. I need Cross to take me home.

I start to cry out his name just as other people from the party come rushing up the stairs. One of the girls comes to help me up, and a couple of the guys pull Cross off Dante. He jerks away from them and comes for me. He picks me up in his arms and starts to carry me down.

As he passes the guy who lives at the condo, he says, "You will answer for this."

The guy throws his hands up and pleads, "Cross, man, I had no idea he was feeding her X without her knowledge, I swear to God."

Cross just barrels past him, and as we get to the bottom of the steps, Dante manages to get up.

He yells down to us, "She wanted it. Her panties are so wet; she was begging for me to touch her."

I tuck my face into Cross's neck and cling tighter to him.

He turns back, and I whimper, "Please don't. I just want to go home."

"I will deal with you later, Calvacanti. Don't think this is over."

I am aching in the front seat of Cross's car. I have no idea how he found me, and at the moment, I don't care. My skin is too hot, and the air conditioner blowing on my body is a sweet agony. I can't make the throbbing between my legs stop, and I can feel every single droplet of sweat sliding down my back. It's a wonderful and an awful feeling.

When we pull into Cross's driveway, I am barely out of the car and up his front steps before I am pulling at the straps of my dress. *Off. I have to get it off now.*

Cross gets the door open, and I burst inside and kick my shoes off. Then, I drop my dress to the floor. He gathers my things as I climb onto his bed. I lie there, almost hyperventilating. I want to crawl out of my skin. It's too much.

He comes over with a bottle of water. "Here, Gabby, you need to drink this. The X is going to dehydrate you."

I moan as I take the cool bottle and rub it on my stomach. It feels good. I am so hot. I want to roll the bottle all over me.

"No, baby." He takes it from my hands and opens it. "You have to drink it."

I sit up a little and let him bring the bottle to my lips. I drink it down.

"That's it, all of it. Good girl."

He starts to get up, and I grab his arm and stop him. Then, I climb into his lap.

"We need to get you in a cool shower, and I want to clean that cut on your head."

I start writhing in his lap. I need friction. My body needs friction. I can feel his cock growing hard beneath me, and I sit down hard on his lap. *Ahhh.* I wrap my arms around his neck to steady myself, and I start moving. He brings his hands to my hips and halts me. I cry out.

"Please, Cross, please. I need you. Please."

I am out of my mind. I have no idea how much of this drug I consumed, and at the moment, I do not care. I just want the ache to go away.

"Okay, okay, I am going to make it better, I promise."

He picks me up, and then he lays us both back on the bed. He is beside me with my back to his chest. I protest because I think he is going to try to get me to go to sleep now, and I can't. I just can't. I am on fire right now.

"Shh, baby, I am going to make it better."

He slides his hand down my side, and I groan. The contact feels so good. Better than any touch I have ever had. I back up into him, and he wraps one arm around me, and the other hand continues. He presses his palm between my legs, and I shudder at the pleasure of the pressure against me. He holds it there. *Yes, oh, yes, that is exactly where I need him.* I start rocking back and forth on his hand, but it's not enough. I need more.

I turn my head back to him, and I beg, "Cross, please."

"Say it again."

"Pleeeease," I whimper.

"No, *Tesoro*. My name. Say my name again."

"Cross," I cry, and he crushes his mouth to mine.

Our tongues wrestle. I am wild. I bite at his lips and suck his tongue into my mouth with a force that makes him groan loudly down my throat. I am fighting for him to ease whatever this need is pulsing through me.

I tear my mouth from his. "Cross, touch me. Oh God, touch me."

He places his forehead against mine, closes his eyes, and he lets out a breath. "Baby, I am afraid, if I do, I won't be able to stop."

"It's okay if you don't stop."

"No, it's not. You've been drugged, and you don't want this. You need this, but you don't want it."

"Yes, I do," I persist. "It's you, Cross. It's always been you."

He sucks in a breath at my words. Words that I mean. Then, he opens his eyes and searches mine. I can't wait for him any longer. I reach for his hand, and I put it where I need it to be. I start moving again. All while looking right into his eyes.

I want this. See how much I want this.

"Shit." He gives in, and I feel his fingers slide into my panties.

Oh, sweet relief.

He starts sliding his fingers through my wetness, and then he rolls me over, so he can pull my panties down my legs. For a minute, he sits there, looking at me, and I think he might stop.

"You are fucking beautiful, Gabby," he says hoarsely.

Then, he spreads my legs wider apart. He runs his nose up my core and breathes in deeply. He hooks one leg over his shoulder and lowers his mouth to me. I feel his tongue run a line right through my folds, and I buck off the bed.

He brings his hands to either side of my hips to hold me in place.

"God, you taste better than I imagined," he whispers.

Then, his tongue does a delicious swirl around my clit, and I cry out. It feels so damn good. He sucks me into his mouth as he inserts a finger inside me, and I swear, I see stars. I start grinding myself into his face, needing more, needing it faster, harder, deeper. He adds another finger and then another, and I explode in his mouth. Like a bomb going off, I scream out his name as I grip his hair and hold him to me. He laps at me, getting every drop, and continues to pump his fingers in and out until I ride my climax to completion.

Wow. I am spent. My entire body is liquid. He crawls up my body and kisses me one more time. I faintly taste myself on his lips. He gets up and heads to the bathroom, and I roll over and pull the covers over me. I am sated and happy. I can feel him sit back down next to me. I think he is cleaning the cut on my head as sleep pulls me under.

CHAPTER
Twenty-Three

Brie

Present

DECEMBER HAS BEEN A HARD MONTH FOR ME. I LOVE THE HOLIdays. It is my favorite time of the year. Back home, the month was filled with extravagant parties and dances and shows. My social calendar would be bursting at the seams. Then, Christmas Eve and Christmas Day would be spent with my large, loud family, attending mass and feasting and exchanging gifts. Magical. This year, it's been work and school and a lot of alone time while the girls spend time with their families and Jake spends time with his. He invited me to church with his parents and sisters, but it's way too soon for that. I need to keep our relationship at a pace I am comfortable with.

Rick and Melanie have had many events to attend, so I have gotten extra time with the baby, and that has been my saving grace. I cannot be sad, looking into his tiny, little face. They have also allowed me to help make his first Christmas extra special. I accompanied him and his mom to the mall for his first pictures with Santa, which he screamed all the way through. I went with them to pick out their tree and spent the night decorating it with them. The tree fascinates him. His little face beams, and he squeals whenever we turn on the twinkling lights. A man after my own heart. He is eight months old now and crawling all over the place, so Melanie cannot place any presents under the tree.

She had a couple under it the night we decorated. When we returned from the kitchen with cocoa, Cassian was sitting under the tree with his little fists full of wrapping paper, and it was headed straight for his mouth. Everything goes straight into his mouth nowadays.

God, I love that kid.

Tonight is going to be special. I am cooking for my friends for the first time. A full-out *Tastes of Italiano* holiday feast, complete with homemade broth and bread-dumpling soup, baccala, handmade fileja pasta, marinara, meat sauce, rack of lamb marinated in red wine and herbs, grilled asparagus, roasted rosemary potatoes, with struffoli and Buccellato cake for dessert. It is the week before Christmas, and I took the entire weekend off, so I could prepare and make every dish from scratch. It is therapeutic.

"Girl. Oh my goodness! It smells amazing in here." Dawn comes bouncing into the kitchen while I am rolling out pasta. "I cannot believe you are making that by hand. You have been holding out on us. If I had known you could cook like this, I would have been making requests."

"Exactly why I did not tell you," I tease.

She sticks her tongue out at me and steals a taste of the sauce that has been simmering on the stove since very early this morning. "Oh, yum. Is it possible to fall in love with a ragu? Because I am pretty sure my mouth just had an orgasm."

I laugh at her and shoo her away from the stove. "Go away. No eating until tonight."

"What? I have to starve all day?"

"Go rummage through the fridge. Just stay out of my bags."

She pouts and grabs a banana and a coconut water.

"So, who all is coming to this shindig anyway?"

"You, Kelsey, Daniel, Julie, Jake and his two sisters, Melanie and Rick, Uncle Matt and Susan and me."

That is an even dozen. Any more, and we would not have room to seat them. As it is, we can accommodate six at the kitchen island, and the other six are going to have to eat in the living room or at the outside table. Luckily, Santa Monica in December is warm enough for outdoor dining. In New York, your food would freeze to your fork before it made it from your plate to your mouth.

"Full house. I like it."

Dawn loves entertaining. She just loves people, period. It is one of her best qualities.

Three hours later, and I am pulling myself together after finally being able to shower. Everything is as ready as it is going to get. Kelsey has Christmas music playing and a snowflake martini in hand when I come down the hall. It's good to see her getting into the spirit.

The breakup has been rough for her. One week after she threw him out, Dawn spotted Bradley out to dinner with Tonya. There was a tiny altercation, which ended with Tonya wearing her dinner home. I wish I had been there to see her covered in lobster bisque. He hasn't stopped calling either. Constantly. How could he possibly think she would take him back after all this? Men are so clueless.

We use the occasion to dress up, so Dawn, Kels, and I stand in front of our tree in our red dresses, and Daniel snaps a few pictures right before the guests start to arrive. One by one, they pop in with gifts in hand. Flowers and bottles of wine. The last to arrive are Jake and his sisters.

"Hey, baby," he says as he wraps me in his arms. "These are my sisters, Brittney and Emily," he introduces me to the two girls, who follow him in.

This I can do. No way am I ready to meet his parents and do the whole family Christmas thing with them, but having his sisters over for a casual dinner party at my apartment, that is a step I am comfortable with.

"Hi, girls. So nice to meet you both. I am glad you were able to make it."

"Thank you for the invite," Brittney says as she hands me a bottle of red wine. "We hope you like red. It's our favorite."

"I love red, and this will be perfect with the lamb. Please give your coats to Daniel, and he'll take them in my room. Then, come in the kitchen and make a drink."

An hour later, and everyone is making their plates. I have Cassian in my arms. The sitter Melanie and Rick had hired for the night had to cancel.

"I am so sorry. We won't stay long," Melanie says as she settles at the island with her plate. "We will just eat and be on our way."

"Are you crazy? You can stay as long as you like. I love having him here. It doesn't bother me one bit."

"So, this is the other guy in your life, huh?" Jake asks.

"Yep, this is my one true love."

"Ouch. Hey there, little guy. That's my girl, you know."

Cassian just turns his big emerald-green eyes to Jake and grins. Then, he snuggles in close up under my chin as if to say, *Mine.*

Jake bursts out laughing. "I guess you showed me." He reaches out and pets the baby's head. "Message received loud and clear, little dude."

Melanie smiles at us. "He is super possessive of his BB."

"BB," Cassian coos, and my heart melts.

"I don't blame you, little man. She is pretty incredible."

He kisses the top of my head, and Cassian grunts in protest. Then, he takes his little hand and pushes Jake away from me. We all erupt into laughter.

"Oh my God, Brie. This food is amazing. It's like eating your nonna's cooking but even better." Uncle Matt barely stops shoveling food in his mouth to give me the compliment. What a huge compliment it is, too, because my nonna is the best cook I know, hands down better than any chef.

"Yes, dear, you should be doing this for a living now. I know tons of socialites who would be willing to pay you a lot of money to cater their parties," Kelsey's mom, Susan, agrees.

"You think?"

"Darling, I know. If you have a business card printed up, I will be happy to pass it along to all my friends."

Another source of income would be great. I don't want to spread myself too thin, but if I could start cooking for a living now, that would bring me one step closer to my dream, and as much as I have enjoyed working at the club, my heart would not be broken if I were in a position to give that up.

"I will have cards printed this week and send them over with Daniel."

"Awesome, darling."

I adore Susan. She and Daniel might have had a rocky start, but she is fierce and unashamedly bougie. She reminds me of a young Joan Collins. I mean, she came to a party at her husband's niece's apartment in a long cocktail dress and fur, dripping in diamonds and rubies. Freaking baller. I want to be her when I grow up.

Around midnight, everything is winding down, and the only ones left are Daniel and Jake and his sisters. The girls are in the kitchen, making to-go plates, when Jake walks with me to my room to gather their coats.

"Hey, I have something for you." He pulls a small box from his coat pocket.

Oh shit, I didn't get him anything. Are we at the place where we buy each other gifts? Crap, I guess we are. Jeez, I am really bad at this girlfriend thing.

I think he notices the panic on my face.

"Hey, it's nothing big, I promise. Relax."

He hands me the box, and I carefully open it. Inside is a beautiful blown glass Ferris wheel Christmas ornament.

"So you always remember our first official date."

"I love it. It's perfect."

And it is. It's thoughtful, sentimental, and inexpensive. I am so thankful he knew not to make a big deal because I am sure he had to fight against his instinct. He is definitely more the grand-gesture guy.

We head back down the hall to the living room.

"Oh, and one more thing."

He turns and reaches in his coat again, and he produces a mistletoe.

I freeze.

Then, I throw my hands up and squeeze my eyes tightly shut. "No. No. No."

I stand there in the dark for a few long minutes. When I open my eyes, the others have come in the room, and all are watching me.

"It's just mistletoe, Brie. I was just going to ask you for a Christmas kiss."

I feel so stupid. Everyone has a look of concern and puzzlement on their faces. I want to turn and run to my room and hide, but I don't.

"I am sorry. I don't do mistletoe. It's just a thing. I had a bad experience with it once." I know I sound ridiculous, but I can't explain it any further. "You don't need it to get a Christmas kiss from me anyway."

"Okay. No big deal."

He crumples the offending branch in his hand and cautiously approaches me.

Everyone pretends to disperse, and the girls start putting on their coats.

He wraps his hand around my neck and tugs me in close. "You okay?"

I just nod.

"All right. I have to get the girls home. Thank you for dinner. It was a great night."

I nod again, still not meeting his eyes. I am so embarrassed.

"Hey, look at me."

At that, I lift my head. "I am sorry about the awkward moment."

He leans in and plants a kiss on my lips. "I got my Christmas kiss, and that is all that matters."

I smile up at him. Thankful that he let me get away with it and isn't pushing.

"I wish I could stay and kiss you all night, but I am the girls' ride."

"Next time," I whisper to him.

He gives me one more long kiss, and they are off.

I wave as they head out the door and down the steps.

When I close the door, Kelsey comes and wraps her arms around me from behind. "That was an awesome party. I say we finish this bottle of wine and put *Elf* in the Blu-ray. The rest of the dishes can wait till tomorrow."

"Sounds great to me."

"By the way," Dawn yells from the kitchen, "you are making the food next Tuesday. You can make taco-filled ravioli or lasagna or something. We will do Italian-themed outfits. What do Italians wear anyway?"

I look down at my dress. "What do Italians wear? We dress just like you do."

She comes into the living room with her nose wrinkled up. "That can't be right. We have to Italian it up a bit."

Kelsey and I crack up.

"Okay, Dawn, I'll get us some A.S. Roma football jerseys or something."

She shrugs. "Works for me. I didn't even know they had football in Italy. Oh! We can do shoulder pads and put those black stripes under our eyes. Maybe we should do helmets instead of sombreros."

"Shh, she'll never know," Kels whispers to me.

And we laugh.

We all change into our matching Christmas PJs I bought for us and settle in for our movie. Daniel, too. I sigh in contentment. These are my people now. *La mia famiglia.*

CHAPTER
Twenty-four

Gabby
Past

I WAKE WITH A HORRIBLE HEADACHE. I REACH UP AND WINCE WHEN I feel the bandage at my temple. It's tender to the touch. I look around with blurry vision and don't see Cross, so I crawl down the bed and tiptoe over to the kitchen. I am so thirsty. I grab a bottle of water from the fridge and walk over to look out the window to see if his car is still in the drive. I see him out front with Nicco.

Great, I guess he knows about my night now. I move closer to the window to eavesdrop.

"I knew. As soon as she said she felt strange and he wouldn't let her leave. I knew that punk had drugged her. I told her to lock herself in the bathroom and not to come out. Somehow, the fucker got her to come out before I could get there."

Nicco is turning bright red with rage. "How did you find her?"

"I called Manny and had him trace the phone number she'd called from. It was Bryant's apartment. I should have known. He is infamous for throwing X parties. I raced to SoHo as fast as I could without killing myself or anyone else. When I got there, Bryant answered the door and acted like he had no idea who Dante was. When I told him he had Tony Mastreoni's baby sister with him, he went pale as a ghost and pointed me upstairs. That's where I found the two of them."

Cross's hands are balled tightly by his sides now, and he is pacing back and forth in front of Nicco's car.

"He had her pinned against the fucking wall with his hand under her skirt. She was begging him to stop. I lost it, man. Completely lost it. I charged at him, and he launched her behind him. She screamed out in pain, and I saw blood running down her face. I just started pounding him. I would have kept pounding him until he wasn't breathing anymore if I hadn't been pulled off of him."

"Why didn't you call me to go with you? I would have finished the fucker myself," Nicco says through gritted teeth.

"I tried to call you. She tried to call you. We both were going to voicemail, and I didn't have time to waste tracking you down."

"Fuck, it's Marianna. She does that shit. Turns my phone off because she doesn't like me getting calls on *her* time."

Cross gives him an *are you kidding me* look.

And Nicco tells him, "It won't happen ever again.

"Where is she now? I'll take her to Marianna's place for a few days to recover, and you and I are going to pay Bryant and Dante fucking Calvacanti a visit."

"No," Cross says.

"What do you mean, no?"

"She is not going anywhere."

"Dude, Angelica is going to flip her shit if she finds her here. Marianna has a spare room and a nursing degree."

"I said no."

They just stand there, staring each other down for a few long moments, and I am holding my breath. Nicco looks angry with Cross for some reason. I make for the door to stop whatever this showdown is because I do not want my stupidity to get them into a fight, but before I can open it, Nicco breaks the silence.

"Now? Are you sure you want to do this now?"

"I have to do this now. I am done with this dance, Nicco. I have been respectful. I have done what was asked of me, but she is not leaving here. She is mine. She has always been mine. I cannot sit back and watch every man she comes in contact with fight to capture her attention anymore, and I damn sure will not let another one lay a single finger on her again."

"They won't make it easy on you."

"I know."

"She might not want this. Have you considered that?"

"Yes."

"Then, what?"

"I'll cross that bridge if I come to it, but for now, you need to call a meeting with your brothers. I need to see them face-to-face. As soon as possible."

"Okay. But, first, are we going to SoHo or what?"

"Definitely. He has her purse and phone, and I want your brothers in on this, too. If his ass is in hiding, we will need all our resources to find him."

"On it." Nicco walks to his car with his phone to his ear.

What the hell was all that about?

My head hurts too much to try to decipher it all. I need to lie back down. I run to the bathroom to pee and stop dead when I see myself in the mirror. *Oh my God.* My hair is matted to my head with dried blood. My left eye is black and puffy, and my right arm is killing me. I peel the bandage off of my temple, and there is a large gash held together by butterfly tape. I feel like I might pass out. I steady myself on the sink. A soft knock comes at the door a few seconds later.

"*Tesoro*, are you okay?"

"Go away, Cross."

"No going away, Gabby."

"Please. I don't want anyone to see me like this."

"I have already seen it."

"Don't let Nicco in."

"Don't think I will be able to keep him out."

I start to quietly cry.

"Let me in, baby, so I can help you."

I sink to the floor and wrap my arms around my knees. I start rocking, and a few minutes later, I hear them picking the lock on the door. Then, I am in Cross's arms, and Nicco is right behind him. I bury my face in his neck to hide as he carries me from the room, but there is no hiding. He sits on the edge of the bed and rubs my back until the tears subside.

"Hey, sis." Nicco kneels down in front of us and speaks softly, "It's okay. Marianna is on her way here to check you out. It's all just surface. It will heal."

I turn my wet face to him. "I am so embarrassed."

"You shouldn't be. You did everything right. I am so very proud of you, and I am so sorry I didn't get your call last night. When I think of what could have happened …" He closes his eyes tight as if imagining it. "Thank God you remembered Cross's number, and he actually picked up the fucking call."

He is angry with himself. He should not be angry with himself. None of this is his fault. I wouldn't have answered a strange number that late either. I reach over and tightly hug him. He gently rubs my hair and hugs me back.

"It is okay. I wouldn't have answered an unknown number in the middle of the night either. This is not your fault. This is all my fault."

He pulls back and looks me dead in the eyes. "No, ma'am. A girl should be able to go out on a date with a man without worrying about being assaulted. This is most definitely not your fault."

"It's Calvacanti's fault. His and his alone," Cross hisses.

After they have me calmed down and Marianna comes to check and redress my head and my arm, Cross informs me that she is going to stay with me for a while, so he and Nicco can run an errand.

"No, please don't go." I cling to him.

"I won't be long, *Tesoro*." He kisses the top of my head. "Marianna is going to make us all dinner, and we will eat and watch a movie when we get back."

"I don't want you or any of my brothers to get into any trouble because of me," I whisper.

He sits down on the bed beside me.

"We have to handle this, Gabby. We want to get your belongings back, and we have to deal with Bryant and Dante now. When we are done, I can guarantee no other girl will ever walk into one of Bryant's house parties without him making extra sure she knows exactly what she is there for."

"What about Dante?"

"I had my go at him last night. Now, it's your brothers' turns. It is up to them what happens to him. I just want to get your things back to you."

"Do you have to tell them?" I am still so ashamed.

"Yes, I already have told them. This is not something I could keep from them."

I swallow my tears. "Please don't let them do anything that will land them in serious trouble. He is not worth them going to jail. Please, Cross, promise me."

"I will do my best."

That's all I can hope for at this point. I can imagine the state Tony is in. He will kill Dante if he is left alone with him. I just know it.

I watch as Cross and Nicco head out to meet him, hopefully, they can keep him at bay. I look over at Marianna, who is starting to chop vegetables. She seems as worried as I am.

"Can I help?"

"Sure, if you feel up to it."

We cook in nervous silence and wait for the guys to return.

CHAPTER
Twenty-five

Brie

Present

I T'S CHRISTMAS EVE. UNCLE MATT AND SUSAN INVITED ME TO COME stay at their home through Christmas. They said I should be with family. I declined. I don't want to impose. I came tonight to eat and exchange gifts with them, but I plan to go back to the apartment and celebrate Jesus's birth alone with a pint of Haagen-Dazs Rum Raisin. I truly am fine. I thought I would have a harder time, but I survived last year away from home, and honestly, this year, I am enjoying my alone time.

Jake left for Aspen with his parents and sisters last night. It's their family tradition to spend Christmas Eve through New Year's Day in Aspen. He wanted to stay behind this year for me, but I encouraged him to go. Traditions are something you should keep. I agreed to him coming home a day early though, so we could ring the New Year in together. That appeased him, and I am looking so forward to it. I am going to miss him while he is gone. My barriers are coming down brick by brick, and my feelings for him are getting stronger every day.

We are gathered in front of the tree and about to exchange gifts. I could not do much, but I managed to find them all a little something that reminded me of them. A spa package at the club for Susan— thanks to my employee discount rate, which I am pretty sure did not exist until Mr. Cloniger decided it did for me—and a pair of vintage Ray-Ban aviators for Uncle Matt because he is too cool for the awful shades he has been wearing.

Kelsey's and Dawn's gifts—handmade earrings by a local artist—are back home. We will be exchanging gifts next week, as Kels is celebrating with her dad and his family tonight.

Daniel opens his gift next, and it is a handmade leather guitar case. I noticed the one he carries around has seen better days, and the zipper is always getting stuck. So, when a man who owned a fetish leather shop in LA hired me for private tennis lessons, I got the idea. His shop specializes in hand-tooled masks and crops and things of that nature, but he could do anything. He told me, while we were playing one afternoon, that he had hand-made a clarinet case for his daughter who was in her middle school band, and that was when I asked if he could do a custom guitar case for Daniel. He agreed to give it a shot, and since it was his first one, he did it for a steal. I had Daniel's initials branded into the side, and his band's logo was emblazoned on the front. I think it is beautiful, and the smell of the new leather when you open it is heavenly.

"Brie"—he reverently runs his hands over the logo—"this is amazing."

"Do you really like it?"

"Like it? Are you kidding me? It's cool as shit," he exclaims as he unzips the case and looks inside. "This must have been expensive."

"Not as much as you might think."

He gives me a look that says he doesn't believe me, and I am so happy I was able to give him something he loves. He has been a lifesaver. Truly. This transition would have been so much harder for me without him.

We continue opening boxes, and they have spoiled me. I am the new owner of a couple of Tarte eye-shadow palettes, a pair of Jimmy Choos, a toggle bracelet from Tiffany with a signature blue enamel cupcake charm, a Givenchy handbag, and a new generation iPhone because mine is on its last legs.

The doorbell rings a few minutes later.

"I think that maybe your last present just arrived, Brie."

Daniel hops up and walks to the foyer. I wonder what he could have gotten me that is being delivered this late on Christmas Eve.

I look at Susan. "What in the world? You guys have already gotten me so much. I do not need another gift."

She just grins conspiratorially as we hear the door open and close.

He walks back in and announces, "It is. Right on time, too."

He steps to the side, and there, standing behind him, with a huge smile on his face, is my big brother Nicco. I leap to my feet and run into his arms. He catches me and then picks me up and twirls me around. A cry of pure joy escapes me, and he puts me down and raises my chin.

"I hope those are happy tears, *cara.*"

They definitely are. As much as I have convinced myself I am perfectly content on my own, I am over the moon to lay my eyes on my big brother.

"Of course they are. But why are you here? Is it only you? Don't you want to be home for Christmas? What about the boys and Marianna?" I start hurling question after question at him in rapid succession because I can't believe he is here.

"Well, for one thing, Marianna and I broke up months ago, and Mamma was more than happy to let me out of family obligations when she heard I was coming to California."

Mamma. I have only spoken to her a handful of times since I left. She is my biggest ally in this move. Although it's silent encouragement at this point. Papa is not happy. He likes his children under his thumb.

I can still remember the day I told them. I had already been gone almost a year. I had run away and hadn't even said good-bye. I sent word through Una that I was okay and that I just needed some time for myself. I let them know that I was going to spend a year backpacking through Europe with some friends I had made during my time in Paris. For over eight months, I had zero contact. No technology. No telephone. Nothing.

He has never forgiven me.

When I came home, I told them I had decided, while on my jour-ney of self-exploration, that I wanted to go to school far away. It just added insult to injury. He forbade me to leave and threatened to have his men come to drag me home wherever I landed. That was when Mamma stepped in. I had never really witnessed her go against my papa before. He was furious at us both, but when she said that, if he did not let me go, then she and I would go, he relented. He did not want me out of his life, but he could not imagine his world without her.

He has not spoken to me since. Not one word.

As hard as it is, it has been for the best. It has made it so much eas-ier to cut ties to my old life.

"How long are you here? Dawn is with her family, and Kelsey is staying here through the holidays, so you can stay with me at the apartment for a week or so."

"Thanks, sis. Actually, that will work out well. I can stay with you while Daniel and I look for a place."

"What? Look for a place?" I ask, confused.

"That's right," Daniel chimes in. "Nicco called and said he was thinking about moving out here, and I told him to get on a plane. I would love a roommate. It's about time I move out of the pool house, don't you think?"

I look back and forth between the two of them. "Are you serious? You are here to stay?"

As thrilled as I am to see him, I am not sure this is something I want. It's hard to be independent when you have a big brother hover-ing, especially one who hasn't cut ties to the people in your past that you have.

"Yes, Brie. After Marianna and I split, I decided I could use a fresh start, too. Moving out here will get me out of a lot of things back home, too."

He gives me a pointed look, and I know exactly what he means. If he is here, looking after me, then he does not have to work for our papa. I am instantly okay with him staying.

"Welcome home, big brother."

He smiles, and I rejoice. One more of us is free. We are a team now. In a way, we always have been.

"Here we are. Home sweet home."

Nicco sets his bags down by the door and checks out the apartment. "This place is nice. I half-expected to find you living in squalor in some run-down shack, being as you have returned every check I have sent you." He looks at me accusingly.

"Taking money Mamma is trying to feed me through you is not me making my own way. I told you both, I wanted to do this on my own."

"So hardheaded," he declares, shaking his head. "There is nothing wrong with family helping you out. As much as you want to be independent, we will always be your family."

"I know that," I say under my breath.

"Do you? I know things got ugly for you in New York, but are you sure running away was the answer?"

"It was the only choice I had. I know you guys did not understand, but I had to go. Please, can we talk about something else?" I plead.

"Yes, we can. That's all water under the bridge now anyway. I am kind of running away myself, so who am I to judge you anymore?"

"All right, so if you are going to stay here—and by here, I mean, in California—we have to set a couple of ground rules, okay?"

"Hmm, let's hear them first before I agree."

"First, no trying to feed me money and no reporting back to Mamma and Papa. You are not going to spy on me for them. *Capisce?*"

"Got it. No spying," he agrees.

"Second—and this is the most important rule—you absolutely do not ever bring *him* up. Not ever. I mean it, Nicco. He does not exist here. Do you understand?"

He looks me dead in the eye and says, "I understand, sis. I did not come here to bring any of that shit to your doorstep. I won't so much as utter his name. Ever."

"Thank you." I blow out a breath I did not even realize I was holding. "Now, I am going to leave you here to get settled in, and I am going to drive down the road to see the baby I nanny for. It's his first Christmas. I told them I would come by on my way home tonight to help tuck him in, and his mom and I are going to read him *The Night Before Christmas*."

"Just like Mamma and Nonna used to do for us when we were little."

"Yeah. It is one of my very favorite Christmas Eve memories," I say with a sad smile.

"Take your time. I am going to take a quick shower and unpack. We will talk more when you get back."

He hugs me once more, and I relax.

"I really am happy you are here, Nicco. I missed you so much."

I leave him at the apartment and head to Rick and Melanie's house. Cassian is already bathed and in his adorable Christmas onesie that matches his parents' pajamas. I snap a picture for them in front of the tree for Melanie to place in the silver *Baby's First Christmas* frame I bought them as a gift.

After I rock him and we read him to sleep, I hold him close for a few extra moments and then gently lay him in his crib.

"Merry Christmas, baby boy. I hope visions of sugarplums dance in your head all night long." I kiss the top of his head, and we back out of his nursery as quietly as we can.

Rick is loading Santa gifts under the tree when we walk back into the living room.

"I wish I were going to be here to see the look on his face when he gets a load of all this loot," I say in amusement.

Rick stands back and assesses the massive display. "We might have gone a wee bit overboard. He is not even a year old."

"Well, he will only have his first Christmas once," Melanie dismisses his comment.

He looks at me and rolls his eyes. "I can't imagine what his first birthday is gonna look like between the two of you."

He is right. At least half the boxes under that tree are from me. Every time I walked into a store the past few months, I walked out with something I had seen and just known he had to have. I am a sucker. What can I say?

Rick heads off to bed, and Melanie and I walk into the kitchen. I tell her about my night and the big surprise.

"Are you good with this?" she asks as she slides a mug of eggnog my way.

"I think so. I am a little apprehensive, if I am being honest, but I cannot explain the elation that washed over me when he walked through that door. I love my brothers, and Nicco and I have always been closest. I just hope he doesn't bring anything or anyone else from my past into my present."

Melanie is the only one here who knows my whole story. She knows all my secrets. It's like she is my surrogate mom. I trust her.

"I, for one, am happy he is here. I know you think you have to be an island, Brie, but you don't. I think having him here will be good for you."

"I sure hope you are right."

CHAPTER
Twenty-Six

Gabby
Past

WHEN THE BOYS RETURN FROM THEIR VISIT TO SoHo, THEY have Tony, Stavros, and Lorenzo in tow. Tony comes through the door, takes one look at my face, and walks right back out. We can hear the explosion of expletives coming from the stoop and then a crash. Stav hurries out after him, and they come in a few seconds later and wrap Tony's hand in ice. Apparently, he punched the brick wall of the garage. Remorse. I feel deep remorse for causing this reaction from my brothers.

Tony notices my distress, and he comes and wraps me in his arms. "Do not be upset, *cara*. It doesn't hurt at all."

"Liar," I mumble into his shirt.

"It might hurt a bit later, but I deserve it for not protecting my baby sister."

I pull back and look up at him. "You have always protected me. This was out of your control. You cannot be there every single second of my life, and even if you could, I would not let you."

He lifts my chin and plants a kiss on the tip of my nose, just like he did when I was little. "I will always try. Always."

I know it is true. For all of them, including Cross.

Marianna sets plates around the island, and everyone eats. The boys are ravenous. I guess beating down your sister's attacker works up a mighty hunger. Once they are sated, Tony, Stav, and Lo say their good-byes, but before they are out the door, Cross pats Tony on the back.

"Tomorrow, yes?"

Tony looks back at me for a long moment, and then he answers, "Yes, Christoff, tomorrow. She is safe here with you for the night?"

"Safest place for her in the world."

Tony nods, and then they are gone, leaving me, Cross, Nicco, and Marianna to watch a movie.

I must have dozed off at some point because, when I rouse, the movie is over, and Nicco and Marianna are gone. My head is in Cross's lap, and he is stroking my hair. It feels nice.

I can't believe Nicco snuck out without saying good-bye. I thought that I might be leaving with them. I guess not. Looks like Cross is stuck with me again. I know I could go back to my apartment, but I really do not feel like getting on the train tonight or asking Cross to drive me all the way back to the city.

"You're awake."

I look up at him and nod. "Did they leave without me?"

He looks at me, confused or maybe bemused at my question.

"Yes, you are staying with me for a while."

For a while? What does he mean, for a while?

I lift my head and turn in his lap. "I appreciate you letting me stay last night and tonight. I honestly don't want to be in the city right now, but I have to go home eventually."

He brushes the hair from my face and gently places it behind my ear. "You are home, Gabby."

"What?" Now, I am the one confused.

He places his forehead against mine, and our breaths mingle as I wait for him to explain. He closes his eyes, and he absentmindedly runs his hand up and down my spine.

"I am done," he starts. "Done pretending that I want to be friends.

169

Done watching you date guy after guy. Done waiting to see if this is what you really want." He opens his eyes and looks deep into mine. "You are mine."

My heart does a flip inside my chest. *What is he saying?*

"I am yours?" I ask.

"Yes. No more games. No more waiting."

"I ... but ... I don't understand."

"Yes, you do."

All of a sudden, I can't breathe. *Is he serious? He thinks that he can just decide that I am staying here, and, poof, it's done?*

I try to get up, and he stops me.

"Look at me, Gabby."

I don't, and I think he is going to get angry, but he doesn't.

He just softly demands again, "Give me your eyes, *Tesoro.*"

I look up into his green eyes, which are alight and intense.

"Do you love me?"

"What? Yes. You're Cross; I have always loved you."

He smiles, and then he asks, "Are you *in* love with me?"

"That's a different question."

"I know. That's why I rephrased it."

I don't want to answer him. I don't want to be that vulnerable again. I look away, but he doesn't let me for long. He puts his finger under my chin and brings my face back around to his. I squeeze my eyes shut. Like a bird with its head in the sand, I don't want him to see me.

"Are you, baby? It's a simple yes or no question."

"There is nothing simple about it."

"I need your answer, Gabby."

"Yes, I am *in* love with you, okay?" I manage to get out without opening my eyes. It's an embarrassing admission. I thought we were past this, yet here I am, a little girl pouring her heart out all over again.

"I tried," I say, and a sniffle escapes. "I tried so hard to fall out of love because I knew you did not want me like that, but I came home, and it all just came flooding back. I can't *not* love you."

I bury my head in his chest. He rubs my back as I let it all out. All the frustration of trying to date away my feelings, trying to hate him so that I wouldn't love him, the hate I feel for Angelica because she has him, the pain of knowing it will never happen. It's all been an act, a brave face for everyone else.

When I finally get it all out and I am just a mess of hiccups and tears, he finally speaks, "Did you hear me earlier?"

"When?"

"You are mine, and if you want me, I am yours."

It starts to hit me—what he has been saying and the conversation I overheard between him and Nicco this morning. He wants me. I am his.

"Do you love me?" I ask.

He smiles one of his unabashed smiles that causes the dimple in his cheek to come forth. I love that dimple.

"I have always loved you, Gabriella Mastreoni."

At his words, I crawl up into his lap and seal my lips to his. Elation. Pure, unadulterated elation is what I feel. I kiss him with everything I have, and he lets me. No pushing me away. No stopping. No guilt. Just us. I pour everything I have into that kiss.

Cross stands to his feet, taking me with him as he walks to the bed platform. My lips never leave his. He has his hands under my hips; he lifts me up on the bed, and we disengage. He lifts his shirt up over his head and tosses it to the floor before he crawls atop me as I scoot back to the center of the bed. Then, he is there, covering me with his body, and I reach up and run my hands over the hard muscles of his chest. I have always wanted to explore him this way. Always wanted to feel my way down his body. He lets me, and I bend my head and run my tongue along his collarbone and up the column of his throat. I find his lips again, and I pull him fully on top of me. I wrap both my legs around his waist, trying to keep him there. I am so afraid that he is going to change his mind and leap from the bed as he tears his mouth from mine.

"I am not going anywhere, baby. I am right here." He reaches behind himself, grips one of my legs, and brings it down. Then, he bolts up to his knees and brings his hands to the hem of my shirt. "Arms up."

I do as I was told, and he pulls the tee from me and flings it aside. Then, he brings his hands down my sides, and I instinctively lift my bottom, so he can remove my shorts. I am lying with him in nothing but my bra and panties, and I vaguely remember the night before with him between my legs, helping ease the ache I was feeling as a result of the drugs. He is wearing the same look of desire now, and the realization hits me that he wasn't just doing me a favor last night. He wanted it. He wants me now. Me.

He runs his hand over my panties, and I tremble at his touch. I want so badly to touch him this time. To feel him. Taste him, but I have no idea what to do.

"Cross, I need to tell you something," I start.

He continues to caress me through my panties, and I can feel them soaking through at his touch.

"What, baby?"

He loops a finger inside the fabric, and I lose my train of thought. I let my thighs fall open wider to give him easier access to me. He takes advantage and snaps the sides of the thong, and it falls apart and away from me. His eyes are focused on me as he runs his finger up and down my lips, getting me wetter and ready and more frenzied. Then, his eyes find mine as he takes his fingers and sucks them into his mouth.

"Mmm, delicious," he growls.

Oh my God, it's so hot. I come up to my elbows. I want to see him and touch him.

"Aren't you going to get undressed, too?"

He chuckles. "My greedy girl is so impatient."

Then, he stands and drops his pants to the floor. He comes back over me. He unsnaps the front of my bra, and my breasts spill out. They are already peaked and ready for his attention. He sucks one nipple, and I arch my chest to meet his hungry mouth. My hand flutters down his back, feeling every muscle, and then dips into his boxers. I squeeze his ass and press him into me. He feels so good—big, hard, and ready. I bring my hand around to the front as he continues to lavish attention on the other breast. I wrap my hand around his cock, and my nipple falls from his mouth as he groans. I slide my hand up and down his length. Alternating between a light grip and a tight one. His eyes are closed, and I see the sweat starting to glisten on his brow. I watch the muscles of his throat tighten and release as he swallows. He gets to his knees again, and I lose my hand on him. Then, his boxers are gone, and he sits there, fully naked. His erection reaching for me.

"Cross, we really need to talk. I have to tell you something."

"Later, baby. No more talking now."

He is over me again, and he takes himself in his hand and guides himself to my entrance. He swirls the tip in my wetness and slowly drags it up to my throbbing bud, and the pleasure that ripples through me is exquisite.

"I have wanted to be inside you for so long, Gabby."

With that, he presses in a little, and I hold my breath. He is about to find out exactly why we really needed to talk.

"That's it, baby. Open for me."

He rocks back and pushes in further, and I go still and let out a small yelp.

He freezes.

No, no, no.

"Fuck," he says between gritted teeth as he starts to pull out of me.

I grab his ass and try to keep him where he is. "Don't stop. Please don't stop."

"Baby, fuck, how?"

He's looking down at me, and I just let it out.

"Because it has *always* been you. Always," I cry.

He brings his mouth back down on mine, hard, and kisses me as he settles once more between my legs. Then, he is inside me again.

173

"This is going to hurt for just a second. Then, I promise I am going to make it feel so good."

I nod because I want this.

One quick, hard thrust, and he is seated completely inside me. It is a delicious, burning stretch, and I love it. It's a good pain. He stays there for a few minutes, letting me get used to the full feeling, and then he starts to move. Slowly at first and then faster. He brings his hand between us and starts massaging my clit with each thrust, and I am drowning in sensation, reaching for that eruption that I know is coming. I plant my foot, and I arch up to meet every move of his hips. When I finally explode, it is intense and loud, and my entire body quakes as it rockets through me. Cross continues pumping in and out till his back bows, and he cries out as his own orgasm is milked from him while I spasm around him. It feels like too much and not enough, all at the same time, and I am a soaking, sated mess when I finally come back down.

We lie there, tangled up in sheets and each other, for a long time before our breathing evens out. He raises his head to look at me, and I see it. I see the love in his eyes. It's always been there. I just did not know that's what it was until this moment.

CHAPTER
Twenty-Seven

Brie

Present

"YOU KNOW, YOU ARE LUCKY I AM HEAD OVER HEELS FOR your cousin because, if I wasn't, I would be lapping at that tall drink of water."

Dawn is back from the holidays with her family, and she was delighted to find we had Nicco as a houseguest. He is bunking on our couch until next week when he and Daniel move into their new beach condo. I guess Papa didn't cut him completely off when he left after all.

"Ew. That's my big brother."

"Yep, he sure is." She sighs dreamily. "Damn, your family sure knows how to grow them."

"You know, he and Daniel are getting a place together, right? You'd better learn to control that drool."

"I know. It will be hard, but I will eventually stop picturing him naked around the house."

"You are such a good girlfriend."

"I know, right? Daniel is so lucky."

Kelsey comes walking in, wearing another dress. It's the third she has tried on for us.

"Veto. It's too conservative for New Year's Eve."

"Dawn, you have said that about every one," she huffs as she stomps back toward her room.

"Well then, stop coming in here, dressed like a schoolteacher. You are on the prowl for a new man to kiss at midnight, remember?" she calls after her.

I giggle to myself, and she turns to me. "What?"

"You just remind me of someone from back home. She used to badger me just like you are badgering Kelsey."

"I only do it because I love her. If I let her sit and mourn her relationship with Brad any longer, she is going to get stuck in that cycle. He has taken enough time from her. He is not taking her confidence, too. I won't let him."

"I know. You are a kick-ass friend."

She turns to me, and her eyes are glassy. "I love you guys. You are the sisters I never had. I would cut a bitch for either one of you."

"Aw, I would cut a bitch for you, too."

I throw my arms around her neck just as Kels walks in, wearing dress number four.

"What's going on?"

"Brie is being a girl again."

We laugh and turn to see Kelsey standing there in a stunning blue cocktail dress with a lace bodice; it flares out into a short swing skirt, which comes right above her knees. She looks good.

"Wow. Now, that is a showstopper."

She looks down. "You think? It's not too much?"

"It's perfect."

We hear the door opening, and we all turn to see Nicco and Daniel walking in, carrying bags of groceries.

"We picked up a few things at the—" Nicco stops mid-sentence when he catches sight of Kelsey standing there.

Uh-oh. This could be trouble.

I get up and go to take one of the bags from his arms.

"Hey, man, you going all the way in or what?" Daniel asks from behind him.

"Um, yeah. Sorry, man." He comes the rest of the way in.

I look in the bag I took. "Wow, you guys did shop."

"I figured I owed you guys for letting me crash here."

He is still focused on Kelsey, and I realize that I have not had a chance to introduce them yet.

"Nicco, this is our other roommate, Kelsey. Her mom is married to Uncle Matt. Kelsey, this is my older brother Nicco."

She blushes under his stare as she walks over and extends her hand. "Nice to meet you, Nicco."

He takes her hand and gently shakes it. "You, too, Kelsey. I appreciate you guys letting me impose a couple of more days."

"It's no problem at all. You are welcome to stay as long as you need." She turns back to us. "So, this one gets the thumbs-up?"

"That's definitely the one," Dawn approves.

"Okay." She walks back to her room.

Dawn turns to Nicco and points her finger at him. "All right, lover boy, you watch yourself. She just shook off a douche bag, and she is a little fragile at the moment. You take advantage, and I will twist your balls off with a pair of pliers while you sleep."

Nicco's wide eyes shoot to mine, and I shrug.

"She's serious, and honestly, I would look the other way."

"I would never."

"Stop." Dawn brings her hand up in front of his face. "Do not even try to tell us we read that wrong. You were struck dumb when you walked in and saw her in that dress. I don't blame you. She's freaking stunning, and if you happen to be standing in her vicinity around eleven fifty-nine p.m. tonight and don't have anyone else to kiss to ring in next year, well then, so be it. You are both grown adults, and truthfully, she could use an Italian stallion to ride, but it's none of my business. Just treat her with care either way. Okay?"

"Yes, ma'am."

She nods at him and then takes our bags and follows Daniel into the kitchen to put them away.

"Well, that was intense," he says to me as he blows out a breath.

"Yep, we are a little overprotective of each other."

"I didn't mean to, uh … did I do anything—"

"Do not even try to play that off, Nicco Mastreoni. Your tongue practically hit the floor when you walked in and looked at her." I roll my eyes.

"You are exaggerating. It is a nice dress. She looked good."

"Uh-huh." I nod.

"Whatever. I am going to use your shower and start getting ready. Where are we going again?"

"To the country club where I work. They are having a huge New Year's Eve gala. I am going as Jake's date, and you are going as Kelsey's guest."

"Guest? So, she"—he points at the door Kelsey just shut behind her—"is my date?"

I turn to him with my hands on my hips. "Her guest, Nicco. You are her guest." I clarify, "You have to either be a member or the guest of a member to get in."

"So, you are this Jake person's guest?"

I walked right into that one. The last thing I want to do is explain my new relationship to him. The relationship that I swore was not going to happen. Now, here Nicco is, and Jake is on his way, so there is no way to avoid the meeting.

"No, I am Jake's date. We have been dating for a couple of months now. It's not too serious or anything yet, but I do like him. Please don't scare him," I plead as I stare at the floor. I can't meet his eyes.

"Hey," he says as he moves toward me. He bends down and looks up at me. "I am not going to say anything to your friend. I promise. As long as he is good to you, that's all that matters to me. Okay?"

"Okay. Thank you," I whisper. "Oh, and by the way, your name is Masters now."

He stops and turns back to me. "What?"

"Masters. I am Brie Masters. That makes you Nicco Masters."

"You are kidding, right?"

"You are the one who wanted to move here and invade my new life. You have to play the part."

"Fine." He rolls his eyes. "But, sis, it doesn't matter what you call yourself. You are who you are, and eventually, that will catch up to you."

Jake and Daniel rented a stretch limo for the night, so we could all drink without having to worry about getting home safely.

The meeting between Jake and Nicco was slightly awkward. My brother is intimidating, even when he is trying his best not to be. His six-foot-four frame stood a head taller than Jake, and he let his Italian accent and bravado fly when I introduced them. He shook his hand for a full two minutes, and I did not miss the tiny twinge of unexpected pain that passed on Jake's face at Nicco's unnecessarily tight grip. I swatted him away and gave him an *I am going to kill you* look that made him grin. The moment was over, and Jake more than got the message. *Do not mess with my little sister's heart,* was written all over his expression.

When we arrive at the club, the party is already in full swing. We grab a table and head to the buffet for food.

"Hi. I don't think we've met," says a girl with a platinum pixie haircut, who just finished loading her plate as I come up to make a salad.

She extends her hand for me to shake, and I reach to take it. I introduce myself when I hear Dawn approaching.

"Oh my God, who let the trash in? You are not a member here, Tonya."

Daniel comes rushing in behind her, and Nicco, Jake, and Kelsey are around the corner.

"Trash? Pot. Kettle," she says as she points between herself and Dawn.

Rage lights up in Dawn's eyes, and I instinctively take a defensive stance between the two. About that time, Tonya spots Kelsey, and she smirks.

"I don't have time to trade barbs with you, Dawn. I have to get back to my date, Bradley. He must be missing me."

With that, she turns and heads back toward their table. I watch as Kelsey's eyes follow her path and see the pain that rocks her when she finds Brad, who doesn't see us, laughing at something the guy beside him said. She turns and walks rapidly back toward the restroom. I hand my plate to Jake, and Dawn and I head after her.

As we pass, Dawn looks up at Nicco. "I've changed my mind, handsome. Tonight, you show my girl the time of her life, and don't let that asshole"—she points in Brad's direction—"anywhere near her."

"This is stupid. I know," Kelsey whimpers as she wipes her eyes with a tissue, trying not to ruin her makeup. "I just can't believe he would bring her here. He knows this is where I would be on New Year's Eve. He hated that I made him come last year. He hates dancing, and he just wanted to stay in and watch the stupid ball thing drop on television."

"He did it just to get a reaction out of you, Kelsey. He is a douche canoe. You want me to deck him?" Dawn is fighting mad.

Kelsey laughs. "No, I do not want you to deck him."

"What about her? Can I please break her nose?"

"No," she breathes through more laughter.

All three of us are laughing now.

"Stop making me laugh, guys," I protest. I can barely breathe in this dress as it is.

We all get it together, and I turn to Kelsey.

"Hey, you got this. You look like a sexy princess in that dress, and you have Nicco on your arm. Bradley is going to have a seizure when he sees you."

"Nicco did not sign up for this. I can't ask him to pretend to like me."

"Are you kidding? I thought he was going to swallow his tongue when he first saw you tonight. I don't think it will require him to do much pretending."

"Right," Dawn adds. "Plus, he is super hot, mysterious, and a tad scary. Just what you need by your side to face the couple from hell."

She sniffles. "You think they are a couple now?"

"What I think is that, whether they are or are not, he brought her here just to mess with you. So, instead of letting him see tears or letting them run you out of here, you are going to let that Italian stallion out there twirl you around the dance floor. You are going to laugh, eat, and drink, and they can go to hell. Now, dry it up, and let's get back to it."

With that, I see the resolve stiffen Kelsey's back, and she dries it up. We head back out to the boys. Crisis managed.

Nicco is standing at the buffet, waiting for us. The boys must have filled him in on the Kelsey, Bradley, Tonya situation because I can see it written all over his face. *Game on.*

CHAPTER
Twenty-Eight

Gabby
Past

THE NEXT MORNING, CROSS AND I WAKE TO BANGING ON THE LOFT door. I look over, and it's five in the morning. I sit straight up and take stock of myself. I am naked and tangled up in the sheets. The banging gets louder and faster, and I look to Cross, who has hopped out of the bed and is pulling on his jeans.

"Go into the bathroom, Gabby. Take a shower or just wait. Stay in there until I come to get you."

"Do you think it's Tony?"

"Not sure. Maybe."

I decide to do as I was told. I wrap the sheet from the bed around myself and scurry quickly into the bathroom. I place my ear to the door and hold my breath, waiting to see if I will have to jump out and in between Cross and one of my brothers to keep them from throwing punches.

"What the fuck?" I hear Angelica shriek. "I have been calling and texting you for the last three days, and all I get back is a *something important came up; talk later* text?"

"Calm down, Angie."

"Calm down? Calm down? Cross, I have been going out of my mind. You missed our date last night. I waited for you for hours before

I went on to the wedding … alone. I didn't even have an answer when people asked where you were. Do you know how embarrassed I was?"

"I am sorry. I didn't mean to leave you hanging like that. The past few days have been"—he pauses, searching for the right words—"complicated."

"Complicated, huh? Well, explain that to me, please. What is going on?"

I feel like I should get in the shower and give them some privacy, but I also very much want to hear what is said. I don't blame her for being upset.

"It's a long story and one that I will tell you, but can we do it later?"

"Later. Why? We are both here right now. Wait. What the hell?" She pauses in her diatribe. "Whose are these?"

Shit, all of my clothes are scattered across the floor of the loft.

"Angie, I—"

"Whose?" she screams.

I decide to go out there and face the music instead of cowering in the bathroom, hiding and letting Cross face it alone. I wrap the sheet tighter around me, and I open the door and step out.

"Mine," I say as confidently as I can.

She turns her angry glare toward me, and I see the hurt and betrayal written all over her face. I feel sick.

She turns back to Cross. "Really? Her? This is about her?"

"I didn't mean for you to find out this way," he says, remorse evident in his voice.

"How long?"

"Last night."

"Last night? You stood me up and"—she sweeps her hand out toward me—"fucked this little girl instead?"

She looks back up at me, and then she does a double take. "What the hell happened to your face?"

I bring my hand up to my bandage and hide my eye with my forearm.

"I told you, it's a long story, and you deserve to hear it all, so if you will go wait in the car, I will be out in a minute. We can go to breakfast."

At that, I snap my head up to him. *What? He is going to take her to breakfast. No.*

"Cross—" I start to voice my protest.

He cuts me off, "Gabby, why don't you lie back down and get some more sleep? It's early. I will be back shortly, I promise."

"I—no," I whine.

He walks toward me, and I start backing up. He stops.

"Are you serious?"

"Please, *Tesoro*. She deserves that much from me."

I stop and let him reach me. He lifts my chin and places a quick kiss on my lips. I look past him at Angelica, who now has tears in her eyes. He is right. She deserves an explanation, and she deserves to hear it in private. As much as I hate to let him get into a car and drive away with her, I have to.

"Okay," I whisper, "but hurry back."

"Promise."

I don't go back to sleep. I can't. I grab my purse that the boys retrieved from Dante, and I plug in my phone, which has no charge. Then, I go rifle through the refrigerator. After making some toast, I start to pace, and I let my insecurity run wild.

What if he changes his mind? What if she cries and he decides that he really loves her and she is the one he wants, not me? What if she seduces him? Was I crazy for letting him go with her?

I hear my phone power up, and then there's a symphony of notifications.

Dozens of missed calls and frantic texts start to come in, mostly from my mother and Adriana. I take a deep breath. I am not ready to face the questions yet. I haven't even thought of what to say. I know that I cannot tell my mother the truth. If she tells Papa, then Dante is a dead man. If he isn't already. Plus, I don't want them to force me to come home, and that is exactly what would happen. Adi, I will tell everything. I just don't want to do it now, not when I am so preoccupied with Cross and Angelica.

I shoot off a quick text to Adi and tell her I am okay, more than okay, and that I will call her later today to explain.

I get back a, *Fine. I might answer if I am not too angry to speak to you by then. Glad you are not dead*, and a middle finger emoji.

I decide a bath is what I need, and I run some warm water and add a handful of Epsom salts into Cross's large sunken, jetted tub. It is honestly the best part of this place. It sits in a nook between the bathroom and the bed platform. Open to the entire loft. He had it added as an afterthought and wanted it, so he could soak and watch the television in front of the fireplace at the same time. I step down into the water, and I realize how very achy I am. Between Dante tossing me around, my night with Cross, and the lack of sleep, my body is screaming. I immerse myself and turn on the jets. *Ah, heaven.* I lean against the cool tiles and close my eyes.

I hear him come in and cross the room about thirty minutes later. I don't move. I don't open my eyes. I don't say a word. I just stay there and wait, afraid to know what transpired between them. Afraid that he will ask me to get my things and go. He was gone a couple of hours. If they weren't making up, what could have taken so long? It doesn't take hours to tell someone you want to break up. It's five little words.

After a long silence, I feel the water sway. Then, Cross's arms pick me up, and he slides in underneath me. He pulls me between his legs and settles me on top of him. We lie there in the water for a while, not saying a thing.

"Are you going to tell me how it went? Because I am not going to lie; I have been here, letting my imagination run wild."

He grabs a bar of soap and a washcloth from the edge of the tub and starts to lather up my arms.

"We went to the diner down the street. She wanted to go to her place, but I knew that somewhere public would be better. We ordered food, and I told her about what had happened this weekend."

"You told her about Dante?" There is a hitch in my voice. I didn't want anyone else to know.

"I had to, *Tesoro*. She saw your injuries, and I really could not tell her the whole story and leave that part out."

"Everyone is going to know."

"She will not tell anyone."

"You don't know that."

"She is not the villain, Gabby. I know you have never liked her, but she is really a good person."

"A good person who hates me."

He sighs. "You are not her favorite person, but she is hurt. I should have talked to her before I let anything happen between us."

"Yes, you should have. We are horrible people."

"That's on me, not you."

"Continue, please," I push.

"She was livid with Dante. She hated that it happened to you. Then, I explained about us. How we feel about each other. How we have always felt about each other. It was … difficult … for her to hear. But she knew. She said, before she even showed up this morning, in her gut, she knew."

"How did she know?"

"Baby, everyone knows. Do you think your brothers are going to be surprised?"

Actually, I do think they are going to be surprised. I was surprised.

"I do."

He laughs in my ear as he moves to wash my neck and chest.

"No, you and I are apparently not very good at hiding our feelings. We never have been."

186

And here I thought, I had everyone, including myself, convinced I was over my crush.

"Is she going to be a problem?"

"I don't think so. She said she always knew that, one day, you and I would find our way to each other. She hoped she was wrong. When you came home from Paris with Antoine," he bites his name out, "she thought maybe she and I had a real chance, but after the summer and the weekend at the Hamptons, she knew it was only a matter of time. I guess I wasn't very good at keeping my jealousy close to the vest after all."

"Your jealousy? In the Hamptons?"

"Yes, when Jeremy started rubbing lotion on you. His hands on your skin. I swear, if Lo hadn't stopped me, I would have ripped his arms right off his body."

"I thought you said Jeremy was a good guy."

"He is. I still didn't fucking like it."

I turn in his arms so that my chest rests on his, and we are face-to-face.

"So, Lo knows, too?"

"Yeah. I tried to play it off like I didn't like a guy touching you for the same reasons he didn't like it, but he knew."

"Oh."

"How did you leave things?"

"I gave back the key to her place, and we finished eating, and then she drove me back here. It is over."

"Just like that?"

"Just like that."

It dawns on me that I am naked in a bath with Cross. I am naked in a bath with him. This is surreal. I lean in and kiss him. I can do that now. I can be naked in a bath with Cross and kiss him.

He slides his soapy hands down my body and palms my ass. I feel him beneath me and glide up and down his hard length.

"Are you sore, baby?"

"Sore?"

"Yes, here?" He slides his hand between my legs and whispers his fingers over me.

"A little," I tell him the truth.

"We will be gentle with you today," he says as he starts kissing down my neck and across my chest.

"Mmm."

"Let's get you out of this tub." He stands with me in his arms and steps out. He lays me out wet on the rug in front of the fireplace and then goes to grab us both a towel. He takes his time, drying me off. He flips me over and starts to run the towel gently over by back. He places a trail of hot kisses down my spine to the dip of my lower back.

"I love your back. It's beautiful."

He peppers kisses on my ass as he continues prowling down my body. My head is in my arms folded under me, and I just feel. When he spreads my legs apart and runs his hands up the inside of my thighs, I moan into the rug, and he chuckles against my skin.

"Is this where it hurts, baby?" He lightly spreads me open and caresses me.

"Yes," I breathe.

"I am going to kiss it and make it all better."

And he does. He laps at me from behind, and it makes it feel all kinds of better.

CHAPTER
Twenty-Nine

Brie
Present

NICCO HANDS KELSEY HER PLATE AND KISSES HER ON THE TOP OF her head. Then, he leads her to the buffet with his hand resting on the small of her back. I glance over at Bradley and Tonya's table, and I see that the message has hit its mark. Bradley is watching the entire exchange with a red face and an intense stare. Kelsey doesn't even look in his direction. She is fully engrossed in my brother's attention. *Good for her.*

We all head back to our table, and Nicco pulls her chair out for her. She smiles back at him, and I pray that this doesn't backfire. Just as we settle in to eat, preparing our stomachs for all the champagne consumption we plan for the night, Bradley approaches the table and clears his throat. Kelsey looks up to him just as Nicco moves in closer and lays his arm across the back of her chair.

"Hey, Brad," she says as nonchalantly as she can pull off at the moment.

"Hey, baby. Can we talk for a minute?"

She winces at his term of endearment but doesn't let the smile fall from her face. "Sure, go ahead."

He looks nervously around the table and then adds, "Privately?"

Dawn starts to stand up, but Daniel places his hand on her

shoulder to hold her in place.

He gives her a look that says, *Kelsey needs to handle this herself.*

She relents and stays seated. Then, she starts to eat her salad while shooting daggers at Brad with her eyes.

"I don't think so. We just sat to start eating, and I don't want to be rude to my friends or my date."

At that, Brad looks at Nicco and his hand that is now playing in Kelsey's hair.

"And who is your date?"

Nicco extends his free hand and introduces himself. "Nicco Masters. And you are?"

Bradley looks affronted that Nicco doesn't already know who he is.

"Bradley Moore. Kelsey's boyfriend."

Nicco starts laughing and then says through his laughter, "Funny, she hasn't mentioned a boyfriend during the past few weeks we've been getting to know each other."

Kelsey looks over at him and beams. "Ex-boyfriend, and I didn't because it wasn't worth mentioning." She shrugs.

"Okay, Kels, you have had your fun. You've brought this Neanderthal to my club and have thoroughly embarrassed me. You have gotten your payback. Now, can we please go somewhere a little more private and work this shit out already?"

"Did he just insult me?" Nicco raises one eyebrow at me.

"I think he was trying to insult Kelsey."

He looks up at Brad. "You aren't very smart, are you?"

"I wasn't fucking talking to you," he whisper-shouts at Nicco. "Kelsey, let's go."

At that, Nicco slowly slides his chair back and stands up. He towers over Bradley, and Brad just stands there, looking up at Nicco's now-angry face.

"Back down, little man. You do not want this to play out in front of these people. The lady politely told you no. If I have to tell you again, I will not be so polite."

Bradley obviously isn't very smart. "Go ahead. This is my club, and if you so much as lay a finger on me, security will have your ass out of here so fast."

"Hiding behind security, huh, Brad? Tell you what; you go sit back down with your sleazy date and let me and my lovely date enjoy our evening, and I will forget this ever happened." He moves in closer. "You don't, and I will have your ass screaming like a little bitch before your security team has a chance to put their forks down."

We all see the fear cross Bradley's face, but his stupid pride won't let him back down.

"Really, Kelsey? This is what you want? This lowlife? I cannot believe you. Do not expect me to still want you after you have been slumming, baby."

Kelsey bursts out laughing at his statement.

"Him?" She points at Nicco. "He's part-owner of a super-successful multimedia advertising company in New York City, and he has come to spearhead their West Coast expansion himself. He is gorgeous and funny and great in bed. If that's slumming, then I am more than willing."

At that moment, Tonya walks up and wraps her arms around Bradley. "Honey, your food is getting cold, and I am getting lonely."

Dawn chimes in, "Speaking of slumming, looks like the trash is getting desperate for some attention. You'd better run along, Brad."

He shrugs off Tonya's touch. "We aren't together like that, Kels."

Tonya huffs behind him, "We aren't together like what?"

He turns on her. "Tonya, can you give us a minute? This is a private conversation between me and my girl."

She looks at our table. "It doesn't look very private. And what do you mean, your girl? You've been in my bed every single night for the last two weeks," she practically screeches at him.

Our table has now garnered the attention of every guest in the ballroom. All eyes are turned toward us.

"Shh, you are causing a scene," Brad hisses at her.

"Oh, honey, I haven't even begun to cause a scene. You are not going to humiliate me in front of all these people. Now, get your ass back to our table. I came as your fucking date. She"—she points at Kelsey—"is the bitch who threw you out of her house, and you came running to me. Telling me how you were done with her anyway and that you wanted me and only me. Remember?"

I look over, and I can see the tears welling up in Kelsey's eyes.

Jake clears his throat, and everyone looks to him.

"Bradley, I am two seconds away from calling my father and having you thrown out of this club, and I do not mean for the night."

At that threat, Bradley's back stiffens, and he finally relents. He says, "This isn't over, Kelsey," and turns to walk away with Tonya on his heels.

We all sit there in silence for a moment, and then Daniel pipes up, "I don't know about you guys, but that was entertaining as hell. Nicco, welcome to the gang." He raises his champagne flute. "A New Year's toast to new beginnings and taking out the garbage."

We clink our glasses in a toast of good riddance.

"Thank you."

Jake and I are on the dance floor, wrapped in each other's arms.

"For what?"

"For pulling out the big guns earlier and getting rid of Brad before Nicco really lost it."

"I could see that he was on the verge, and as much as I would have loved to see him have his way with Moore, I knew that wasn't what Kelsey or you needed tonight."

I cuddle into him as we sway to the music. He really is a good man. I catch Nicco looking our way. He has a sad smile on his face. I know that everything that happened back in New York was hard for him, too. Maybe we both can heal.

"Isn't that the girl from the pool the other day?" Dawn asks when I make it back to our table.

"Which girl?"

"You know, the redhead who used to date Jake or wanted to date Jake," she adds.

I turn to scan the room, and I spot Carlie in the corner, talking to Tonya. They are wearing matching scowls while watching Nicco and Kelsey dancing. Oh no, nothing good is going to come of those two conspiring.

"Yeah, that's her."

"Fabulous. Two bitches for the price of one."

The DJ comes over the loudspeaker and announces that the countdown to the New Year has begun. As the entire crowd starts to count aloud, we all gather together on the edge of the dance floor. Jake wraps his arms around me from behind, and when the clock strikes midnight, he spins me around and dips me low into a breathtaking kiss. I cling to him as he pulls me back up, and we join the chorus of "Auld Lang Syne" with all the others.

I look over and spy Nicco and Kelsey. He has one hand wrapped in her hair and the other holding her to him. Her arms are around his neck, and they are kissing. Not a friendly New Year's Eve kiss, but an intimate, longing kiss. He picks her up off her feet and walks her back toward our table.

My eyes meet Dawn's, and we give each other a wide-eyed look that says, *Eep. What do we do?*

We silently decide to let those cards fall where they may.

We are all sufficiently drunk on bubbly and tired from shaking our booties on the floor all night, so we head outside to wait for the limo to pick us up. It's a chilly night, and Jake is holding me close to shelter me from the night air. He is warm and solid, and I like having him wrapped around me. I feel safe. As crazy as it sounds, safe is scary for me. I am much more comfortable on high alert.

Once we are home, we say our good nights, and Jake heads to my room.

Nicco watches him disappear and then turns to me. "I like him."

"Good. I like him, too."

"I never thought I would see you happy again. Maybe moving out here was the right thing for you."

I move to the closet and bring him the spare blankets and pillows I stashed for him. I move to make the couch up.

He comes over and takes the pillows from my hands. "Go on to bed. I got this."

I give him a stern look. "You are sleeping in here, right?"

"Of course I am," he says, avoiding my eyes.

"I am serious, Nicco. I am not opposed to the idea of you and Kelsey, but it's too soon for her."

"Not everyone has to move at a snail's pace like you, sis. Maybe a night with me is exactly what she needs to put that asshole out of her mind. I can remind her just how fucking desirable she is and that she does not ever have to take shit from another man."

Well, all righty then. It is hard to argue with that.

"Fine. Just make sure it is what she wants."

He gives me an offended look. "Like I would go there with a girl, any girl, if I wasn't sure it was what she wanted."

"I didn't mean that. I just mean that she's a little mixed up right now. I want you to be extra sure she isn't going to regret anything in the morning."

He gets a wicked grin. "Never had a girl wake up with regrets yet."

Dear Lord, my brothers and their over-inflated egos. I roll my eyes.

"Okay, lover boy, just be quiet? These walls are kind of thin, and the last thing I need is to fall asleep to the sound of you and one of my best friends."

"Same. I swear to God, if there is anything coming from your room, I will kick him out myself. I like him, but I have my limits."

Great, I should have had the limo driver drop us off at Jake's house. Oh well, we have waited this long. What is one more night?

I slip into bed beside Jake after I have showered and changed. I think he has already drifted off to sleep, so I try to be as quiet as a mouse, but as soon as I am settled in, I feel his hands snake around me and pull me into his body.

"I was beginning to think you had abandoned me in here," he whispers into the dark as his hands start roaming my body beneath my tank.

"I just had to set my brother straight on a few things before I jumped in the shower."

He chuckles. "Kelsey is a big girl. She can handle him all by herself."

"I know. I just wanted to make sure he was careful with her heart. Mmm."

I moan as one of his hands wraps around my breast and starts gently kneading it while he kisses his way up the back of my neck and across my shoulder. His other hand is flat against my stomach and firmly holding my back against the front of his body.

"Jake," I pant, "we can't tonight. My brother is in the room next door, and I just …"

"Shh, I know. I just want to touch you."

He moves his hand down to trail his finger across the top of my shorts. I want so badly for him to explore lower.

"I am going to stay on top of these. If I don't, I am afraid I won't be able to stop myself."

He continues kissing my neck and shoulder, and the sensation has me curling my hips back into him. I can feel his erection against my backside, and I want so badly to turn around, but I don't. I lie still and let him explore. He removes his hand from my breast and moves it under my tank. He now has my nipple between his fingers, flesh on flesh. His other hand moves lower, and he caresses me between my legs.

"Jaaaake," I call with a shaky voice.

"I know, baby," he whispers and moves his hand back up to my stomach. "Turn over."

He removes his hand from my shirt, and I do as he said. He pulls me close, and I put my head on his chest.

"Close your eyes, pretty girl. We have all the time in the world for that."

Then, he kisses my forehead, and as much as I want to continue, I can already feel my eyelids getting heavy. I snuggle in close and instantly fall sound asleep.

CHAPTER
Thirty

Gabby
Past

I AM PACING WHILE I WAIT FOR ADRIANA TO PICK ME UP. CROSS'S meeting with my brothers was postponed, but they are now at a pub called Murray's, a few miles from here.

I overheard Cross on the phone with Nicco, making the arrangements, while I was in the shower, and as soon as he left, I called Adi and told her to come get me and to call a couple of our girlfriends in New Rochelle to accompany us. The boys will not make a scene in front of all of us. At least, I hope not.

I did the best cover-up job I could on my eye and hid the bandage at my temple with my hair. It is still visible but not too bad. I decided I would tell everyone that I had lost my footing while carrying schoolbooks and taken a tumble down the last couple of flights of stairs at our apartment building. With our walk-up and my clumsiness, it sounds like a feasible explanation.

When Cross finally gave me back my purse he had retrieved from Dante, there were thirteen missed calls and voicemails from Adi. The first few were teasing because she thought I had decided to spend the night with Dante. The next few were angry because it was rude to stay the night with Dante and not call my roommate to let her know I was doing so. The last few were frantic and worried because she could not reach me or Dante, and she thought I must be dead in a ditch some-where, being as I wasn't calling her back. I felt horrible because it had never occurred to me to call her in my drugged and battered state. If the shoe were on the other foot, I would have been a wreck, trying to find her as well. When I did call her at last, she was a sobbing mess on the phone, and by the time I got the entire story out, we were both sobbing messes.

I hear her car pull up, and I meet her at the door. When she sees my face, she bursts into a fit of tears.

"I am going to kill that motherfucker," she says as she wraps me in a tight hug.

"I am not sure he is even alive. Cross will not tell me anything about what happened when he and the boys went to get my things."

"Whatever they did to him is not good enough."

I doubt that is true. I am sure my brothers dealt out sufficient pun-ishment. I just hope that Dante is still alive and breathing and walking on two legs. I also hope that I never lay eyes on him again.

We drive over to Murray's in Adi's car, and the other four girls meet us there. Stacy already has a table for us near the front and a round of drinks on the table. I start scanning the place as we sit. It's a large pub and one my brothers have spent many a night in. The owner's son went to school with Stavros, and he has been letting the Mastreoni men call this place their home away from home for over a decade.

The pub is full. It is always full. It has a large mahogany bar against the back wall, and there are tables filling the space in front. Off to the right is a huge opening leading into the other side, which houses four large pool tables and a few dartboards. High-standing pub tables are scattered around the pool room, and to the left and a few steps up is loft-style seating for larger parties that overlooks the main bar. That's where I spot them.

"Excuse me, ladies. I see my brothers up there, and I am going to say hello."

"Oh, tell them to come say hi," Noelle says as I start to walk off. She has always had a crush on Stav.

"Sure thing."

I make my way to the stairs. None of the boys have noticed me yet, so I walk quietly, hoping to gauge the situation. It's tense, to say the least. Tony, Stavros, and Lorenzo are wearing matching scowls that are aimed at Cross. I am not going to stand for anyone else coming between us. Lilliana already cost us four years.

"How long? How long has this been going on?" Tony roars.

"How long have I loved her? Or how long have we been together?"

"Both."

"I have loved her since the day I met her, but that love changed into something else around the time Nicco and I got home from college."

"When you got home from college? She had to be, what? Fourteen? Fifteen?"

"It changed, but I did not act on it. I just knew that it was not the same brotherly love I had had for her all those years. In fact, I started actively avoiding her for the most part until she was sixteen or so, and she started seeking me out. I had hoped it would go away, but by then, she was feeling it, too, and making it a little harder for me to avoid her. When she upped and left for Paris, I thought that was that. I left her alone because I thought it was what was best for her."

"And now?"

"I cannot fight it anymore. I can't, and I don't want to."

"I don't like this. You are too old for her." That came from Lorenzo.

"She is almost twenty-one. It's different now."

"Do you think Vincenzo is going to think it's different? Do you think he will be okay with you and his daughter?" Stav asks.

"Honestly? I do not care. I am here to talk to you guys out of respect, but whether you give us your blessing or not, it doesn't matter. It is done. No going back now. Tony, you know me. You have known me most of my life. No one will love her more than I do, and no one will protect her like I will. No one."

I have heard enough. As good-intentioned as they are, who I do or do not choose to date is not their decision. It is mine and mine alone. It is time they understand that.

"Hi, fellas," I say as I come up next to Cross.

"Baby." He sits up and puts his arm around my back. "What are you doing here? Are you alone? You shouldn't be out alone."

"I am not alone. The girls called and asked me out for drinks, so they came and picked me up. Besides, you can't keep me locked away in your home forever. I have to start living my life again. I won't let him take that from me."

His eyes soften, and he pulls me a little closer to him.

"The girls just happened to call and ask you out for drinks here, tonight?" He totally has my number.

"Yep."

"Bullshit. You need to let me and your brothers work this out."

When he realizes what I am wearing, he pulls back and turns me around.

"What is this?" he says as he tugs at the hem of my slip dress.

"It's a dress."

"It's a shirt," he states firmly.

"No"—I laugh—"it's a dress."

"Where is the rest of it?"

He is crazy if he thinks he is going to start telling me what clothes I can wear. There is absolutely nothing wrong with this dress. Yes, it's short, and, yes, it is backless, except for a series of thin straps that criss-cross down my spine. But it covers all the important parts, and I like it. I hear snickering coming from across the table, and I look to see all four of my brothers trying hard to hold in their laughter.

"What do you guys find so funny?"

They all look off in different directions. They know this will not end well.

I turn my attention back to Cross. "There is nothing wrong with this dress. Besides, I thought you liked my back?"

"I do"—he slides his hand across my bare back—"but I don't like every guy in here seeing it and deciding they like it, too. And, after the past couple of days, I am sorry, baby, but I am on edge when it comes to you. I cannot help it."

At his admission, I lean into him and drop some of the attitude. I know this has been hard for him. For all of them actually. Every one of them carries guilt over what happened even though it had nothing to do with them. I guess, no matter how old I get, they will always see me in pigtails and curls.

Cross continues in a soft tone that only I can hear, "And, right now, I have to convince your brothers to let us be together without shooting me in the head. The last thing I need to be concentrating on is you in this dress."

"Okay." I give in. "Take your shirt off."

He has a tee on under his button-up, so I come up with the best solution I can.

"What?"

"Give me your button-up."

He does as I asked and removes his shirt, leaving him in a white V-neck. I put his shirt on over my dress, and it swallows me whole. I tie the ends in knots and roll up the sleeves. I look ridiculous, but at least I am covered better.

I splay my arms out in front of him and do a quick turn. "Better?"

"Better."

I bend down and brush a light kiss across his lips. "Do not get used to this. You act like a caveman again, and I will go out in nothing but my underwear next time."

Now that that's taken care of, I turn my attention back to my brothers. Tony is looking between the two of us with an odd expression on his face.

"What?"

"Nothing, *cara*. Nothing at all."

Cross draws my attention back to him. "Go enjoy your drinks with the girls. Your brothers and I need to finish our conversation. I will come and get you and drive you home when we are done."

I walk over to Tony, and he bends over to place a kiss on my cheek.

"Take it easy on him, Tony. I love him."

He searches my eyes, trying to see the truth behind them. Then, he gives me a small nod.

"I know, but I still have to make him suffer a little. Keep him on his toes."

"Just a little?"

"Yes, *cara*, just a little. He still has to declare himself to Papa, so he has to save some courage for that."

I roll my eyes because he is not wrong. Papa could take the news very well or very, very bad. There is no way to tell.

I make my way around the table and kiss each of my brothers.

When I make it to Nicco, I whisper in his ear, "I hope you are his ally in this."

"I haven't decided yet. Are you sure this is what you want?"

I give him an incredulous look. Of course I am sure. Christoff Scutari is all I have ever wanted.

The girls and I are able to finish several rounds before Cross and the boys emerge.

Noelle and Stacy were struck dumb when they found out that Cross and I were finally together. Apparently, he is right; everyone did suspect it would happen eventually.

When we get home, Cross heads to the living area and turns on the game. I follow, and when I get in front of him, I start to slowly undress. He diverts his eyes from the television and focuses on me. I am nervous. I have never taken charge before, and the girls encouraged me to try it. They even gave me a few pointers in seduction over drinks.

Cross stays silent as I fumble through my little striptease, his eyes intense.

Once I am completely bare, I drop to my knees and approach him. His eyes follow my progression. I crawl between his legs, and he widens them to accommodate me. I reach up and start to undo his belt and then his zipper. He lifts his hips for me, and I slowly drag his jeans and his boxers down his legs and let them hit the floor. He is fully erect and ready for whatever I have in mind.

I take him in my hand and start to gently slide my hand up his length. He grows even thicker as I stroke him. I bring him to my mouth, and I swirl my tongue around the tip of him, just like the girls instructed. He brings one of his hands to my face and then puts it in my hair as he intently watches me. I take his balls into one hand, and I begin to gently knead them as I lick my way from tip to base. I relax as much as possible and breathe through my nose as I move up and take him fully into my mouth. I start to suck as I move my hand up and down and take him deeper and deeper.

"Fuck, baby." He bucks off the couch and guides my motion with his hand in my hair.

His excitement fuels my lust, and I take him as deep as I can. He hits the back of my throat, and I choke slightly.

"Gabby," he gurgles my name, and I know that I have him just where I want him.

As much as I would like for him to finish in my mouth, that will have to wait for another day. I want to feel him inside me. I move back, and he releases his hold on my hair. His cock pops out of my mouth.

I climb up into his lap, and I straddle him on shaky legs. I am not sure exactly where to place my hands, and I sit there, not meeting his eyes, trying to decide my next move.

"Hey, baby." He draws my attention. "You are naked on top of me. Nothing you do can be wrong at this point. I am so fucking hard; anything you do, I promise I will like."

His words give me the confidence I need, and I rise up on my knees. I reach between us, and I take him in my hand and guide him to my entrance. I slowly start to bring myself down on him, and I moan as his cock stretches and fills me. I reach for his hand and bring it to where we are connected.

"Do you feel that?" I look in his eyes.

"I feel it, *Tesoro*."

"You are inside me; we are connected."

"We are."

"You fit me perfectly. I was made for you, Cross," I whimper.

"Fuck, baby."

He leans forward and kisses me. I kiss him back with all I have.

After a few minutes, he says in a rough voice, "Baby, I need you to move."

I was so lost in the feel of him inside me; I forgot that part. I bend backward and clasp my hands on his thighs to balance myself. Then, I start sliding up and down on him, riding him faster and deeper until he is hitting the exact spot I need him to reach. I am completely lost in my own pleasure when I feel him bring his fingers to my clit and massage me as he takes over and starts thrusting his hips up to meet me. My orgasm hits me hard, and it causes my body to shake from top to toe. He finally loses his patience and bears up. He flips me onto my back on the couch and starts thrusting harder and harder. A second orgasm rockets through me a minute later, and he follows me. He pulls out, and his seed spurts hot and hard against my stomach. He takes his hand and rubs it into my skin. Watching his hand and then bringing his eyes to me.

"I love you."

"I love you more."

CHAPTER
Thirty-One

Brie
Present

JAKE LEFT EARLY THIS MORNING. HIS PARENTS' PLANE LANDS AT LAX in a couple of hours, and he wanted to run home before picking them up.

I grab a blanket and lie on the suspiciously empty couch to watch the recording of *Dick Clark's New Year's Rockin' Eve* and the ball drop. I had fun last night, but nothing compares to New Year's Eve in New York City. The crowd, the music, the food, the decorations, and the excitement in the air … it's just magical.

I bet Adriana was dressed to the nines and flitting her way from posh party to posh party. Probably on the arm of some tall, dark, and handsome guy. As angry as I was with her when I left, I still miss her so much. I wish I could call her, but I am not sure she will ever forgive me for leaving. It's better this way anyway. Adriana is a family princess. She intends to stay and marry the man of her papa's choosing and live the glamorous life as the head of a dynasty. The exact opposite of what I want.

An hour later, Kelsey's door slowly creaks open, and Nicco tiptoes out in only his pajama bottoms. His hair is mussed, and he is yawning as he makes his way to the living room on silent feet. When he finally sees me, he stops dead in his tracks. He looks back down the hall and then shrugs with a sheepish smile.

"Come on in. It's not like I don't know where you were," I say as I pat the seat beside me.

He walks over and sits down. "I bet Tony and Stav are in that crowd somewhere," he says as he nods toward the screen.

"They haven't missed a New Year's Eve in Times Square for as long as I can remember."

"No, but things are different this year. It's still a tad"—he carefully chooses his words—"volatile back home."

"Are they okay?"

I don't know why I am asking. I really do not want to know any of the details of the aftermath.

"Oh, yeah. After the big shake-up, Tony became Papa's right-hand man. He actually assumed a lot of power, which is good. The other families respect him, and everything has stabilized for the most part."

I am going to hate myself for asking this next question.

"What about the Scutari family?" I pick at my nail as I ask, and I don't meet his eyes.

"I thought you told me not to ever mention his name. He doesn't exist here, remember?"

I look up at him and scowl. He knows how much I hate having my words thrown back in my face.

He laughs. "It is not like it was in the 1960s, sis. The families show respect and work together, and as long as no one steps out of bounds, things are fine."

I stand abruptly and start walking toward the kitchen. "I don't want to talk about this anymore. Do you want coffee?"

"Sure. I am going to jump in the shower real quick. Save me a cup?"

"Okay."

Why did I ask him? The inner workings and hierarchy of organized crime are things I do not care to understand. I make coffee and try to shake off the entire conversation.

Kelsey scoots into a barstool about fifteen minutes later. She keeps her head down and will not meet my eyes. I slide a mug under her nose, and she lets out the breath she was holding.

"Do we have to talk about it?"

"Not if you don't want to."

"I just don't want this to be weird. Okay? I know that I just met your brother, and I know that last night was just two people enjoying each other for the night." She blows the liquid in her mug and brings it to her lips. "I needed that. I could not have faced Bradley and Tonya last night without you guys, and having Nicco playing the part of a charming, handsome date? It was the icing on the cake, Brie."

"Look, you guys are adults, and you know what you are doing. So, it's none of my business. I love you. I love him. If you two end up together, I will be thrilled. If you don't, then I hope you at least enjoyed yourself and made a good memory last night. But I absolutely, positively do not want any details. Ever."

"I do!" Dawn interjects as she comes in, still wearing her dress from last night.

"You do realize you are home, right? You should not be doing a walk of shame through your own apartment," I dig.

She looks down at herself and shrugs. "Daniel wanted me to leave the dress and shoes on last night. He has a high-heel fetish. I guess I passed out right after. To be honest, I don't remember much after him cuffing me to the bed. Anyway, back to you and those details." She wags her eyebrows at Kelsey.

"Dawn, seriously," I protest.

"Jeez, just pretend like she is talking about any random hook-up and not your brother."

"I don't think I can do that." I cringe.

"Oh, get over it. Your brother is an Adonis. He has lots and lots of dirty sex with an array of women. Kelsey happens to be one of those lucky pieces of ass, and she is going to share all the sordid details with her besties because that's what we do."

I stick my tongue out at her, and she returns the gesture with her middle finger.

"Now, go ahead, Kels. Tell us all about the stud, and don't forget to grade his girth, stamina, form, and describe the face he makes when he comes."

"What is girth?" Kelsey asks.

"You know, the size of his member."

Kelsey wrinkles up her nose. "You want me to talk about his size in front of his sister?"

"Yes. He is an Italian stallion, and I need to know if he is hung like one, so spill—and also his come face. Don't forget that part."

"Why would you want to know that? You have never shared details about Daniel's come face with us."

"Ugh, Daniel's is similar to his surprise face but more like he is in severe pain. It is kind of frightening, but I have gotten used to it."

We hear someone clear their throat and look up to see Nicco and Daniel standing in the doorway.

"Bad timing, guys. Go back and try again in, say, fifteen"—she cuts her eyes to Kels and adds with a question in her voice—"twenty minutes?"

"Sorry, ladies, we are hungry. You are just going to have to discuss Nicco's sexual prowess and my horrific come face later."

"I didn't say horrific, but honestly, the first time, I thought you were having a seizure. I started to call 9-1-1."

We all start laughing.

Nicco walks over to Kelsey and kisses the top of her head. "Good morning, sleepyhead."

"Good morning," she says, looking up at him with a big grin.

"What are the plans for today?"

"We usually spend New Year's Day in our pajamas, eating junk food and watching the *Rose Bowl Game*."

"Girls after my own heart."

Kelsey blushes and gives me an *eek* look. Uh-oh, I think it's too late to try to stop this train now. I sure hope my knucklehead brother knows what he is doing.

A few hours later, and we are prepared for our afternoon of gridiron fun. We have buffalo wings, chips and salsa, pigs in a blanket, loaded tater tots, ham 'n' cheese sliders, and cold beer on ice. All the essential football snacks. Us girls are in the kitchen, finishing up the prep, when a knock comes at the door.

"Hey, bro. Can you grab that? It is probably Jake."

Nicco gets up and heads to the door.

"You have got to be fucking kidding me."

We hear Bradley's angry voice, and we all drop what is in our hands and run to the living room. He is standing in the threshold, holding a bouquet of pink carnations. Nicco's amused expression has Bradley turning an alarming shade of purple.

He wrenches his neck to look around my mammoth brother and narrows in on Kels. "Really, Kelsey? He spent the night?"

"I sure did."

Ignoring my brother's gloating proclamation, he continues to address Kelsey, "You've made your point. I messed up. I am here to apologize and put this rough patch behind us."

"Rough patch?" Dawn looks at me. "Did he just call lying and cheating on her a rough patch? Dude, a rough patch is her getting pissed that you keep throwing your socks on the floor."

"I said I was sorry," Daniel chimes in. "Do I need to get a bouquet of lame-ass carnations?"

"I moved the hamper from the bathroom to an inch from your side of the bed, and you still throw them on the floor. Beside the fucking hamper. Who does that?"

Bradley gives Dawn a murderous look and then cuts his eyes back to Kelsey. "Kelsey, you cannot be serious with this"—he looks Nicco up and down, trying his damnedest to find something to insult—"brute."

At that, we all start laughing collectively.

"Lamer than the flowers, dude." Dawn shakes her head.

"As amusing as this little show is, I really need to speak to my girl alone."

"I am not your girl anymore, Brad. I stopped being your girl the minute you stuck your pencil dick in Tonya. No, you know what? I stopped being your girl the minute you started openly flirting with my fucking roommate. I tried to brush it off. I tried to reason that you were a guy, and what guy wouldn't flirt back when a girl was being so suggestive? But you wanna know who wouldn't? A guy who loves me; that's who wouldn't. So, I am sorry you ended up with the trash that you don't want to take home to Mom and Dad, but that's not my problem."

"See, Kelsey, you did it. Pencil dick is an example, describing Bradley's unimpressive girth. Now, let's finish this little scene, so we can get back to you filling us in on this here stud's girth."

"Are you kidding me with this?"

We hear Jake's voice coming from outside.

"Brad, look at that guy." He points to Nicco. "He would tear you in half without breaking a sweat. You fucked up. Lost your girl. Time to accept it and move on, my friend." He pats Bradley on the back in a sympathetic show. Then, he shoulders past him and into the apartment. He fist-bumps Nicco. "Hey, man. Let's get this party started." Then, he reaches up and slams the door shut in Bradley's face.

Nicco turns to me with a wide grin. "I really like him, sis."

So do I. More and more every day.

CHAPTER
Thirty-Two

Gabby
Past

M Y BROTHERS HAVE BEGRUDGINGLY ACCEPTED THAT CROSS AND I are now together. Not that they ever really had any say in it. Maybe when I was sixteen, but not now. I am my own person, and I make my own decisions. At least, I did. Now, Cross thinks my decisions are his business, and I guess, in a way, they are. He gets a say, but he is not going to boss me around. Our current discussion is about my living situation. He wants me to move in with him straightaway. I want to finish out the school year in the city with Adriana. Besides, we still have to face Papa and Mamma before we can make any major moves.

"I would just feel better if you were here at night, so I knew you were safely tucked in with me."

That does sound nice, but I can't let him know that.

"I have always been perfectly safe at my apartment. What happened did not happen there."

"No, but he knows where you live. He could follow you home. Anyone could."

"Are you trying to scare me? Because, if I let him steal my life and make me terrified to do the things I love, then he gets to abuse me over and over again. Can't you see that?"

He deflates a little. "I don't want you to be afraid all the time, *Tesoro*. I would just feel better if I knew you were safe every night."

I wrap my arms around him, and he rests his chin on my head.

"How about I spend every Tuesday night here since I don't have a Wednesday morning class? And then, Friday and Saturday nights, I am all yours. Plus, I promise to call you every night that we are not together and let you know when I am safely locked in the apartment with the alarm set?"

He sighs. "I guess that sounds reasonable—for now."

All the men in my life treat me like I am made of glass. It's annoying but also wonderful.

Papa called a family dinner in honor of our new relationship. Obviously, he took the news of me and Cross much better than expected and considerably better than Mamma. He actually seems very pleased at the announcement. All that worry for nothing.

Mamma simply hugs me tightly and says, "I hope you know what you are doing, Gabriella."

"All I know is that I cannot run from it anymore, Mamma."

She gives me a sad smile. "Then, we start now and pray that he decides against the path of your fathers' and makes his own way for the two of you." She takes my face in both her hands. "All I have ever wanted is happiness for you. You know that, right?"

"Of course I know that, Mamma."

He makes me so very happy. She must see that on my face because she nods and kisses my cheek. Then, in silence, she and I peel apples for the pie we are baking for the family dinner.

Everyone comes for dinner—Papa and Mamma, Cross's father and his brothers and his grandparents, all my brothers, and Nonna and Nonno. It is a huge celebration. Papa even starts calling Cross son.

"Welcome to the family, child." Una embraces me. "I have never seen my grandson so carefree. I feel like he has been holding his breath since you were just a young girl, and now, he has finally let it out."

"Thank you, Una. I think maybe we both have been holding our breaths."

She smiles at me and brushes the back of her hand across my cheek. "You are good for him, Gabriella. His destiny."

Her words warm me. I want to be his safe haven, just like he is mine.

After dinner, we walk back toward Cross's loft. I wrap my arm around his middle and lean into him as we stroll.

"Are you happy, baby?"

"Uh-huh," I confirm.

"The night went really well. I think your brothers stopped giving me the evil eye about halfway through the night."

"You know, at this point, they are only doing it to mess with you, right?"

"I know. I will take my licks like a man."

The night is beautiful. A crisp, cool October night in New York.

"Cross, you want to go swimming?"

"Swimming? What? Now?"

"Yeah, we can go down to the hot springs."

"We don't have suits with us."

"I know," I say with a wicked lilt.

He immediately turns us back toward the woods and heads for the springs. When we get there, we check to make sure no one else is around, and I start stripping. I get my clothes off before Cross, and I take off running and jump in the water. It's so warm, and it feels glorious. A few minutes later, Cross jumps in after me. I swim over to him and wrap my arms around his neck.

"You know we have no towels, and we are going to freeze while walking home, right?"

"So? We are warm right now, aren't we?"

He rests his hands on the small of my back and pulls me in closer. "We are."

I kiss his nose. Then, I kick out of his grip and start swimming. He gives chase, and we play in the water. Splashing and laughing and soaking in the warmth.

About an hour later, we are settled on the side of the spring, wrapped up in each other, and we hear footsteps crunching through the leaves.

"Christ. Really, man?" we hear Nicco's voice boom through the clearing before we see him and Marianna making their way with a basket and bags in tow.

I laugh and try to hide myself behind Cross's big frame.

"Sorry, Nicco. We didn't realize anyone else would be out here tonight."

"This sucks. It is not like when you were with Angie." He cuts his eyes to me in a silent apology. "I can't hang out with you while you are skinny-dipping with my sister, man."

"I know. I will be sure to let you know when to steer clear in the future."

"Ugh, now, the thought of you two naked in that water is burned into my brain."

"Did you guys happen to bring any towels with you?"

"Yes." Marianna elbows Nicco in the side. She comes to the water's edge and hands us a couple of towels.

"I'll start a fire," Nicco grumbles as he lumbers off.

"He'll get used to it." Marianna grins at me. "It's just weird right now, you know?"

"I get it."

Cross and I get out and wrap up in the large towels. Once we get dressed, we make our way to the fire. He sits on a log we used as a bench around the pit the boys dug out years ago, and I settle between his legs. His arms are around me from behind, and he is rubbing his hands up and down my arms, trying to warm me. I lean my head on his thigh, and I look through the flames to Nicco. He is closely watching us, and he gives me a hint of a smile. For all his complaining, I know my big brother is happy for me. Happy for us.

CHAPTER
Thirty-Three

"ANYONE SEEN MY PHONE?" NICCO BELLOWS DOWN THE hall.

It's moving day. He and Daniel finally found the perfect place for them at Venice Beach. It's about twenty minutes down the road from our apartment.

"Where was it the last time you saw it?" I ask.

"I don't know. I had it last night. I am going to check Kelsey's room again."

"Tell her to call it real fast," I yell down the hallway.

A few seconds later, I hear a faint buzzing coming from between the couch cushions. I fish it out and hit Accept Call.

"Aha! I found it. It was under the couch cushions," I declare in victory.

Silence.

"Hello?" I singsong into the phone.

"Gabby?"

Oh no. No. No. No.

I stay on the line. I should hang up, but I am paralyzed.

"*Tesoro*," he whispers across the line in a strangled voice.

Nicco comes back in.

"It's not in there. I have looked everywhere. Maybe it's in your car." He stops as he gets a look at my face. "What's wrong?"

A small sob escapes me against my will.

"Gabby, I am sorry. I did not know you would answer the phone …"

I do not hear the rest of what he says because Nicco has made it to me and taken the phone from my hand.

"Hello? Fuck. Hey, man. No, I misplaced my phone, and she was helping me find it."

He gives me a look that says he is sorry, and he walks to the kitchen and out onto the back deck. I go to my room and shut the door.

This is exactly why Nicco moving here was a bad idea. I was stable. I was okay. At least, I thought I was. Now, grief crashes over me, wave after wave.

I am not sure how long I sit there before a soft knock comes. I wipe my eyes and stand up. I open the door a hair.

Nicco is standing there, looking contrite. "I am sorry, sis."

"It's not your fault. I should not have answered your phone, especially without looking at the caller ID. I just thought it was Kels calling, so I could follow the ring and find it. I answered without thinking."

It could have been anyone. Mamma or Papa, one of my other brothers, or Cross. It was a stupid move.

"We haven't talked about him, but he and I …"

"You are still friends. I get it. You always have been."

"We always will be, but I promise I won't bring it to your doorstep. Honestly, that's the first we have spoken since I came here. I really am looking for a fresh start of my own."

I just nod.

"Hey, Brie, Melanie is here," Dawn calls as she comes in the front door.

Shit, I forgot that I was going with her to take Cassian for his twelve-month shots today. He turns a year old in less than a month. I

217

can't believe it.

"Isn't that the lady you babysit for?" Nicco asks.

"Nanny," I correct him. "I am a nanny, not a babysitter."

"Nannies live with the family and watch the baby every single day. You are a babysitter."

"Whatever," I say as I pass him. I grab my phone and purse and head for the door before Melanie and Cassian can make it up. I need to get out of this apartment.

"I take it, I don't get to meet them?" he calls after me.

"Maybe next time," I call back.

Once I am in the courtyard, I can finally breathe again. Melanie is standing there with the baby.

"You look like you saw a ghost."

"More like heard one."

On our way to the pediatrician, I fill Melanie in on my morning.

"Oh, jeez, Brie. Honey, I was afraid something like this would happen when that brother of yours showed up."

"I know. Me, too, but I learned my lesson. No answering Nicco's phone. Ever."

"Do you think he had any ulterior motives for moving here? I mean, it just seemed so out of the blue."

I think about it for a minute.

"Maybe. Papa could have sent him here to check up on me, but honestly, if that were the case, he could have sent any number of his soldiers and not exiled one of his sons. It just doesn't add up. Perhaps his breakup with Marianna sent him running, just like how everything that had happened with me sent me running. They were together for years and years. I barely remember the time before they were a couple. It had to be hard."

I want so desperately to believe that Nicco was sincere when he said he, too, wanted a fresh start. I hope that he has no ties to the family business and that none of that has followed him here to taint our lives or our new friends' lives.

Melanie doesn't look convinced. "I hope so, for your sake. You are doing so well. You have made friends, you are working, you have a new boyfriend. I don't want you to revert back to that girl who was always curled into herself."

"The one thing that I know beyond a doubt is that Nicco loves me very much. He wants me to be happy as much as, if not more than, anyone else."

"Good," she says like her fears have been eased. "Are we going to get to meet him?"

"Eventually. Right now, you guys are still my safe haven. The one place I can run. The only ones who know my whole story from all sides, and I don't know if I am ready to share you guys with Nicco yet. Where will I run when things like this morning happen?"

She reaches over and pats my knee, and I know she understands what I am trying to say. I thank God daily for her and Rick. In a lot of ways, their friendship has saved me.

We arrive at the doctor's office, and I get the baby from his car seat and hold him close. Shot days are hard for us. I think I cry harder than he does. It sucks when he is so little and can't understand what is happening, and his mother and I—two of the three people he trusts most in this world—hand him off to get pricked and prodded. I bet, in his mind, it is a betrayal. It slays me every time, but I keep coming because I don't want Melanie to have to do it alone.

"Here we go, little man. You are going to be okay. Mommy and I are going to be with you the whole time. I promise it will only take a second. When it is over, we are going to hold you tight, and we are going to go to Jeni's Splendid Ice Cream to get you the biggest cone they have. Then, we are going to go to the splash park, and you and I are going to jump through the water," I whisper to him the entire walk to the office.

As soon as we walk into reception and his eyes see the desk and Miss Linda, he bursts into big crocodile tears and buries his face into my tee. It breaks my heart.

After the terror is over, the three of us do get ice cream and go to the splash park close to their home. Cassian is not quite walking on his own yet, so I hold him in my arms as we stomp through the water sprouts and run through the arched fountain.

He giggles and keeps shouting, "Gin," for again, so I know that he has forgiven us.

"So, what are we doing for the big birthday?"

"I am not sure yet. I was thinking a safari theme maybe. Or Candy Land. I have always wanted to throw a Candy Land theme party. I went to a baby shower once that was Candy Land theme, and it was amazing. I always said, if I ever had a shower of my own, I would want that one," Melanie explains, and I know we are kindred spirits.

I would love to help her throw Cassian a Candy Land birthday party.

"Let's do it!"

"You like that idea?"

"I love it, and there is so much we can do." I start plotting. "We can have a huge cake made to look like King Kandy's castle. We can have a candy bar set up with goodie bags where guests can make their own candy gift bags to take home. We can make huge lollipops out of PVC pipe and Styrofoam we cover in see-through color-tinted plastic. We can fill huge clear plastic bags with smaller helium-filled colored balloons to look like gumballs. Oh, we can even dress like Princess Frostine and Princess Lolly, and we can dress Cassian as a tiny Jib. Do you think Rick would dress up as Mr. Mint?"

She starts laughing. "I like where your head is."

"Our boy only turns one once, and we have to make it extra special. Do you want to check out some bakeries now?"

"Absolutely."

We spend the rest of the afternoon together, planning the most epic first birthday party ever thrown.

When they drop me back off at the apartment, I am in a much better mood. That baby is always the best medicine.

The apartment is empty, and the girls left a note on the kitchen island, saying they are at the boys' apartment in Venice, helping them get everything unpacked. They want me to join them when I get home. After work today, Jake was going to help move the furniture that Uncle Matt had bought the guys, so he is probably still there as well. So, I grab my car keys and head out.

CHAPTER
Thirty-four

Gabby
Past

BLISS—THAT'S THE ONLY WAY TO DESCRIBE THE PAST FEW months. I finished up my classes and ended the year on the Dean's List. Adriana moved back home, and I moved in with Cross for the summer. He is working for his papa, running one of his legitimate businesses, and his papa is so impressed that he is giving him more and more responsibilities. I have been working at Papa's club, giving private tennis lessons to children and young adults because I want to earn my own pocket money without having to ask Papa or Cross every time I need something. I have grand plans of doing a little redecorating in the loft.

"What do you think of these?"

I show Cross the beautiful wine-colored leather barstools I found online. They have to be custom-made, but I think they would be gorgeous at his island.

"They look nice," he says distractedly while watching a Yankees game on the television.

"I was hoping for something more enthusiastic than nice." I sigh. "I'll keep looking. Would you prefer a brown or something? They have them in a tobacco color."

He turns to look at me. "A what?"

"Brown? A different color?"

He seems to realize what I am talking about.

"I am sorry, *Tesoro*. I wasn't paying attention. Show it to me again."

I turn the screen back toward him, and he considers them for a moment.

"They seem awfully fancy for this place."

"I am trying to make this place more homey."

He reaches for the remote and turns the game off. "I have an idea."

I give him my full attention.

"Why don't we find a piece of land of our own and draw up plans to have your dream house built? Instead of you trying to dress this place up, let's save it for a place that is ours."

"You want to build a house with me?" I ask him in shock.

"Of course I do. Did you think I was going to make you live in this loft behind my father's home forever?" He grins. "It doesn't have a second bedroom, and the bed it does have doesn't even have walls around it. How will I be able to ravage you without our babies walking in on us?"

"Our babies?"

"Yes, ma'am. I want a houseful of babies who look just like their mamma."

"A houseful, huh? Exactly how many are we talking?"

He pretends to think for a moment. "Eight or ten."

"Eight or ten? You do realize that means that I would be pregnant for a decade or more."

He flips me onto my back and places his big hand on my stomach. "I think you would be sexy, pregnant. Knowing that a part of me is growing inside of you"—he places a kiss right below my belly button—"I don't think there could be a greater gift in this world than babies half-you and half-me."

"Well, we have to wait until I am out of school and have had at least a couple of years to get a restaurant off the ground before any babies."

"I know. Doesn't mean we can't start building the house to fit them all though. What do you say?"

"I say, we start looking for land."

"Wait, he wants to build you a house? Isn't that a little premature? Shouldn't he be in the market for a ring first?" Adi asks as she sips her cocktail.

We met her and her latest conquest out for dinner. Cross and … Derrick? I think that is his name. They are playing a game of pool while we wait for our food.

"We haven't talked about a ring, but he said he wants me to have ten of his babies, so I am fairly sure we will eventually get there."

She chokes on her drink. "Ten babies? Is he insane? You are not a puppy mill, for Christ's sake. Dude, your body will never recover. He will be looking at saggy tits and stretch marks for the next fifty years."

"That won't happen."

"The hell it won't—unless he plans on sending you down to Dr. Miami for one of those fabulous Mommy makeovers."

"Who is this Dr. Miami?" Cross butts into our conversation as he follows the server who is bringing our plates.

"Her saving grace if you are serious about this ten-babies business."

I roll my eyes at her ridiculousness.

"What I want to know is, when do you plan to put a ring on it?"

"Adriana!" I scold. I cannot believe she just asked him that.

He just grins at her like he has a secret and looks at me. "Is she always going to be this nosy?"

"Probably. She has no boundaries."

"It's true. We are a package deal. You should have considered that before you went and laid claim on my best friend. She was mine first."

"Oh no, I believe she was mine first."

"Please don't fight over me. I have enough love in my heart for you both."

"Yeah, but you can only live in one place. This asshole stole my roommate. I know there is zero chance that you are moving back to the city with me when school starts in the fall." She pouts.

About that time, Cross's phone starts ringing. He looks at it and sends the call to voicemail. Two seconds later, it starts ringing again. Another send to voicemail. Then, my phone starts ringing. I grab my purse and check, and it's Papa. I look to Cross as his phone again starts ringing. We both answer this time.

We head to my parents' house. When we arrive, my parents, grandparents, my brothers, and Cross's grandparents are all there. Mamma comes barreling toward me and collapses in my arms. We are still confused and have no idea what is happening.

"Thank God you are okay," she cries.

"Of course I am." I look to Tony. "What's happening?"

"I think we all need to sit down in the study." Papa corrals us, and once everyone is seated, he explains, "Tonight, there was an attack on the Scutari family. While leaving dinner at Amici, Cross's father and his brother Emilio were gunned down. Marcello is alive but seriously injured. Emilio did not make it."

I tightly squeeze Cross's hand and look over to see he has gone completely pale. Una is now sobbing into his grandfather's jacket, and Mamma is clinging to Lorenzo.

Papa gives it a moment to let what he just said sink in and then continues, "Atelo was making a business run in Queens. He, too, was shot at from a passing vehicle, but he was able to take cover and slip away, unharmed." He turns to me with panicked eyes. "That's when we started frantically looking for you two. Ah, *bambina*, I have died a thousand deaths tonight."

"Why, Papa? Why is this happening?"

"We aren't sure. There has been some ... unrest ... lately, and Marcello has made some enemies."

I was raised in this life, and nothing like this has ever touched us. I know that Papa and Mamma have sheltered me. I look to Mamma, and I see it. I see in her eyes all that she wasn't telling me when she sent me to Aunt Mitzi. She wasn't just worried about my heart; she was worried about my safety if I were with Cross.

My mind is awhirl with questions. I clear my throat and ask Papa, "What do we do now?"

"First, we get you somewhere safe."

"Me? Why me?"

Mamma is the one who answers in a small, angry voice, "Because, sweetheart, everyone knows you are Cross's now, and if they want to hurt him, they know they can do it through you."

"Why would they want to hurt Cross? He doesn't have anything to do with this. He doesn't work for his father. He's not a soldier like Emilio and Atelo." I am growing more and more frantic as I try to make sense of it all.

Cross speaks, looking at the floor, "Because I am the only one left. If they want control of Scutari territory, of Scutari business, then they want to wipe out anyone who might challenge them." He looks up and meets Papa's eyes. "You will protect her?"

"I will protect her." Papa nods.

Cross stands. "Take me to my father."

I stand, too, and grab his hand. I am going with him. No way am I letting him face all of this alone. His father might not make it. Emilio is dead. We have no idea where Atelo is.

"I am going with you."

"No, *Tesoro*. You have to stay here and do what your father and brothers tell you to do."

I look around the room at all the somber faces. They will stop me.

"No. I go where you go. That's the deal now," I protest.

He takes my hand and pulls me out of the study and into Papa's office. "Gabby, baby, I need you to stay here, please. I have to go and check on my father, and I have to find Atelo. I cannot be worried about you on top of that. Please, I promise that I will come get you as soon as I can."

I wrap my arms around him. I am scared. I have never been this scared before. *What if he walks out that door and someone starts shooting at him?* I would rather us both be gunned down than to lose him.

"What if something happens to you?"

"It won't."

"You don't know that," I insist.

He tightly holds me for a few moments, kissing my forehead over and over again. Then, he pries my arms open and deposits me into Una's waiting arms.

"I will be back soon. I promise."

Tony and Stavros flank him.

"We are going with you, Cross. Lo and Nicco are staying here with Gabby and Mamma, and our grandparents. Papa is headed to meet with the other family heads."

"I appreciate it," he says as he grips Tony's hand and then Stavros's.

At least he won't be alone. He heads for the door, and Tony stops at me.

"I'll make sure he's okay, *cara.* I promise."

I nod to him, and they all walk out.

We huddle in the living room, like we are waiting out a storm. All of us women. Adriana and her mother showed up about an hour after the boys left. Adi's father was one of the men meeting with Papa, and he sent them to us with an armed guard. Nonno, Nicco, Lorenzo, and Cross's grandfather are drinking brandy and keeping their eyes and ears open. Mamma and Nonna and Una made sandwiches and coffee and brought down blankets and pillows for everyone. Adi and I have been curled up together on the sofa and watching the news, waiting to see if anything will be reported.

It has been the longest night of my life. I keep my phone tucked close to my side, and I check it every few minutes for any word from Cross. I want to call or text him, but I know I can't. He doesn't need me to add to his worries right now.

Sometime around three a.m., I must drift off to sleep.

I rouse when a hand runs through my hair. I look up, and Cross is standing there. He looks exhausted. He looks grief-stricken. I get to my knees. I pull him into my arms, and I hold him. I hold him while he weeps silently. I hold him while he accepts what has happened. I hold him as my own heart shatters into a million pieces because I know—I just know—nothing will ever be the same again.

CHAPTER
Thirty-five

Brie
Present

CASSIAN'S FIRST BIRTHDAY PARTY IS OVER-THE-TOP AMAZING. Melanie and I really outdid ourselves. I even hired a photographer to capture the entire event. It is my gift, being as the child already has more toys than he could ever play with. She captures every precious moment—from his arrival and the excited look on his little face when he sees the gumball balloons to his eyes dancing and him clapping as everyone sings to him before Rick helps him blow out his candle to the epic mess that is him after we strip him down to his diaper and let him have full access to his smash cake. Unfettered joy—his, his parents', and mine.

How did a year go by so quickly? It seems like only yesterday I was introduced to this miraculous little bundle, and now, he has a mouth full of teeth and is only days or weeks from taking his first steps. I really hope I am there the day he decides to take off on his own two feet. Melanie jokes that, if he stands up and she thinks he is about to take a step, she will gently push him down if I am not around.

After I help Melanie clean up and bathe Cassian and rock him to sleep, Jake comes to pick me up.

I mentioned once that I wanted to visit Wild Horse Winery & Vineyards because they made my favorite pinot noir. Turns out, Paso

Robles is drivable from Santa Monica, so we are headed there for the long weekend to enjoy a few wine tours and some much-needed alone time. Between my jobs, school, Nicco being in the house, and Jake's work schedule, it has been hard to spend more than a few stolen moments together here and there.

"There's my girl." He plants a kiss on my lips as he takes my overnight bag from my hands and places it in the trunk of his car.

Every time he pulls up in this car, a thrill shoots through me, and now, we get to take the top down and drive up the coast. I am so excited.

"How long is the drive?"

"About three and a half hours if we take I-5, but I was thinking of taking the long way and stopping in Malibu for dinner. What do you say? Are you up for a long adventure?"

"Absolutely."

Thirty minutes later, we are pulling into a place off the PCH called Moonshadows. It's a spectacular seafood restaurant with a large outdoor dining area that is built on stilts and into the ocean. Jake reserved us one of the large outdoor beds that overlooks the water. It's dark out, and the deck is softly lit in blue lights. The water is lapping up and splashing on the Plexiglass that surrounds us. It's so romantic.

"How exactly are we supposed to eat dinner on this bed, Jake Mason?"

"The server will bring the food out on large trays; don't worry."

"How did you find this place?"

"My dad used to bring us a lot when we were kids. We have a beach house in Malibu, and we would come up and spend the summers. Every year, on our way in and out, we would stop here. I remember how exciting it was for us, being able to watch the dolphins play while we ate dinner. Look out there." He points out into the dark sea. "Can you see them? They always stay close."

I come up to my knees and search the water. I finally see the fins. "Wow, that is so cool. They are beautiful."

"So are you," he says, looking up at me.

After dinner, we keep heading north. The drive is breathtaking. The California coastline really is something to see. We finally make it to Paso Robles around nine o'clock, and we check in to our hotel. The Paso Robles Inn is a quaint hideaway with beautiful rooms featuring large spa tubs on private balconies. As soon as we unload our bags, I walk out to check out the tub. A nice long soak sounds amazing right now. I turn the water on to let it fill, and I am instantly hit with the foulest smell imaginable.

"Jake," I call, "I think something died in the pipes."

He walks out with an amused look on his face. "Nothing died. That's just the water."

"It smells like rotten eggs. Do you not smell that?"

"Paso Robles is known for its hot springs. The water for the tubs is fed straight from them."

"Okaaay, I know exactly what hot springs are—we had one in our backyard back in New York—but this water smells rancid. It's not supposed to smell that way."

"Yes, it is. These hot springs are sulfur springs. Not all hot springs have a high mineral content, but the ones in this area do. The people here believe the sulfur has medicinal properties, and bathing in the water is supposed to be very therapeutic."

I wrinkle my nose. "Ew, gross. Who would want to get in it? I don't think I would last long."

He makes his way to me and wraps me in his arms. "You will love it, and after ten minutes in the water, you don't smell it at all anymore."

"Really? So, we will smell horrific, but we won't notice?"

He laughs. "Something like that."

"I don't know. Couldn't we have just gotten a room with a normal-smelling hot tub with regular water?"

"No, ma'am. You have to have the full Paso experience, and bathing in putrid water that makes you feel better and possibly cures cancer is one of the highlights."

"All right, but if I puke, it's your fault, and you have to take care of me without complaint."

"Terms accepted."

I step out of his arms and start to remove my jeans. He stands there, intently watching me.

"Aren't you getting in, too?" I ask.

"Yes. I just want to look at you for a minute. Do you realize, this is the first time we have been completely alone?"

I haven't thought about it, but he is right.

"Well, Mr. Mason, what will we ever do to entertain ourselves?"

He lunges for me, and I squeal and run around the other side of the tub.

"Nowhere to hide, pretty girl. You are all mine tonight."

I remove the rest of my clothes and toss them at him as he prowls toward me. I am cornered, so I don't even bother to fight, I let him pick me up in one fell swoop and deposit me in the water. Then, he quickly undresses and joins me.

"So, do you still smell it?"

"No, but I think it's because the fumes have burned the lining of my nose out."

"Complaining, complaining. You are going to wake up tomorrow, feeling amazing, and you will be thanking me."

"I certainly hope it's not just the water that has me waking up, feeling amazing."

He lifts an eyebrow at my innuendo. "Oh, I can think of a few things that I can do to aid the water in making you feel all kinds of good, Miss Masters. In fact, why don't we get out of this tub and into the shower now, so I can show you some of them?"

He stands and offers me his hand, and then he helps me from the tub. We go back inside and immediately to the shower to wash off the stench. Jake stands in front of the spray and starts to wash his hair first. It affords me the opportunity to appreciate his backside. I run my hands around him and up his chest while I trail kisses up his back. He lets my hands explore for a while, and then he rinses and turns to face me.

"Time to clean you up," he says as he lathers his hands with soap. Then, he starts to wash every square inch of me. Once he has me thoroughly clean, he places me under the spray to rinse, and then he leans over me with his hand resting on the stall above my head. "I want so badly to lift you up against this shower wall and fuck you until you are screaming my name."

"Why don't you?"

"Because this is real life, and I would probably lose my footing and drop you to the floor and knock myself out on the way down. I can't have that be the memory you always carry of our first time together."

I start giggling at the visual. The movies always make shower sex seem so easy and hot, but the truth is, the mechanics can be tricky. At least the foreplay of the shower is pretty damn spectacular all on its own.

"Then, why don't we get out and see if your luck fares better in that big ole bed out there?"

"Yes, ma'am."

We get out and towel off, making sure to tease each other as we do.

He kept his promise. I will wake up in the morning, feeling all kinds of good, but for now, I leave him lightly snoring and sneak out to the balcony on silent feet. Tonight was incredible, everything I thought it would be. Jake is sweet and patient, and every touch, every kiss, and every stroke was gentle. He played my body like a well-oiled instrument. The weight of it hit me after we were both sated, and I was cuddled in his side, so I had to escape before the tears came, before he heard me mourn, because, tonight, the last tie that bound me to the past was snapped in two. The last thing that made me *his* and only his. Now, I am truly and wholly Brie Masters.

I cry for what feels like hours. It is cathartic. Once I have it all out of my system, I return to the room. I return to Jake, wrapped in blankets, peacefully dreaming away. This is my future and exactly where I want to be. I tiptoe back to the side of the bed and crawl under the covers with him.

He stirs. "Hey, baby. Where did you go?"

"I just had to pee," I whisper, and then I quickly kiss his lips. "Go back to sleep."

He pulls me close and tucks me into his side. Within a few minutes, he is back in a deep sleep. I snuggle even closer and close my eyes, exhaustion drawing me under, and for the first night in a long time, I do not dream of Gabby.

CHAPTER
Thirty-Six

Gabby
Past

THE DISRUPTION IN BOTH OUR FAMILIES HAS BEEN EXCRUCIATING. We buried Cross's oldest brother last week. His father is still recuperating from a gunshot wound with bullet fragments lodged in his spine, which have left him paralyzed from the waist down. Atelo has left the country and will probably never resurface. Neither Cross nor Papa will tell me the details on what happened to cause this domino effect. All I know is that Papa has taken Cross under his wing, and the two are constantly in meetings. I have barely laid eyes on Cross in weeks.

After the shootings, he had my things moved back to my parents' house. I protested, but he said that he was going to be away a lot, dealing with the aftermath, and he did not want me staying in the loft alone. So, for his peace of mind, I relented.

Now, from the kitchen, I hear his voice in Papa's study, and I go to him.

"Hi," I say as I softly knock at the entryway to the study. "I didn't know you were here."

He is seated across from Papa and Adriana's father, and he doesn't even look my way when he speaks. "We are busy right now, Gabby."

I come fully into the room. "Busy with what? For how long? I would like to speak to you."

"Not now, Gabriella. We are in the middle of something," Papa answers, and it infuriates me. I wasn't addressing him.

"In the middle of what exactly?" I raise my voice, which I rarely do to my papa.

Adriana's father sternly looks at Papa. "Is she going to be a problem?"

She? Is he referring to me? How am I a problem?

"No," Cross and Papa say at the same time.

"I will handle this, gentlemen. Please give me a moment."

Cross gets up and crosses the room toward me. When he gets close, he takes my arm and briskly leads me to the kitchen, out of earshot. His touch is hard and cold. He has never touched me like this before. When we get to the kitchen, I wrench myself from his hold.

"Were you going to even tell me you were here?" I accuse. "I haven't heard from you in days. Days, Cross. And here you are, under my roof, and you don't even bother to tell me."

"This isn't a social call, Gabby. It's business."

"Business. Right. Everything is business lately. And since when am I a social call? I am not a social call. I am your girlfriend. The one you are in love with, remember?"

He looks away for a minute, and when he turns back to me, his face has softened. "I am sorry, *Tesoro*. Everything has been chaotic, and I haven't had a moment to breathe. I don't mean to treat you like you don't matter. It's just … other things are more pressing right now."

"More important than seeing me?"

He wraps his hand around the back of my neck and presses his forehead to mine. "Not more important, just more pressing."

I feel the tears welling up, and I am trying to keep them at bay. I know this has been hard for him, and I don't want to add to the boulder on his shoulders.

"You feel clammy. Are you okay?" he asks with concern evident in his voice.

"I have been sick for a couple of days now. Papa had a doctor come out yesterday. He is so paranoid right now. He wouldn't let Nonna take me to the doctor's office. I feel like a prisoner here."

"What did the doctor say?"

"They think it's the flu. They gave me Tamiflu and told me to drink liquids and rest."

He sighs heavily and kisses my forehead. "I hate that I can't be here to take care of you."

"I am feeling much better. Besides, I don't want you to take care of me. I just want to be with you. Please, can't you stay awhile?"

I know I sound and look like a child as I wrap my fists in his shirt, trying to keep him there. I am just such a wreck right now. Full of anxiety and fear. Everything feels sideways.

"I can't, and I need to get back to this meeting."

I whimper at his words.

"How about tonight? Pack an overnight bag and come to the loft."

At that, I let him go and look up with a huge smile on my face. I can wait a few more hours for time alone with him at the loft.

"Tonight."

He leans in and kisses me, and then we hear Papa at the door.

"If you two are done, we need to get back to this."

I look over at Papa. He has sadness in his eyes. I didn't realize he and Marcello were such good friends. This entire situation has taken a toll on him.

I let myself into Cross's loft around six. Mamma fought me on coming. She didn't think it was safe. When I told her I was going whether she liked it or not, she insisted on her driver bringing me rather than me driving myself. I sure hope the unrest that is surrounding us all dissipates soon because I cannot take much more of this weird behavior from everyone.

Once I unpack my bag, I rummage through the refrigerator to see what I can scrounge up to make us for dinner. I figure Cross will be exhausted when he gets in, and I doubt he will want to go back out. I don't want to either. I just want some alone time with him.

I piece together a meal with what we have available, and I set it in the oven to keep it warm. I decide to take a quick shower and change before he arrives. When I am toweling off, I realize I forgot my night-gown, so I open Cross's T-shirt drawer and grab one. I pull it over my head.

There is a small velvet box tucked underneath his shirts, and I pick it up and open it. Inside is the most stunning diamond ring I have ever seen. It is emerald cut and has a halo of smaller diamonds. I instantly snap it shut. *Oh my God, he is going to propose, and I just ruined my own surprise.* No wonder he has been acting so funny lately. His plans were derailed by these horrific events. As elated as I am, I carefully place the ring back into his drawer and cover it back up. I don't want him to know I found it.

I look at the clock, and it is now a little past eight, so I text Cross to see when he will be home. I go to lie on the couch to watch television and wait. Being ill has really taken it out of me.

Eventually, I drift off to sleep. When I awake, it's four in the morning, and there is still no sign of Cross. I grab my phone, and all of my messages have gone unanswered. I dial his number, and it goes straight to voicemail. Now, I am frantic. Something must have happened.

I dial Nicco, and he answers with sleep in his voice.

"Do you know where Cross is?" I am a panicked, hysterical mess at this point.

"Gabby? No. He is probably at home, sleeping."

"No, he is not. I am at his loft. He told me to come spend the night with him, and he never came home. I have sent him several texts and called a few times, and his phone is going straight to voicemail. God, what if something happened to him?"

"Calm down. I'll see what I can find out. Just stay by your phone."

I go to the stove, remove the ruined plates of food, and throw them in the trash. Then, I start pacing.

About forty-five minutes later, the phone rings, and Nicco's number flashes on the screen.

"Please, please, please," I cry into the phone instead of a greeting.

"He is fine, sis. I was able to get Stav on the phone, and he is with him and Tony. He said they got held up on some business and that they won't be home until sometime tomorrow. Just stay put, and he will call you a little later."

Fuck that.

"Thanks, Nicco. Sorry I woke you up for that."

"No problem. Asshole should have called you instead of letting you sit up all night, worried. It was a dick move. I think he is just overwhelmed."

"Yeah, probably. I'll let you get back to sleep."

I hang up, and I grab my bag and change quickly. Then, I call a cab. No way am I staying here now. Let him worry when he arrives to find me missing.

I hop in a cab and head to the city. I stop at an ATM and get cash to check into a hotel. I know better than to use a card. Papa would have me tracked down in an instant. They can all go to hell for all I care.

I am exhausted, my head is pounding, and my stomach is rolling by the time I get to my room at the Stanhope. It's seven in the morning, and I just want to cry myself to sleep and hide from it all.

My phone rouses me a few hours later. It's Cross calling. I don't even get it sent to voicemail before Nicco's and then Mamma's numbers ring through. I turn it off, and then I pull the covers over my head and drift back off to sleep.

Hours later, there is a banging on the door. I lift my head and look at the clock. It's eight p.m. I slept all day.

"Go away," I call out because I don't want maid service, and I didn't order food.

"Open this door, Gabby."

Cross. It's Cross. How did he find me?

"No. Go away!" My voice is scratchy, and I need water, but I don't feel like getting up. My head is pounding. I cried myself to sleep, and I haven't eaten. I am a mess, and I just want to be left alone.

"Gabby," he pleads. "Open the door, so I don't have to break it down."

I stand on shaky legs and wrap the comforter around me. I wade to the door and open it, leaving the chain lock in place. I peek out. He looks as bad as I feel. *Good.*

"What do you want?"

"Fuck." He lets out a relieved breath. "Why haven't you answered your phone?"

"Same reason you did not answer yours last night. I am busy."

"Really?" His relief has turned to anger. "You want to play childish games right now?"

"No, I don't want to play anything. I want to be left alone. I don't feel good. I am too tired to do this right now."

"Let me in." He leans his head into the door. "Baby, please let me in."

I finally relent and close the door to release the chain. He pushes in, and I collapse into his arms. He picks me up and carries me to the bed where he lays me down. I fall right back to sleep.

"Wake up, *Tesoro.*"

I feel him brushing the hair from my face.

"Food is here, and you need to eat."

I open one eye and look up at him. He is beside me on the bed, and he has a tray of food across his lap. He is in his boxers, and his hair is wet, like he just took a shower. I move to sit up.

"I am thirsty," I manage to say.

He reaches to the side of the bed and grabs a bottle of water. He hands it to me, and I down it in one swallow.

I get up to go to the restroom, and I know I am weak. I take a look in the mirror to assess myself, and I am a mess. My hair is sticking to the side of my head, and my eyes are puffy and bloodshot. Great, the first opportunity I have had to be alone with Cross in weeks, and this is what he gets. I splash water on my face and use the facilities. I am actually feeling much better.

I walk out to face him and crawl back in the bed. I lay my head on his shoulder and wait without saying a word.

"You scared the shit out of all of us yesterday," he starts, his tone gentle. "Do you have any idea what I went through when we figured out you were missing? I damn near lost my mind, Gabby. I didn't know if you had been kidnapped or if someone had shot you in the fucking back and left you for dead in a ditch. I did not know where you were headed, so I had no idea where to start looking. I was frantic. Your mother and father lost their minds. Your brothers lost their minds. We practically tore the city apart."

Remorse sinks into my bones. I did not think this through.

"I was angry and hurt. You did not come home. You knew I was waiting for you, and you did not come home. I was worried, too. You weren't returning any of my texts or calls, and I … I pretty much thought the same thing you did." I don't look at him as I finish. "Nicco said he finally heard from Stav and you were taking care of business. Yeah, right. What kind of business needs attention all night? It was four thirty in the morning. I was sick and I was hungry and I was angry."

"I told Nicco to tell you I'd be home in a few hours. Why would you come to a hotel?"

"I did not want to stay there any longer, and I did not want to go back to Papa's."

"Gabby, you cannot just take off like that."

"I am sorry," I whisper through my tears. "I just …"

I cannot even finish the sentence because he is right. It was a self-ish thing to do. Especially after all he just went through. Adding to his worry was not fair of me.

He leans over and kisses the top of my head, and then he hands me half of a turkey sandwich.

"Eat, baby. We have to get you home before all of New Rochelle descends on us."

"How did you find me?"

"Your father had your cell phone traced."

Well, I hadn't thought of that.

Note to self: if you ever want to truly run away, ditch the phone.

"I see the wheels turning. Don't even think about it. Don't ever run off without leaving me a way of finding you."

CHAPTER
Thirty-Seven

Brie
Present

SUMMER IS AROUND THE CORNER, AND I HONESTLY CAN'T WAIT. Kelsey's mother made good on her promise, and I have been booked with several catering jobs. It feels great to be making some extra cash, doing something I love. Between that, keeping Cassian, giving lessons at the club, final exams, spending time with Jake, and helping to plan Dawn's graduation party, I have been so busy. Too busy. Something has to go, and as much as it pains me, I have to talk to Mr. Cloniger because, of all those things, the club is the only one I can let go of.

"Time to pay the piper," Dawn says as we pull up to the club.

I am practically hyperventilating in the passenger seat.

"For goodness' sake, you look like you are about to confess to murder, not quit your part-time job."

"I just feel horrible, quitting on him. He gave me this job when I really needed it, and I just hate to disappoint him."

"You are a part-time tennis instructor. It's not like you are the CFO, leaving him in a bind. Jeez, Brie, I think you are over-inflating your importance to the entire organization."

I stick my tongue out at her. "You are such a bitch sometimes."

"I know, right? I have no idea why you guys are still friends with me."

"I guess we like bitches."

"Yeah, we do!"

Mr. Cloniger is very understanding. He said he knew it was coming because I had been turning down more and more private lessons. He also assumed I was spreading myself too thin. He was actually quite happy for me when I told him about the catering, and he said to let him know if I needed an internship in the kitchen down the road because he would be happy to provide a recommendation for me.

After turning in my parking pass and cleaning out my employee locker, I head to the office to get my last paycheck and then to the bar to meet Dawn for lunch. She grabbed us a table while I spoke to Mr. Cloniger.

"How did it go?"

"As well as I could hope. He made it very easy for me."

"Told you. All that anxiety, for nothing."

We order food and a couple of waters and sit and chat about the graduation plans.

"So, Mom rented the entire Sonoma Wine Garden for the night. We will have food on the garden patio. The band and dance floor will be in the dining ballroom. The DJ will set up in the bar, which leads out to the ocean deck, and the champagne, desserts, and coffee will be on the Sonoma deck."

"Wow. She is going all out."

"Yep. Her only princess is finally graduating. She has to make it the social event of the year."

"So, what is our budget?"

"We have no budget. We just pick out what we want and charge it to Daddy's black card."

"Oh, this is going to be fun."

"You bet your ass it is. As soon as Kelsey gets here, we are heading out to taste-test every bakery in Santa Monica."

We finish our food and chat more about the party specifics while we wait for Kelsey. Nicco is supposed to be dropping her off any minute now.

I run to the restroom while Dawn waits for our server, and I see Jake leaving the men's locker room with another member. I didn't know he was here. He must have gotten off work early. I head toward him as he turns to his companion and speaks. When I get closer, I see the man's face, and I freeze. *What the fuck?* The man looks up. His eyes meet mine, and he grins. The bastard grins.

I turn and take off running through the club. I head straight for the front door and tear toward the parking lot. I don't even know where I am going. I just know I have to get far away. Arms grab me from the side, and I scream.

"Whoa. Where are you going? Did you not hear us calling your name?"

Nicco. Oh, thank God it's Nicco's voice.

I throw my arms around him.

"Brie, what's wrong?"

"He is here. He's here, and he is with Jake."

"Who is here?" Nicco starts scanning the parking lot.

"I have to get out of here." I struggle to get out of his hold.

"Stop and talk to me, sis. Who is here?"

I look up at him. "Dante."

A look of surprise registers on his face.

"Are you sure? It wasn't just someone who looked like Dante?"

"Who is Dante?" I hear Kelsey asking from behind Nicco.

I am shaking now. "It's him. I could never confuse him with someone else, Nicco. I will never forget that face."

"Where are they?" he demands.

"When I saw them, they were headed out of the locker room. Nicco, I have to get out of here."

He turns to Kelsey. "Take her home. I'll meet you guys there shortly."

She nods, and we head to her car as he takes off toward the club. She already has her ear to her phone.

"Hey, it's me. She is out in the parking lot with me. Nicco is on his way in. Toss him your keys and come get in my car with us. I am parked to the right of the club, behind the Pro Shop. We have to get Brie out of here. I don't know, but she's pretty freaked out. Just get out here, and we will figure it out later."

She ends the call, and we climb into her car. She doesn't ask any questions. She just starts the car, and we wait in silence for Dawn to appear. Once she hops in, we speed out of the club parking lot and head toward home.

"Do you want to talk about it?" Kelsey finally asks.

"Yeah. I mean, everything was fine, and you got up to go to the restroom but never returned," Dawn adds.

"Who is Dante?"

"Dante?"

"Yes, when we were walking into the club, she came flying out the door, and Nicco caught her. She said she saw Jake with someone named Dante, and as soon as the name left her lips, Nicco looked like he was going to rip someone's head off."

"So, who is Dante?"

"He is a very bad person from my past in New York," I confess. "He is not supposed to know where I am. I don't know how he found me."

"Is he the reason you ran away from home?" Dawn asks cautiously.

"Not really, but he is a part of my life I would like to forget. A part that still scares me."

"You say he is bad. Is he dangerous?"

"Yes."

"Well, don't worry; Nicco will handle it," Kelsey encourages.

"He was with Jake," I whisper.

"That doesn't necessarily mean anything."

"Yes, it does."

"You don't know that."

But I do. I do know it. There is no way it's a coincidence. The world doesn't work that way. Betrayal washes over me. Red-hot betrayal. How did I let this happen to me again? I put my heart out there, just to have it shattered again.

I take my phone out, and I send a text to Jake with three little words.

We are over.

Then, I turn it off, and I climb out of the car. I walk up to our apartment, flanked by my friends.

Once we are inside, Kelsey's phone starts ringing.

I walk into my room and kick off my shoes. I grab a blanket, and then I head to the living room. The girls are sitting there, watching my every move.

"Nicco says they were gone by the time he got in there. They must have left together."

"Are you okay?"

"I will be. This isn't my first rodeo with heartache, and if I could survive the last time, believe me, I can survive anything."

Honestly, I am more mad at myself than anything. For falling for Jake. For letting him in. For trusting again. I knew better.

Twenty minutes later, Daniel is at the door.

"Jake has been texting and calling me. He got your text, and he is freaking out," Daniel says after he settles in and Dawn explains what happened. "I told him to stay at the office, and I would come check out what was going on." He asks me, "What should I tell him?"

"Nothing. I am done, Daniel. Just tell him I am done."

I say my good nights, and I head to bed. When I get to my room and close the door, I stop and look at myself in the mirror hanging on the back of the door.

No matter how many miles I put between myself and home, I am still running. I am so tired. I am not even sure who I am anymore. Am I Brie, or am I still Gabby? Because, right now, I see Gabby staring back at me. I think I fall somewhere in the middle. A little bit of both of me.

CHAPTER
Thirty-Eight

Gabby
Past

ONCE I HAVE EATEN, CROSS TAKES ME HOME. WHEN WE ARRIVE, I have to face the equivalent of a firing squad. Papa is beyond angry, Mamma is beside herself, Adriana is furious, and my brothers ... well, they actually seem a little sympathetic. Papa pulls Cross aside and into his study first, and then he calls me in.

"Do you have any idea what you have caused?" he roars.

I flinch at his tone. He has never spoken to me like this before.

"You are not a child anymore, Gabriella."

"I know that."

"Do you? Because you are acting like a brat."

I hang my head and take a deep breath. "I am sorry I scared everyone. I just needed a break. I haven't felt well, and I am tired of being imprisoned and ignored."

"We have kept you here for your safety. We have ignored you because there are bigger things to attend to than your hurt feelings," he shouts.

I look up at him and demand, "Then, tell me what those things are. You cannot treat me like a child and then scold me for acting like one. I am tired of being kept in the dark."

Papa cuts his eyes to Cross and then nods once. "Christoff is assuming the role of acting head of the Scutari family. We have been working to help transition power from Marcello to him. It's a dangerous business because there are enemies who don't want to see him take control. He has the backing of the other families in this, but many feel that his relationship with you is a liability."

"What? Why? Because I took one day for myself?"

"No, because you were not groomed for such a life. You are immature and reckless, which you proved today. Adriana told her father, who told everyone, that you despise the business and that you told her you would never be your mother and be a compliant family wife."

"Why? Why would she say that?"

"Because it's true," Cross finally speaks. "You don't want this. You never wanted it."

"Neither did you."

"No, I didn't, but I have no choice now."

"Yes, you do. You always have a choice. We can leave. You and I, we can leave together and go somewhere and start over," I plead.

"I can't, Gabby. There is no one else, and I can't run like a coward."

"You can. Atelo ran."

"Exactly, and I can't leave my father and grandparents here to face this alone. If I assume power now, I can protect them."

"Okay." I turn to Papa and repeat, "Okay, so we stay."

It is not the life I wanted, but I will make it work.

"You do not understand, Gabriella. There is no *we* anymore."

"What do you mean?" I turn my eyes back to Cross. "What does he mean?"

"It's over, *Tesoro*."

"What's over?"

I know the word that he is going to say before it hits the air.

"Us."

Pain ... blinding pain rips through me.

"No. Why?"

He takes a few steps forward, and I start retreating.

"It is what's best now."

At that, I charge at him. My fists pound into his chest. "What's best? You-you love me. You said you loved me!"

He takes my blows and does not move.

"Why would you let them do this? How can you let them decide? We were going to build a house. We were going to have ten babies. We were going to be a family. Say it. Say you love me." I stop hitting him and look up at his face. "Say it, please."

"Enough," Papa interrupts. "You will stay here until it is safe. Then, you will return to the city with Adriana, and you will finish school like you planned. You will get over this."

"I won't. I won't go anywhere with her."

"You will. You must appear to be moving on. Like the relationship with Christoff was a summer fling. You need to quickly move on with your normal life, resume dating. Marcello's enemies need to see you looking like—"

"Nothing. Like I don't matter. I am nothing," I finish his sentence.

I look to Cross, and he is stoic. His face is blank, and his eyes have shut down. He just stands there, silent.

I stare at him for a long moment. Then, my stomach starts rolling, and I lose my lunch. Right there in the study, I am retching, and Papa calls for Mamma. She comes running in, and Cross bends down and begins rubbing my back. I jerk away from him.

"Do not touch me. You do not get to touch me ever again," I sob. "You promised. You promised me. You are a coward."

He pulls his hand and backs up. I look around the room at everyone. Papa, Mamma, Adriana, Cross, and my brothers. I hate them. Every one of them. I stand, and once I have my balance, I flee, Mamma calling behind me. I make it to my room and slam the door shut. I lock it and then fall on my bed. A puddle of grief. This cannot be happening again.

I have spent the last week confined to my room, refusing to talk to any-one, except Nonna, and making exactly two phone calls. One to Cross. I need to have one last conversation with him. I left him a message and told him he had one more chance to choose us, and he needed to call me today. He didn't. Now, it's time to put my plan in motion. I refuse to stay here and be a pawn any longer. One that Papa and Cross can move around the chess board as they see fit. Move here. Do this. Stay there. No more.

I look at the clock, and it says two a.m. I slip from bed and toss a few necessities into my backpack. I grab my jacket. I leave my cell phone on the nightstand. Then, I creep downstairs on silent feet and head to the alarm panel and disarm it. I take one last look around the kitchen. A place where I watched my mamma cook and where my nonna taught me how to make pasta from scratch. I look at the big dining room table where we sat and ate as a family, and I picture my brothers, loud and happy around it. I say a silent goodbye to the people I love most in the world and my childhood home. Then, I slip out the back door.

I make my way down the drive and a few blocks over to the car waiting at the Stop sign. The back door opens, and Una steps out. I called her two nights ago to ask for her help. She was the only one I could trust. She has lost her daughter and, now, two of her grandsons, and I knew she would understand. At least, I prayed she would.

"Do you have your passport?" she asks.

I nod as I get in the back seat with her.

"Good. I have made all the arrangements." She pats my hand. "I opened an account for you and deposited plenty of cash. It should last you a while. Here is the information." She hands me a large envelope. "There is a new cell phone in there. It's a burner phone, and it is to be used for emergencies only. Do you understand?"

"Yes, ma'am. Emergencies only."

"Do you have the letters?"

I pass her several letters that I wrote, stating that I was alive and well and having the time of my life. Another letter was left in my room, explaining that I had decided to spend the year abroad with friends I'd met in Paris because I wanted to backpack through Europe and clear my head.

"I will have friends mail them from Scotland and France and Spain, one a month for the next few months."

"Thank you, Una."

"Everything is going to be okay, Gabriella. You are doing the right thing. I know it doesn't feel like it now, but your heart will heal eventually."

I want to believe her, but she is wrong. My heart will never recover from this betrayal, and I don't want it to. I want to feel this pain forever, so I know to guard my heart better.

CHAPTER
Thirty-Nine

Brie

Present

NICCO CONFRONTED JAKE. HE FOUND OUT THAT DANTE HAD APproached him before we met and said that he was a friend of my father, who was a very wealthy businessman in New York. He told him I had run off to California and that I was a naive girl whom he was very worried about. He offered Jake a lot of money to get insider information about me. He knew his dad was the club's president, and he thought it would be easy for Jake to befriend me and report back. So, Jake did just that. He thought he was actually helping a father keep an eye out for his daughter, and he was making some cash on the side. No harm, no foul.

I am devastated. Even though he stopped giving Dante any information months ago, he never told me. His entire pursuit of me had been an act. He got close to me on purpose to spy on me for Dante. A man who had been stalking me for years. A man who'd drugged and tried to rape me. His obsession has somehow followed me all the way to California.

For weeks, Jake has tried to see me or talk to me. I have shut him down at every turn. Daniel asked me to hear him out because he believes he really is in love with me and that he was just tricked by Dante before he knew me. That might be the case, but he has had all the time in the world to confess it all to me, and he didn't. My safety was in jeopardy, and I had no idea. Even Dawn and Kelsey, Melanie and Rick and the baby, anyone I was growing close to could have been a target. If there is one thing I have learned, it's that love can hurt people. My love can hurt people.

"Are you sure you don't want to at least hear him out?" Melanie asks.

"I am sure."

"I hate to see you shut down like this. You were just starting to open up and live again."

"I should have known better."

"Do you think he was still feeding this Dante character info?"

"No, but that's not the point. He lied to me. He got close to me with an agenda, and I did not see it. I let his charm and his good looks weasel his way in. Maybe he eventually did fall for me, but none of the beginning was genuine. I just can't, Mel. I just can't."

"I get it. He really messed up."

"No, I did. I really messed up, and I know better."

She looks at me with sadness in her eyes. I know she wanted this second chance for me.

"Where is this Dante person now?"

"I don't know. Nicco can't find him. He had the number Jake was given traced, and it led to an apartment in Los Angeles that belongs to Dante's father's business, but it is empty."

"That's disturbing."

"Everything about Dante Calvacanti is disturbing."

"What are you gonna do now?"

"I am going to go home and get ready for Dawn's graduation and after-party."

"That sounds like a great plan."

"You guys are coming, right?"

"We will be there. We have Rick's mom coming to stay the night, so we can actually hang out with the grown-ups past midnight."

Graduation was boring and lasted forever. The speeches dragged on and on and on. I swear, if it hadn't ended when it did, Kelsey and I were going to end up making a break for it, but alas, we stayed till the bitter end because we are awesome friends and also because Daniel was our ride, and he refused to leave.

After standing around while Dawn's mom took a zillion photographs, we are finally on our way home to get ready for the big shindig. We plan to party the night away, and then, tomorrow morning, Dawn and Daniel are off on a three-week graduation trip to Monaco, all paid for by the proud parents. She is so lucky. I would love to have three weeks to lie on a beach in Monte Carlo and shop and eat and explore. However, I still have one last year and a lot of money to save before I can travel. California beaches will have to do for now. Not that they are anything to sneeze at. Home is pretty spectacular.

"Come on, guys; let's go," Dawn urges.

She is dressed in a stunning gold cocktail dress, and she has her hair pulled into a low chignon on the side of her head. She is wearing a glittery tiara. She looks every bit the California princess. Kelsey's dress is black with hot-pink polka dots on the skirt, which sounds awful, but on Kelsey, it is gorgeous and fits her personality to a T.

She picked out a bronze cocktail dress for me with black lace inlay. She said the color looked amazing against my olive skin. It has a low neckline and a short skirt to show off my long, tan legs. I'm wearing my hair down in a beach wave, and I've kept my makeup simple with a few extra coats of mascara and a nude lip stain. I stand in front of the mirror, and I think Jake would have loved this dress. When I carried it in after our trip to Beverly Hills to shop for dresses, he begged me to try it on for him, but I wouldn't. I told him he was just gonna have to wait to see the final result tonight.

"Coming," I yell as I take one last look at myself and grab my clutch.

When we arrive, the band is already playing, but they stop and then start playing "Unwritten" by Natasha Bedingfield as Dawn twirls and blows kisses at the crowd. Everyone is clapping, and she is soaking up all the love and attention.

Kelsey and I head inside to grab a plate. Our favorite steak and seafood restaurant, Larsen's, catered, and we have been anticipating the food all day.

The food is amazing, and the drinks are amazing. We are all on the dance floor, having a great time, when I spot Jake entering the ballroom. *Wonderful.* He stands on the side of the dance floor, watching us. Nicco pulls in close to offer me support if I need it, but I don't.

"I am good," I tell him. "I guess it's time to hear him out."

I march off the floor toward Jake. Maybe Melanie is right, and he deserves the chance to explain.

"What are you doing here?"

"Well, I was invited," he slurs.

Great, I can smell the overwhelming aroma of whiskey on his breath. This should go well.

"Jake, I know we have to have a conversation, but I don't think now is the time."

He looks around the room, and his eyes come back to me. "I am sorry, Brie. I am so damn sorry."

"I know, and I believe you. I am just not ready to forgive you."

He nods as if he understands. "I deserve that."

"I don't know if you deserve it. I am just very mixed up right now. I need time."

"I can give you that. You know where to find me when you are ready to talk. If you are ever ready to talk."

A redhead in a risqué blue mermaid dress slinks up beside him. Carlie. *Unbelievable.*

"Did you bring her here?"

"She just gave me a ride. I was at the club, drinking and trying to decide whether or not to come tonight. She offered to bring me because I couldn't drive myself."

"Really?" I hiss. "You have got to be kidding."

"What? I needed an ally, walking into the lion's den."

"You are a jackass."

"No, I am not. There is nothing going on here."

"You know what?" I look at Carlie. "Enjoy yourself."

"Oh, I intend to."

I stomp off the dance floor.

I am so sick of meaning so little to people who mean the world to me. I am so easily discarded or replaced. I want someone who is willing to fight for me as much as I am willing to fight for them. I want someone who thinks I am worth the fight.

"Did that asshole bring a date?" Dawn asks as she charges toward Jake and Carlie. "Oh, hell no."

I catch her arm and pull her back. "Don't. It's not worth ruining your dress or your party over."

"I disagree. I think, if you let me punch her just one time, it will bring this party up a notch."

"He is drunk. Nothing you say is going to make a difference."

I look over, and Carlie is wrapped around his arm. His eyes are still on me. Such a jackass.

"I don't want him to ruin your night either. It's supposed to be a celebration for all of us."

"He won't. He came here, hoping to get my attention, but we aren't in high school anymore. I am done."

"In that case, let's dance."

She grabs me and Kelsey and pulls us up on the stage into the spotlight. Then, she yells for the DJ to play Cee Lo Green's "Fuck You." The three of us dance like no one is watching as we sing the lyrics at the top of our lungs. We end up holding on to each other, laughing our asses off as the room erupts in applause. We take a slow bow, and I scan the crowd, hoping Jake and Carlie have left and, at the same time, hoping that they haven't, when my eyes fall on a tall shadow watching from the corner.

A shadow in a three-piece suit. A shadow and a pair of piercing green eyes that I would know anywhere.

Oh my God. I stand there, frozen to the spot. *What is he doing here?*

Nicco is standing in front of the stage, looking up at us, and his eyes fall on me.

"Brie, what's wrong?" He turns his head and starts looking in the same direction.

Cross.

Epilogue

Cross
One Week Earlier

"A**RE YOU FUCKING KIDDING ME?**"

I cannot believe what I am hearing. He must have a death wish. When I tell Tony that Dante has followed Gabby to California, he will kill him himself, and it will be a slow and painful execution.

"No. She came running out of the building, completely freaked out. She looked right through us. I started calling her name and chasing her. When I grabbed her, she lost it. It was like she had seen a ghost."

"Where is he now?"

"I don't know. By the time I got it out of her and ran in to find him, he was gone. I followed a few leads I could gather, and everything was a dead end."

"What about Mason?"

"He said Calvacanti approached him when Gabby started working at the club. He introduced himself as Lucas. He knew Jake's father was the president, so he assumed he could get access to private information. He lied to him and told him that he was a friend of her parents and that they were worried about their young daughter who was so far away from home."

"He fell for that bullshit?"

"Yes. At first, Dante said they were willing to pay an outrageous sum of money for peace of mind, but they didn't want her to know they were keeping tabs on her. He wanted Jake to befriend her and get close to her. Once he met Gabby and saw how headstrong and independent she was, it all seemed plausible."

"So, the entire relationship has been a lie? Damn it, Nicco. She trusted him."

"I know. She's devastated."

"Again."

"Again. But I don't think the entire thing was a lie. Once they started dating and he started really caring about her, he stopped giving Dante anything substantial, which agitated him. He said Dante got unpredictable, showing up all the time, demanding more intimate personal info that no parent would. He tried feeding him unimportant stuff to pacify him. Her address, her work schedule, classes, her friends' names—shit like that."

"None of that is unimportant. He could have been waiting for her after work or followed her home and grabbed her," I roar.

"I know that. Thank God he didn't, but all that is stuff he could have easily found out on his own. Jake knew that. He was playing the part, so Dante would not go seeking someone else to do his bidding. I don't know what he was waiting for, what he wanted exactly. Eventually, Jake had enough. He cut off all contact with him and made sure security at the club had his name and description and would not allow him access. But, somehow, he got past them that day, and he cornered Jake in the locker room. That's when Gabby saw them—when he was trying to get him out of there."

"He never thought to tell her? Warn her or her roommates that some lunatic was stalking her?"

"No. He honestly thought Dante worked for her parents, but when Gabby wouldn't share any details about her family, he assumed they were just rich, controlling assholes. He was waiting for her to open up, which she was starting to do a little, and he thought, if he said anything, she would close back up."

"He made the wrong decision."

"I know that, and you know that. He didn't know."

"She deserves better."

"Yeah, well, she has always deserved better than she's fucking got."

There is a long silence between us.

"Sorry, man. I just … I hate seeing her crushed like this again. She was finally starting to seem happy."

"I hate it, too. All I want is for her to be happy and safe. It's why I sent you to her."

"What's the next move?"

The next move is finding Dante Calvacanti and making him regret the day he was born, and then I will deal with Jacob Mason.

"Sit tight for now and just watch over her. I have to make come calls, and I will be in touch."

I end the call and throw the phone across the room. It shatters into pieces, and Una comes running in.

"What's happened?"

"A situation in California. Can you book me on the next flight to Los Angeles?"

She just stands there. I can tell she wants to say something, and I wait.

"Are you sure that's a good idea, Christoff?" Her worried eyes are boring into mine.

"I have to handle this, Una. I needed to go to her anyway. She has to know, and I want to tell her in person. She deserves to hear it from me."

"She will hate you."

"She already does."

Acknowledgements

Where do I begin? They say it takes a village to raise a child. I say it takes a village to create a book. Here is my love letter to my village.

Colleen Hoover, this book exists because of you. Sitting on a rooftop in Los Angeles, I told you about a story I had in my head. I asked, "don't you think someone should write this?" Your reply was, "yes, sounds like you should write it." I explained that I wasn't a writer and I couldn't do it. You just kept telling me I could and that I should. So I went home, and I did.

Gloria Green, you were the first person to read any part of this story. When I sent you the file, I had already decided that if you thought it was shit, I would shelf it, and not speak of it again. I will never forget your excited phone call to me, at 5:25 pm, from a grocery store parking lot. You finished it. You loved it, and you were proud of me. That is the moment I knew Gabby and Cross's story had to be published. Let's not forget that you also helped create the perfect cover because you are the supreme model hook-up.

To my early readers: Amanda White, Jessica Barnette, Christy Hutchins, Angela Jones, Michelle Hunter, Mindi Adams, and Brandee Veltri, I can not tell you how valuable your input was. The excited texts at all hours of the night were my favorite. I trust you all as readers and as friends. I am sorry for keeping the secret from some of you until after you read, although, a couple of you were suspicious from the beginning. Perhaps the most encouraging and unexpected of all the early feedback came from Michael McNamee. I still can not believe you read this book, Mike.

If you all could have seen the early versions of this manuscript, man, it wasn't pretty. All I can say is Jovana Shirley with Unforeseen Editing and Judy Zweifel with Judy's Proofreading are goddesses. Very patient goddesses. I still think commas are from the devil, Jovana.

What is a book without a spectacular cover? Scott Hoover took a few notes and the beautiful couple, Taylor Rhodenbaugh and James Pulido, and made my vision of Gabby and Cross come to life with his gorgeous photos. Then, Sommer Stein applied her design skills and, well, magic happened.

Autumn Gantz with Wordsmith Publicity, there is no way I would have made it through the publishing process without your help. I wrote the story and then had no idea where to go from there. You took me by the hand and led me step-by-step through the process. You are a rockstar at what you do but more than that you are a fantastic friend. I am so lucky to have you in my corner.

David Miller, thank you for always having my back and supporting my dreams. You make me feel like I can do anything. You are my anchor, my rock and the best thing that has ever happened to me. I am so happy God chose me to be your wife. Sorry about all the nights you had to pick up dinner, the days you had to wear dirty socks to work, and for all the conversations you had to have with yourself while my mind was lost in my fictional world.

Lastly, there are the countless friends I have made in the indie community over the years. Friends I consider family. Authors, bloggers, and readers I love and admire. There are too many to name, but I will name two, Corinne Michaels and K.A. Linde—Black & Gold 4Ever!

About the Author

Amber Kelly is a romance author that calls North Carolina home. She has been a avid reader from a young age and you could always find her with her nose in a book completely enthralled in an adventure. With the support of her husband and family, in 2018, she decided to finally give a voice to the stories in her head and her debut novel, Both of Me was born. You can connect with Amber on Facebook at facebook. com/AuthorAmberKelly, on IG @authoramberkelly, on twitter @ AuthorAmberKel1 or via her website www.authoramberkelly.com.

Made in the USA
Middletown, DE
12 June 2019